DIRTY LOOKS

A J.J. Graves Mystery

LILIANA HART

ALSO BY LILIANA HART

JJ Graves Mystery Series

Dirty Little Secrets

A Dirty Shame

Dirty Rotten Scoundrel

Down and Dirty

Dirty Deeds

Dirty Laundry

Dirty Money

A Dirty Job

Dirty Devil

Playing Dirty

Dirty Martini

Dirty Dozen

Dirty Minds

Dirty Weekend

Dirty Looks

Dirty Liars

Dirty Valentine

Addison Holmes Mystery Series

Whiskey Rebellion

Whiskey Sour

Whiskey For Breakfast

Whiskey, You're The Devil

Whiskey on the Rocks

Whiskey Tango Foxtrot

Whiskey and Gunpowder

Whiskey Lullaby

The Scarlet Chronicles

Bouncing Betty

Hand Grenade Helen

Front Line Francis

The Harley and Davidson Mystery Series

The Farmer's Slaughter

A Tisket a Casket

I Saw Mommy Killing Santa Claus

Get Your Murder Running

Deceased and Desist

Malice in Wonderland

Tequila Mockingbird

Gone With the Sin

Grime and Punishment

Blazing Rattles

A Salt and Battery

Curl Up and Dye

First Comes Death Then Comes Marriage

Box Set 1

Box Set 2

Box Set 3

The Gravediggers

The Darkest Corner

Gone to Dust

Say No More

Laurel Valley

Tribulation Pass

Redemption Road

Midnight Clear

Forgiveness River

Atonement Trail

To Scott—I love you.

Children are the world's most valuable
resource and its best hope for the future.

~John F. Kennedy

See that you do not despise one of these little ones. For I tell you that in heaven their angels always see the face of my Father who is in heaven.

~Matthew 18:10 (ESV)

PROLOGUE

She loved games.

The girl put her hand over her mouth to stifle a giggle. Hide-and-seek was her favorite, but she had to be quiet if she wanted to win. She peeked through the crack in the secret door, watching her grandmother to make sure she was really asleep.

She gnawed at her lip, wondering if she should check on Grandma. She hadn't been feeling well and she'd said she just needed a little rest, but the girl knew Grandma had caught the stomach bug because her face had turned a horrible shade of green when Molly had brought up dinner.

The girl pushed the door open a crack,

thinking she could tuck Grandma under the covers a little better and maybe get a sweatshirt and her house slippers. Her pajamas were thin and the passageways were chilly. Even as she had the thought a violent shiver racked her body.

The decision made, she started to step out of the passageway and back into the bedroom when she heard footsteps from the hallway. She hurriedly closed the secret door and ran down the narrow steps.

She didn't know how many were playing the game, but the grown-ups liked to play as much as she and her siblings and cousins. It was one of the best things about coming to Grandma's house. Everybody liked to play. It was most fun when they were all there together. But this time, it was just her.

There was another noise, what sounded like a door closing, and she squeezed her body into a crevice, wiping her damp hands on her pajama pants. And then when she thought enough time had passed, she ran as fast as she could down another flight of stairs and to the secret door that led to Grandpa's office. She wasn't supposed to be in there, but Grandpa wasn't home so probably no one would notice if she used the doors that led out onto the patio where he liked to smoke.

Grandma didn't like it when he smoked, and he thought no one could see him on the private patio. But she could see him just fine from her bedroom. Sometimes she could even hear him talking on his phone and saying lots of bad words when she opened the windows.

She stifled another giggle as she crept into the dark office, her feet sinking into the thick rug as she made her way behind the desk and toward the door. Technically, she wasn't supposed to go outside, but the rain had stopped and she was just going to run back around to the front of the house and slip in the kitchen door. Besides, there was still daylight left, and if she was the last one found then she'd win the game. And then maybe Molly would give her something besides soup. Like a chocolate chip cookie. She made the best cookies. Even better than her mom's.

The girl grasped the black metal handle of the door and opened the door, freezing when the hinges creaked loudly. She could barely breathe as she waited, her ears straining for someone to come in and catch her. Her heart thumped wildly in her chest, and she looked down at her bare feet, wishing she'd put on her shoes.

But there was no time for such regrets. She gathered her courage and pushed the door open the rest of the way, and started running. She was outside and halfway around the house, just about to breathe a sigh of relief, when arms came around her and tossed her into the air. She squealed with laughter.

"Oh, man," she said, looking up into the face of her captor. Disappointment filled her. "How'd you find me? I was so quiet."

"You're predictable. You always take the same route. You've got to mix it up a little. And I won't tell your grandfather you were in his office again."

She blew out a sigh, already thinking about where she would hide the next time. Maybe she'd climb out a window and go down to the stables. They'd never find her there.

"You won't find me next time," she said.

"That's what you always say. Come on. Let's go see your horse while it's still daylight."

"Oh, can I?" she asked, jumping up and down. "I've been wanting to go see her, but Grandma said I was too sick. But I'm better now. Pinky promise. And I've been so bored. I've read all my books, and I practiced my golf swing, and I didn't throw up my dinner."

There was a chuckle. "Come on. We'll go down in the car. Last thing we need is you catching a cold."

"I should put on my riding clothes," she said, looking down at her pajamas. She was starting to shiver with the sun going down, and it looked like it might start to rain again.

"No riding tonight. If Molly catches you out of your room she'll have your neck. Maybe you can ride in the morning if the weather is nice."

The girl kicked at the ground and watched water droplets scatter across the grass, knowing there was no point in arguing. Molly would tell her she was too sick to be out and about, and that she'd catch her death being out in the damp. Molly liked to fuss.

"Okay," she said. "Let's go before it gets too dark. It's been ages since I've seen Megan Thee Stallion."

"It hasn't been ages. And I can't believe your grandmother let you name one of her horses that."

"That's what Daddy said," she said. "He said Grandma keeps her head buried in the sand to the ways of the world now that she's retired. He said she doesn't have near enough to do and it's making her crazy. But Grandma said the horse was mine and I could name her what I wanted to. Megan doesn't have the hind legs to be a contender, but she's just right for me."

There was another chuckle as she hopped

into the back seat of the black Land Rover and didn't bother buckling her seat belt. It smelled of polished leather and sandalwood and she bounced slightly on the seat. She was excited. She'd been cooped up in the house way too long.

She hummed to herself as they drove through the tree tunnel, and she pretended, just as she had when she was a very little girl, that it was the secret entrance to a magical place of fairytales and dragons and knights on white horses. Grandma's house was always like coming to a magical place.

Lost in her song, she didn't notice when they didn't take the turn toward the stables. They passed the garages and through a thicker covering of trees.

"Where are we going?" she asked. "You missed the turn for the stables."

"I just need make a quick errand. It won't take long."

She watched curiously as they approached the gate, but there was no guard stationed there like usual. A button was pushed and the iron gates slid open, and the Range Rover rolled through smoothly. She rubbed her hands together nervously. She'd never been taken on an errand before, and the sky was getting darker.

"Here we are."

The Range Rover pulled up next to another car similar to the one they were in, but she couldn't see the driver. The windows were too black. She heard muted conversation, and then the back door opened and there was a man standing there, and a sigh of relief went through her.

"Hey," she started to say, but then a hand came over her mouth and darkness covered her eyes. She tried to struggle and scream. Her foot connected with something solid, and she thought she heard a grunt, but she didn't have on her shoes and kicking hurt her toes. It was getting hard to breathe and she clawed out wildly as panic and the instinct to survive took over.

"Ouch, you little brat," the man said, and he punched her in the stomach hard enough that she couldn't draw in a breath.

She couldn't breathe or scream and there was nothing but darkness all around her. Her arms were yanked roughly behind her back and something was pulled tightly against her wrists so she couldn't move. Couldn't fight.

She whimpered as she was dropped onto the hard ground. She tried to get her legs under her. To run. But the man grabbed her by the hair and dragged her. And then he slipped something cold and hard around her neck and pulled hard.

"Careful. She's already got a buyer. And he'll be pissed if she's too roughed up when he gets her."

"Yeah, I got it," the man said. "Just like last time. Get in the car and shut up, brat."

He picked her up and tossed her into the back seat, but she barely felt the pain in her shoulder as she landed on the seat. It was easier to succumb to the dark.

When she woke again she didn't know where she was or how long she'd been gone. It was still so dark. And cold. But at least there was nothing over her eyes, and she was able to breathe a little easier.

She curled up on her side, a whimper escaping as her battered body protested movement. The man who dressed like her daddy was a very bad man. He looked like he should have been nice, but his face had been like a monster, contorted and evil. Her clothes were gone. And flashes of the bad man hitting her and touching her all over flashed in her mind. She couldn't get it out of her mind. He'd hurt her so bad, forced himself inside of her so she thought her body would tear in two.

Grandma would notice she was gone. And Molly. They'd come find her. And her daddy would hurt the bad man. He would probably punch him in the face. Thoughts of her daddy hurting the bad man helped clear some of the horrors from her mind.

She needed to think. She needed to be like one of the girl spies in the books she liked to read. What would a girl spy do? Try to escape? Try to find someone to help? Try to remember every little detail for the police?

First she needed to figure out where she was. Maybe there was a phone or a neighbor. Wherever she was, it smelled funny, and it made her nose burn when she breathed in deep. But at least her eyes were adjusting to the dark.

There was a dollhouse in the corner and stuffed animals on the floor. Somehow it seemed worse that she was in another little girl's bedroom. She hadn't remembered being brought here. She only remembered waking up when the man was on top of her. Tears pricked her eyes but she refused to let them fall. She hadn't cried. Not when all the bad things were happening to her. She didn't think she'd ever be able to cry again.

She could hear voices somewhere in the house. No, not voices. A television. She gingerly crawled off the bed, unable to control the whimpers that escaped, and she went to the window to look out. She peeked through the frilly curtains and opened the blinds, but it was dark outside. There wasn't even a streetlight. Only the moon that was half hidden behind a cloud.

Her body shuddered with cold, and she was starting to feel sick to her stomach again. Just like she'd felt after Junie's birthday party. She'd thrown up cake everywhere. Bile rose in her throat and she swallowed it down. She couldn't be sick now. He'd hear her and he might do bad things to her again. No matter what, she couldn't let him do the bad things to her again.

With that determination in mind she went to the closet, looking for her clothes. Or any clothes. But the closets were empty. Her breaths were coming faster and faster and she stumbled on her way to the door to see if there was a lock. There wasn't. He'd be able to walk in anytime he wanted and hurt her again.

Soft mewling sounds came from her throat as the panic began to overwhelm her. She frantically searched the room looking for anything that might protect her. That's when she saw the white wooden chair in front of the vanity table.

She dragged it across the carpet, too weak to pick it up, and she put it under the knob. The sounds coming from her mouth were almost animalistic as she realized she was trapped inside the room.

She pressed her ear to the door, trying to listen, trying to hear if the bad man was coming for her again, but her heart was pounding too loudly in her ears.

A phone rang, a loud shrill sound that cut through the sounds of the television, and she almost screamed in response. She clamped her hand over her mouth. The sounds from the television disappeared and she heard the man's voice. She *knew* the man's voice. She'd never forget the words he'd said as he was hurting her, telling her what a pretty girl she was as he held his hand over her mouth to muffle her screams.

He was talking louder now, mad, and she ran back to the window, pulling aside the curtains and moving the blinds. If she could just get the window to open.

Her fingers fumbled twice with the latch, but she finally got it. And she pushed with all her might until the window rose with a whoosh. His voice was getting louder now. And then the knob rattled and the door banged against the chair.

She couldn't stifle her shriek of fear. The cold night air blasted her in the face and the holly bush scratched the side of her cheek as she climbed out the window and started to run. She didn't know where she was running. She just knew he was behind her and if she stopped running he would catch her. And she could never let him catch her. Not again.

Running was her only hope.

CHAPTER ONE

I ONCE READ SOMEWHERE THAT LIFE WAS A SERIES of lessons that had to be lived to be understood. Over the last thirty-something years, I've lived a lot of lessons. It was the understanding I had trouble grasping. Because under no circumstances could anyone explain to me why I was standing over the body of a young girl—an innocent life taken violently and needlessly.

My name is J.J. Graves, and...for the first time in as long as I could remember, I wasn't sure I was going to be able to stand for the dead. My chest was tight—it was a struggle to draw in a breath—and my eyes burned, though I wasn't sure I was capable of tears.

There were shadows in my periphery—I only had eyes for what was in front of me—though I knew there were other officers and techs on scene. Just like I knew that there were tears streaming down Officer Benson's cheeks as he cordoned off the area. He had a daughter about this girl's age.

There was an underlying rage simmering inside the veteran cops working the scene.

Usually crime scenes were ordered chaos. There was chatter and noise and movement. Everyone had a job to do, but after a while, the job became monotonous. The longer and more often first responders worked these kinds of scenes, the more desensitized they became to the humanity of it. We always had to remind ourselves of the humanity. It's what kept us grounded. It's what kept us sane. And sometimes not so sane.

But this crime scene was different. It was quiet—eerily so—and there was a slow-motion quality about everyone's movements, as if reality hadn't quite caught up to our brains.

It had been a wet spring, one for the record books, and we'd had thirty straight days of rain as we moved into the first week of April. The ground was soggy and damp from the early morning fog, but there had miraculously been no rain overnight to wash away blood spatter and physical evidence.

I was the coroner for King George County, Virginia. Some of the cops affectionately called me a *last responder*. There was a responsibility that went along with the title. It was my job to be a voice for those who no longer had one. It was my job to collect the evidence and put together the puzzle of what happened to victims so criminals spent the rest of their lives behind bars. My job was to bring justice.

But looking at the small and broken body of an unknown girl, I wasn't sure there was any amount of justice I could bring her. Nothing would be enough.

"You okay, Doc?" Martinez said low and under his breath so no one else overheard.

I started to tell him I was fine, but I stopped myself. I'd been around cops too long. Cops and feelings didn't exactly go hand in hand. Expressing emotions was considered a sign of weakness.

"I can't say that I am," I admitted.

He blew out a breath. "Yeah. Me too."

"It's always harder when it's kids," I said. "We're supposed to protect the weak and the innocent. But there are still people in the world who can do this to a child. I'll never understand it."

"There's been a battle between good and evil

since the beginning of time," Martinez said. "My abuela always says to remember that there was murder when there were only four people on the planet. It's a battle good will continue to fight for as long as we're on this earth."

"You sound a little like Reverend Thomas," I said.

"Hey, I was an altar boy," he said. "I know my stuff."

"Your abuela should be proud."

"She is," he said. "Which is why I'm her favorite instead of my no-good cousins."

The conversation with Martinez had given me enough time to settle and to see clearly.

"I guess it's me and you on this one," I said, finally able to look him in the eyes.

Martinez had earned the nickname of GQ Cop in the squad room once he'd been promoted to detective and no longer had to wear a uniform. He was smooth and charming and charismatic, and he would probably make a great politician one day. He had Latino good looks—a strong jaw and dark, hooded eyes that women found irresistible. His hair was stylishly cut and his face shaved smooth.

He wore an expensive dark gray suit, a silvery gray shirt, and a tie with hints of lavender and silver in a checked design. It was barely six o'clock in the morning and he looked like he'd stepped out of a magazine. The press loved him as much as women did.

I looked down at my own standard-issue dark blue coveralls with *Coroner's Office* stenciled across the back, and was glad they covered up the old gray sweats I'd managed to pull on when I'd rolled out of bed that morning. I wore a baseball cap that had the KGSO logo embroidered on the front to cover my bed head.

I shivered, wishing I'd had time to make coffee before I'd left the house, but it wouldn't have done much more than warm my hands. I'd left my fleece-lined windbreaker in the car and was regretting the decision now. The constant rain had kept the overnight temps unseasonably cool, and it was still in the mid-forties, though the brisk wind made it feel colder.

Looking between the two of us, it was obvious Martinez and I were not cut from the same cloth. It would be interesting working with him solo for the first time.

I had no idea where Martinez got his money from, and to my recollection, no one had ever bothered to ask. All I knew was that he couldn't live how he did on a cop's salary. I figured it was probably better not to ask questions. I liked

Martinez and he was a great cop. No point in ruining a good thing.

"I guess that makes us partners," he said, squinting against the pale sunlight that was trying to eke its way through the clouds. "Just so you know I always like to drive, and I hate eating sandwiches for lunch."

"Good," I said. "Because I like being driven around, and I also don't like to eat sandwiches for lunch. Sounds like a match made in heaven"

"The sheriff and Cole are stuck in the Simmons trial all week," he said, pulling out a piece of chewing gum from his pocket and unwrapping it. "Lucky bastards." He stuck the gum in his mouth and put the wrapper back in his pocket.

"Yeah," I said, scanning the scene. "It's a big case. Very high profile. Lots of media attention. *National* media."

"Pain in the ass," he said, shaking his head. "Could be weeks before they're out of there."

When I'd gotten the call from dispatch the bed had been empty beside me and the sheets cool. I'd been no stranger to cool sheets over the past few days. Preparing for the Simmons trial had been more than enough to occupy Jack's time, along with his regular workload. But it had been for the best. Things were strained between us at the moment, and I think both of us were relieved the trial was giving us time and space.

The last year had been the best and worst of my life. Jack and I had come through so much and we were at the height of our professional and personal lives. I had no idea why it felt like things were falling apart. Maybe there had been so much bad in my life I didn't know how to process when things were good.

Some people didn't wear peace well. Maybe I was one of them.

Despite all the good in my life and my marriage to Jack, there were things we didn't have answers to. Like why two people who loved each other and whose heart was family, were having such a hard time starting their own. Or in reality, why *I* didn't seem to be capable of conceiving.

I'd always heard the saying about sins of the father. And my father had a great many sins so maybe there was some truth to it. It was just one of the many questions I'd asked that I had yet to get answers for.

The rift between me and Jack was my fault. *All* my fault. I knew it in my mind, but I didn't know how to right the ship, so to speak. This last round of false hope and pregnancy tests had broken my spirit, and I just hadn't pulled myself out of the quicksand yet. And Jack hadn't offered to pull me out either. I was guessing he was dealing with his own pit to crawl out of.

Jack would be occupied with the trial for the rest of the week, so I had at least that long to try and figure out a way to apologize and make things right again.

I watched the black Suburban we used to transport bodies navigate through the media vans and past the police barricades. The media was relentless this morning. They'd showed up close behind the first officers on scene and it had been a fight to maintain the integrity of the scene and respect the victim's privacy since we didn't have an identification and no family had been notified. The techs had constructed a half wall of sorts to block the victim to prying eyes since she was in a public park.

If Jack had been here he'd have put the fear of God in every one of those reporters, especially since the victim was a minor, but Martinez had done a pretty good job in Jack's absence and all the cameras and fresh and polished reporters stood behind the barricades so they could go live for the six o'clock news.

Lily was driving the Suburban, her face partially hidden by a baseball cap and a pair of dark aviators, but I could see the half smile on her lips as a cameraman dodged out of her way.

Lily was working for me as assistant coroner while she was finishing up medical school to become a pathologist, and I was lucky to have her. She'd go on to a bigger city and a higher paying job at some point, but for now she was a gift to King George County. She had a brilliant mind that people overlooked because of her beauty.

Sheldon Durkus sat in the passenger side next to her. He was my assistant at the funeral home, but more often than not he got roped into helping me on the forensics side of my job description. I'd been a medical doctor working in the ER at Augusta General up until my parents had died a few years back, though it had turned out they'd faked their deaths and had been secretly working for a foreign government to smuggle in everything from weapons to drugs. It had also turned out they weren't really my parents and I'd been stolen as a baby. That might traumatize most people, but to be honest, I'd been relieved to find out I didn't share their blood.

All that to say, I'd inherited the family funeral home, and then Jack had helped me get hired on with the county as coroner so I could pay my most of my bills after the FBI froze all my assets. They came in and took apart my life and business just to make sure I was an innocent party where my parents were concerned. I *was* innocent, by the way.

I hadn't inherited Sheldon along with the funeral home. He'd showed up on my doorstep like a stray puppy looking for a job, and somehow, I'd become responsible for him. He was young and knew the craft, and he was great with the dead. It was the living he wasn't so good with.

I gestured to Lily where I wanted her to park, and then watched as she and Sheldon got out and went to the back to get prepped for transport. They were already dressed in their coveralls, but it would be a while yet. I hadn't even started the preliminary report.

I drew in a deep breath and grabbed a pair of latex gloves from my bag.

"It's been a while since we had a kid," Martinez said.

"Peter Winslow was the last," I said automatically. "You never really forget them."

My breath was coming in cold puffs as I blew into one glove and slipped it on, and then the other. An old trick from my ER days.

The grass was damp with dew, so I squatted down next to the victim, and tried my best to compartmentalize what I saw. Pure science. No emotion. Emotions were paralyzing.

"She's not been moved?" I asked.

"This is how responding officers found her," Martinez said. "The call came in from an early morning jogger." He read from his phone where he'd taken notes. "Kelly Sandborn is her name. She's sitting in the back of the ambulance with the blanket wrapped around her."

I looked in the direction where the ambulance was parked and the woman sitting on the back, taking the occasional huff of oxygen. She looked to be mid-thirties or forties. She was in good shape, and she was decked out in Spandex leggings and a long-sleeved Spandex shirt in hot pink.

"She doesn't look like an idiot at first glance," I said, shaking my head.

"Right?" Martinez asked. "Why the hell was she jogging alone at five in the morning in a mostly deserted area? Maybe this will be a wake-up call for her."

"People generally don't think they'll become a statistic. Especially in a place like Bloody Mary, but this isn't the small town it used to be."

"Tell me about it," Martinez said. "DC has started bringing their crime here."

I knew this to be true. Over the last year Jack had created a white-collar-crime division and hired cops from bigger cities with the experience to deal with it. Developers and politicians had tried to make King George County their playground, and Jack was having no part of it, which put a very large target on Jack's back from some very powerful people.

I pulled my camera from my bag and took several shots so I could remember how she was positioned and then I got a couple of close-ups of the trauma and bruising on her body.

"Rigor is fully set in," I told him. "All the rain we've been having has kept temps in the forties, so that could accelerate rigor and factor into TOD, so it'll be a little wider range of time."

I couldn't cover the body until I'd taken all the samples I needed, and I could tell it bothered Martinez that she was still exposed. My lungs burned and I kept reminding myself to breathe. Everything had to be done right. I documented her body temp in my notes. Checked her eyes and mouth.

Martinez grunted and shifted his feet, his expensive dress shoes beaded with water. "Ms. Sandborn said she always runs this route. She and her husband live in one of the new condos on the square. She takes Anne Boleyn all the way down to Jane Seymour, and then cuts across the empty lot on the corner to get to the park. She would have had a direct line of sight of the vic as she jogged around the corner, but it's pretty misty this morning, so she was almost directly under the park light before she saw her. Sandborn said it was like the girl was being spotlighted."

"Pretty ballsy of our killer," I said. "To leave her right under the park light like he did."

Martinez grunted in agreement. "Seems to me like he didn't care about being seen and didn't care how fast she was found. There are plenty of trees in this park, so he could have dragged her out of the way. But he left her on the perimeter where anyone driving or jogging by would see her."

I looked at my watch and calculated the time. It was a few minutes past six. "I'd put time of death somewhere between nine and midnight," I said. "Bloody Mary is all tucked into bed at that time of night. Especially on a Monday. All of the local restaurants are closed. There are no sporting or church events."

"Almost like he knew that," Martinez said. "What about sexual assault?"

I sighed, trying to focus my attention away from the trauma her skull had sustained. "There's evidence of blood and semen. We're not going to be short on DNA evidence."

"Yeah, I figured," Martinez said, and I could hear the anger in his voice. "She's so small. You think you've seen the worst of things, and people still manage to surprise me."

"She is small for her age," I said, carefully massaging the rigor out of her jaw so I could stick my finger in her mouth. "But she does have upper and lower molars, so she's probably close to twelve at the least.

"Blunt force trauma to the head," I continued. "Overkill. There's a lot of rage in those blows. Significant trauma to the skull. But she was also strangled. Look at the bruising around her neck and the broken capillaries in her eyes. Contusions and abrasions cover most of her body. Ligature marks around the wrists and ankles signify she was bound. Even her heels are raw."

"Indicating she was dragged," Martinez said, taking notes.

I looked up and around the playground area —a place that should have been filled with children and laughter—noting the wood chips at the bottom of the slides and the loose pebbles under the swings.

"I'll take samples to send to the forensics lab in Richmond and see what comes up," I said. "But she's got particulates embedded in the skin. Probably gravel or sediment from the sidewalk. She hasn't been moved since she was killed. Livor mortis has set in."

I lifted her body slightly so Martinez could see the purplish hues of her skin where the blood had settled along her back and thighs. The human body always told a story. Flesh and blood and bone were as descriptive as the pages of a book.

"Any idea what did this kind of damage to her skull?" I asked, but Martinez didn't respond.

His gaze was scanning the crowd that had gathered on the outside of the police barricade. Then he looked toward Officer Plank and gestured him over.

"Yes, sir," Plank said, hurrying to us and standing at attention.

We all had a soft spot for Plank, even though he was still a rookie. He was the boy next door, and all of us were a little baffled at how he'd ended up in uniform instead of coaching Little League or settling down with a wife and living the picket-fence life.

But that rookie shine was beginning to tarnish, and he'd proven himself when the bullets had started to fly. Gone was the naïvety in his eyes, and in place was a harder outlook on humanity that had taken away some of his approachability—cop eyes. I grieved a little for that.

Despite the cop eyes, he was still fresh faced

and pink cheeked. His hair was freshly cut and his uniform starched so stiff it could have stood up by itself.

"Let's check out the crowd that's gathered to watch us work," Martinez told him. "Get names and contact information. Several of them are still in their nightclothes so I'm guessing they live close. Start with that tall guy standing at the back. He's giving me the creeps."

I couldn't see who Martinez was talking about while I was kneeling down, so I stood up to see over the privacy partition that had been erected.

My gaze scanned the crowd of older people, at first not seeing the man that Martinez had singled out. There was still a hazy mist in the air and it was the time between dark and light when everything was in shades of gray. But then the man came into partial focus. He stood next to a tree, dressed in black and blending in with the tree bark. I couldn't clearly see any of his features, but he was a head taller than those standing around him.

"Yes, sir," Plank said, and headed off to follow orders.

I knelt back down by the victim and Martinez came with me and sighed.

"I kind of miss the old Plank," he said. "This job really sucks."

"Yeah, but you wouldn't do anything else," I told him.

"Isn't that the truth," he said, shaking his head. "What does that say about me?"

"That you're the perverse creature we've always known you to be," I said. "Besides, somebody has to catch the bad guys. Better us than letting all hell break loose."

Martinez snorted out a laugh and rubbed his hand over his face. There was a resoluteness about him, a determination to face the horror of what one human being could do to another. He made himself look at the victim, to not shy away from the atrocities. The girl deserved that much. But I knew from experience we'd all pay for it later. In our marriages. In our dreams. In sex or thoughts of suicide. In the bottles of alcohol that awaited some at the end of a hard day. First responders all dealt with trauma differently. Whatever vice they chose, I noticed it usually wasn't the healthiest way of dealing with things.

"We found several large rocks covered in blood and brain matter," Martinez said, pointing to the yellow numbered evidence tags spaced along the ground.

"Several?" I asked. "So he used multiple rocks to bash her head in?"

"That's what it looks like."

"Well, that's different," I said. "Any evidence of more than one killer?"

"Not that we've found," he said. "The rocks were all lining that flower bed there. Maybe in the struggle he was just grasping for something to hit her with. Those rocks are covered with blood. They would have been slippery. So he loses one and then grabs another."

"Wouldn't have been much of a fight," I said, looking at the wounds with my flashlight. "The first blow would've incapacitated her. She wouldn't have been fighting back then."

"Maybe he was just so caught up in the moment he couldn't stop," Martinez said. "What kind of man leaves his DNA and fingerprints all over the place?"

"A stupid one or one who isn't in the system."

"Yeah, that's what I'm afraid of. Maybe a combo of both. This looks frantic. Not calculated. Maybe his first kill."

I grunted in the affirmative. "What about a ligature? Find anything he could have strangled her with? Or whatever he'd bound her wrists and feet with?"

"Nothing so far, but I've got guys canvassing

the area checking trash cans and dumpsters. It's trash day in this neighborhood so it would have been easy for him to shove any evidence in a nearby bin. We would've been out of luck if the trashmen beat us to it. They usually start their rounds about this time. If he got rid of evidence we'll find it. She's covered in blood. He would be too."

"She did put up a fight," I said. "She's got particulates and skin under her fingernails." I carefully bagged both of her hands. "And she's got defensive bruising along her forearms. See the pattern?"

I held my arms up in an X over my chest to demonstrate. "He hit her with something," I said. "Not his fist. See how the bruising almost wraps around the arm. Like a whip, but wider."

"Belt," he said. "I've seen those marks before."

"People tend to grab whatever is closest in a fight. If she surprised him and tried to escape out of a vehicle or house he would have grabbed whatever he could to make her stop. A child in her condition would draw notice if they were out in public. Looks like a couple of fingers are broken too," I said.

"I knew I should have put in for vacation last week," Martinez said. "I could be drinking margaritas in the Florida Keys and flirting with tiki bar waitresses. It sure would beat the hell out of this."

"You probably have kids you don't know about all over the country," I said, trying to lighten the atmosphere. It would be too easy for both of us to spiral down, and I knew from experience it was a lot easier to go down than it was to come up.

"Not me," he said, shaking his head. "I took care of that a couple of years ago."

My head snapped up in surprise. "Get out! You got a vasectomy?" I asked, keeping my voice quiet. "But you're so young."

"No regrets. My family is crazy complicated, and I've never wanted to add to the madness," he said. "Besides, this job isn't good for families. How many guys on the force are paying child support and never get to see their kids? It's a rare woman who can put up with being married to a cop. Though don't tell my abuela. She's very Catholic, and she'd probably disown me if she knew there was no Mrs. Martinez or great-grandchildren in her future."

I'd never actually met any member of Martinez's family, so his secret was safe with me.

His phone rang. "Martinez," he said. It was a short call and Martinez didn't say anything else other than, "Thanks," before he disconnected.

"That was the station," he said. "No missing persons or abductions have been reported in the tri-state area in the last seventy-two hours, and there's nothing in the system with a description matching our victim from previous filings. She's a Jane Doe as of now."

"She's not a street kid," I said. "She's healthy and seems well nourished despite her small stature, and she's got orthodontia. That doesn't come cheap. It shouldn't be too hard to find an identity."

"From your mouth to God's ears," he said. "She's not from Bloody Mary or we all would have heard about it by now."

That was a true statement. Bloody Mary only had a couple of thousand people in it, and every one of them was a nosy busybody. Citizens in Bloody Mary knew enough about their neighbors to make the CIA blush. If one of our local kids had been missing we all would have heard about it.

"There's not much more I can do here," I said, packing my bag. "Let's get her back to the lab."

I gestured for Lily and Sheldon to come over with the transport board. The gurney would be too hard to roll through the grass and there were so many evidence tags along the ground I didn't want them to disturb anything.

I stood up and took off my gloves, dropping them in my bag, and then I moved over to stand next to Martinez to make room for Lily and Sheldon. The sun was struggling to break through the heavy clouds, and I could tell by looking we were in for another wet day. If the crime-scene techs missed something while they were searching this morning, it would most likely be lost forever.

As if my thoughts had been projected aloud, a long, low rumble of thunder sounded in the distance.

"Great," Martinez said, looking up at the sky. "Have I mentioned how much I hate this rain? I need the sun. Look at my skin. Does this look like the skin of a man who can do without the sun? This place is depressing."

"More than forty-five percent of adults struggle with depression in Seattle because of the lack of sun," Sheldon said. "There is a suicide every eleven minutes."

"I can believe it," Martinez said.

Sheldon's Coke-bottle-thick glasses were fogged, and there was a thin bead of sweat on his upper lip. It was still chilly outside, so I could only assume it was nerves making him sweat like a racehorse.

Sheldon hated coming to crime scenes. Seeing a body so fresh after death and not on a cold slab in the lab didn't sit well with him, though he hardly ever threw up anymore. Sheldon had spent his childhood reading random trivia as some kind of coping mechanism. He always had information to share that was in no way helpful for whatever our current situation happened to be. But I also knew spouting useless information was probably keeping him from tainting the crime scene with his own DNA.

"I used to like the rain," Lily said, carefully lifting the small body so they could maneuver the body bag around her. It was important to catch any particulates that might fall off in the bag so we could examine them in the lab. "It's always helped me to focus and study. But after the last month I'm starting to change my mind. Cole and I drove down to Greenville for the weekend to see a concert and I thought I'd died and gone to heaven when the sun came out."

"Cole has terrible taste in music," Martinez said. "All country, all the time."

Lily's mouth quirked in a half smile, her cheeks pinkened by the wind that had started to pick up. "I'll admit I didn't like it at first. I think it's an acquired taste. But after I started listening to it for a while I figured it wasn't any different than watching reality TV. Lots of drama going on in those songs. Think of it as reality TV for the radio."

"I knew Cole would be a bad influence on you," Martinez said, shaking his head. "You missed your chance. I would have treated you like a queen."

Lily snorted and said, "I think there's a country song that says the same thing. I'll send it to you so you can drown yourself in your sorrows."

She and Sheldon lifted the body bag and placed it on the board, securing the victim with wide yellow straps. When they shifted I saw a glint of something in the grass.

"What's that?" I asked, grabbing one of the gloves from my bag and, without putting it on all the way, I used it to pick up a delicate heart necklace.

Martinez still had his gloves on and gently took the necklace from me, examining the simple gold heart on both sides.

"Daddy's girl," he said, reading the inscription on the back of the necklace. "The chain is broken."

"It probably snapped while the killer was strangling her," I said, furrowing my brow in thought. "She was still wearing this necklace at the time of her murder. What about her clothes? Where are they?"

"We've not found any," Martinez said, brow furrowed. "I've got guys canvassing the streets and nearby dumpsters, but nothing has come back so far."

"We did find a baseball cap," Lieutenant Daniels said. "It's an adult man size. About fifteen feet from the victim. I did find a trace of blood on the bill, so we'll send it to the lab and see if it matches our victim."

She'd been crouched down only a few feet from us, cataloguing items they were taking into evidence. Daniels and her crime-scene team were the best, and we'd worked several cases together. She was a short plump woman with dark skin and beautiful tawny eyes, and she'd recently added blond to her braids.

"Fifteen feet isn't far," Martinez said. "Wouldn't have been hard for it to fly off in the struggle."

"So she either ran to the park naked or he stripped her here before he killed her," I said. "No matter which scenario you go with he was asking for someone to notice. Maybe he was in a hurry when he took her clothes and he didn't notice the necklace. But you saw the blood spatter pattern across her body. She was naked before he killed her."

"I see what you're getting at," Martinez said. "She's got defensive wounds. She fought like a wildcat. He's in the middle of the park trying to get her subdued, but she's not making it easy for him. Taking her clothes and raping her at that moment would have been the last thought in his head. He would have been in panic mode. And in panic mode you make stupid decisions."

"Like forgetting your baseball cap and leaving your DNA all over the scene." I looked around the park, at the houses that surrounded the area. "Where did she come from?"

"He wasn't worried about being sloppy," Martinez said. "He kills her in the middle of a public park, violently, where anyone could drive by or walk by and see. Hell, one of the neighbors could have stepped outside for a cigarette and the killer would've been spotlighted. Not to mention, he left fingerprints on the rocks he used to bash her head in. The techs pulled several latent prints from them."

"Maybe not stupid. Maybe just a complete psychopath and not concerned about consequences," I said.

"Comforting," Martinez said.

Regent Park was a small community park a few blocks from downtown and the funeral home. It was the first and oldest park in Bloody Mary, and the homes around it had been built in the last half of the 1800s. They were all narrow, two-story homes with red-brick chimneys, black shutters, and nothing but a stoop leading to the front door. If I had to guess the median age of the people living in the area I'd say anywhere from seventy to a hundred and twenty, plus or minus a few years.

"You think someone's surveillance camera could've picked it up?" I asked.

"That's the hope," Martinez said, looking at the houses that were most visible from our location, but he didn't sound hopeful.

Martinez held the locket up between two fingers and looked at it closer. And then he used his thumbs to open the heart locket. Inside was a small picture of the girl at my feet, though it seemed to be taken a couple of years prior. Her smile was bright and she sat on the lap of who I could only assume was her father, but they shared the same smile. They were both blond and blue eyed and on the verge of laughter. It was a sweet photo.

"Oh man," I said, taking a closer look at the man in the photo. "Why does he look familiar?"

"I was hoping I was imagining things," Martinez said. "Is that Councilman Lidle?"

"Oh," I said. "Yep."

"Hell."

"Yep," I said.

"My mother wrote him a strongly worded letter once," Sheldon said. "She said she wasn't about to let her hard-earned tax dollars be used for him to cut down trees and build ugly wind farms. She said he doesn't have the sense that God gave a goose."

"White people say the weirdest things," Martinez said.

I didn't know Councilman Lidle on a personal level. I tried to stay out of local politics unless Jack needed me to be at an event to eat rubber chicken and smile like I was happy about it. But I'd heard Jack mention Lidle's name on plenty of occasions. Lidle was all for the big developments and bringing progress like wind farms to King George County. Unfortunately for Lidle, Jack and the Lawson family owned most of the land he wanted to see developed.

"Let's check out the neighbors and see what they have to say," Martinez said.

I'd never worked one-on-one with Martinez before, so I was curious what it was like to do the job with someone other than Jack.

"You're the boss," I said. "Lily and Sheldon can transport and unload our vic. But I'll head back to the lab after we're done here so we have a definite identification and can notify next of kin."

"Maybe we'll get lucky and her prints will be in the database," Lily said. "More parents have started having their kids fingerprinted with the rise in trafficking over the last decade or so."

"We can hope," I said, and watched them walk away with precious cargo between them. They loaded her into the back of the Suburban and then slowly made their way back through the police barricades and press line.

My heart was heavy. I didn't know what we were about to step into. Politics usually wreaked havoc with truth and justice. But I knew what my job was, and I knew that the little girl whose life had been so viciously taken was where my loyalty belonged. And though I liked Martinez and figured he'd be fun to work with, I missed Jack.

CHAPTER TWO

THUNDER RUMBLED AGAIN, THIS TIME CLOSER THAN it had been before, and I hitched my bag over my shoulder and walked with Martinez toward the police perimeter.

The park was a perfect square, and there were four houses on each side of the square that faced the park. We moved toward the four houses that were in a direct line of sight from our victim and I noticed the crowd of onlookers had gotten larger, despite the upcoming threat of rain.

It wasn't hard to pick out Plank in the crowd since he was a good head taller than most of the onlookers. We caught his attention and he disentangled himself from the group of people he'd been interviewing to intercept us.

"How does he keep his uniform so straight and clean?" I asked as he walked toward us. "Even dodging bullets and wrestling suspects to the ground he always looks fresh."

"He could be a model for the uniform company," Martinez said. "A couple of guys at the station call him Baby Fresh. I've got twenty bucks in the office pool that says Plank is eventually going to snap and punch someone in the face for calling him that."

"No way," I said, shaking my head. "That kid is stone cold. I've never seen anything get under his skin. Last time a prisoner spit on him Plank offered to stop and pray with the guy."

Martinez whispered out of the corner of his mouth, "Yeah, but I'm still holding out hope for the face punch." Then he turned his attention to Plank and said, "Find out anything interesting from the crowd?"

"They all live in the neighborhood," Plank said, his cheeks redder than normal because of the wind. "I got names and addresses for all of them. The only house that's not represented is that little blue one on the corner."

We all turned as one and looked at the neat blue house with white trim and barren front steps.

"No woman lives there," I said.

"How'd you know?" Plank asked.

"Looks at all the other houses on the street," I said. "The way these houses are built don't lend themselves to a lot of curb appeal, so people set out their flowerpots and hanging baskets and put wreaths on the door because there are no porches. The blue house is nothing but concrete steps. So I figure a single guy has to live there."

"Good call, Doc," Plank said. "The neighbors said his name is Kent O'Leary. Quiet. Stays to himself. No one knows what he does for a living, but they said he must work weird hours because he's in and out at odd times. He never comes to quarterly picnics the neighborhood puts on here in the park."

"Let's see if you can track him down," Martinez said.

"Yes, sir," Plank said. "I'll run him as soon as I get back to the station."

"What about the rest of the neighbors?" I asked. "Anything helpful?"

Plank sighed and relaxed his guard as he pulled out his phone so he could read his notes. "The least helpful group of old people I've ever met."

"Yeah, that makes sense," I said. "I recognize Mrs. Dowdy. She was my third-grade teacher.

Horrible woman. She used to chew snuff and then spit it in a jar she kept in her desk."

"I heard about her," Martinez said. "But I didn't move here until my freshman year of high school so I didn't have the pleasure of having her as a teacher. But Bobby Jenkins told me she made a kid drink that spit jar as punishment one time."

I had to swallow to keep from gagging out of reflex. "I heard about that. I wouldn't be surprised at all."

Plank cleared his throat and, if possible, looked even more embarrassed. "Yeah, she mentioned that she knew you, Doc. Said to tell you your posture is still as bad as it always was."

"Horrid woman," I said under my breath. I could still feel her ruler on the back of my knuckles. "She's hunched over like an old crone and she's going to criticize my posture?"

Plank looked down at his notes and continued, but I saw his lips quirk in a smile. "According to the ringleader—that would be Edith Norton over there in the pink robe and knitted cap—they all came outside about the same time to see what was going on when the sirens came through. Edith and her husband James live in the white house directly across from line of sight of the victim. She was pretty upset how fast the responding officers got the privacy screens up."

I shook my head in disbelief. "People have no human decency anymore. Everything is a show for entertainment."

"It's why our jobs just get harder and why the crime rates are spiking," Martinez said. "Someone gets hurt and the first thing people do is pull out the phone to record instead of offering to help."

Plank nodded, but continued his report. "Edith said they moved here from Allentown a few years ago when they retired, but they're considering moving somewhere else because King George County is becoming just like the city with high crime rates and price gouging."

"I'll make sure to offer my assistance on moving day," Martinez said, rolling his eyes. "What else you got?"

"The others corroborated the story," Plank said. "They all heard the sirens about the same time and came out to see what was going on. But the frail-looking woman with the giant coat and crooked hair was late to the party. Her name is Joanne Crowley. She saw the live feed on the five thirty news and recognized her house. She's mostly deaf so she didn't hear the sirens. Said she had to wait until her biscuits were out of the oven before she came outside."

"I thought I saw a crumb on your uniform," I said, flicking an invisible speck from Plank's shoulder.

He looked down at his spotless uniform, and then looked back up at us, a guilty expression on his face. "She wouldn't take no for an answer. She makes biscuits just like my great-grandma."

"She looks like she'd be a hard one to fight off," Martinez said. "A good breeze would probably blow her away. What about the tall guy who was standing at the back? Was that Kent O'Leary? He seemed quite a bit younger than the others. Looked like a loner."

"Not O'Leary," Plank said. "I asked the others and no one had ever seen him before. He slipped through the crowd and disappeared as soon as I started walking toward him. I had Winslow and Grainger see if they could circle around and spot him, but he was like a ghost."

"We'll add him to our list," Martinez said. "We should be able to go back and check the media footage. If Joanne saw her house on the news then they've probably got a shot of our mystery guy too. We can put out a BOLO."

I knew what Martinez was thinking. This had been a very public murder in a very public place.

The psychology behind the need for publicity more than likely meant that the killer wanted her discovery to be public as well. Why wouldn't the killer want a front-row seat to all the action to make sure things happened as he'd planned?

"What about last night?" Martinez asked. "Anyone hear or see anything suspicious?"

"According to Edith," Plank said, "she and James are early to bed and early to rise. They were both asleep by nine o'clock. The others had a similar story. One lady said her grown son is living with her while he's going through a divorce and he came home late last night, but she wasn't sure what time. She said the only reason she heard him come in is because the mudroom door is right next to her bedroom and it squeaks. He left for work this morning around four."

"Interesting timing," Martinez said. "So this guy comes in some time after nine and leaves the house at four, which is right in the middle of our window for the murder, and he just casually leaves for work without seeing our victim laid out on the same street he lives on? We can put him at the top of the list of persons of interest."

"His name is Jackson Sparrow," Plank said, straight faced. "His mother's name is Myrtle."

"Jack Sparrow?" Martinez asked, clearly not amused. "Are you kidding me right now, Plank?"

"I don't kid, sir," Plank said. "At least not when there's murder on the line."

I looked down so Plank wouldn't see my smile. He really was so sweet.

"Sparrow works at Richmond International as a baggage loader," Plank said. "He gets off at three o'clock."

"It's an hour fifteen drive from the airport with no traffic," I said. "That'd put him back in Bloody Mary around four thirty in the afternoon, give or take. So where was he between then and whenever he came home last night? Most of the bars and restaurants are closed on Mondays in this area."

"It'll be the first question I ask," Martinez said. "But I'm not driving to the airport and wading through that circus to question him. We can wait until he gets off work and we'll swing back by."

The crowd of older people, minus the lone guy who'd disappeared, were still standing huddled together at the edge of the park. Most of them wearing a mixture of their nightclothes and winter coats. A woman with steel-gray hair was holding a carafe and pouring out hot coffee into Styrofoam cups, and a couple of the men were setting out lawn chairs. It looked like they were in it for the long haul.

Martinez looked at me. "Looks like we need to change course since Plank got us a bead on line-of-sight neighbors. We can follow up with Jackson Sparrow this afternoon. For now, the most important thing is to get a positive identity on our victim so we can start interviewing her family."

I nodded and said, "I'll head back to the lab now. I should be able to have something to you soon."

"What do you think the chances are that Sheldon and Lily will keep the news to themselves that the victim could be Councilman Lidle's daughter?"

"Honestly, I think Sheldon has already called his mother and Lily has already texted Cole."

Detective Cole and Lily had been dating for about a year, and they'd recently taken the step of moving in together. About a week ago Cole had proposed to Lily and she'd turned him down. It had been touch or go for a couple of days because Cole had never asked a woman to marry him, and he wasn't used to being turned down for anything. But Lily had told him to ask her again in a few weeks once he had a chance to decide if he hated seeing her makeup on his counter or the way she chewed her food in the mornings. Lily had a lot of wisdom for someone her age. Cole had agreed with her, so as of now, the relationship was still going strong.

Cole wasn't known for his long-term relationships. Not to mention the fact that he was seventeen years older than Lily. But they were managing to make it work. And no one had been able to claim the pool at the sheriff's office that Cole would move on to the next twenty-something model and leave Lily in the dust. I loved Cole like a brother and he was one of Jack's closest friends, but he was hell on women. Apparently, that was a quality certain types of women looked for in a man. Go figure.

Martinez sighed and said, "Yeah, I figured as much. But I was holding out hope."

"I'll get you an identity fast," I promised him. "I should be able to finish the autopsy before lunch."

"Good," he said. "You're buying."

CHAPTER THREE

The first drops of rain started to fall just as I turned onto Catherine of Aragon. Lily had parked the other Suburban under the portico so they could transport the body inside, so I parked right behind her and made a quick dash to the side door.

I let myself in and hung my jacket and bag on one of the hooks in the mudroom, and then walked into the kitchen. It was still early, just after seven thirty, and the funeral home wouldn't open for another couple of hours. Fortunately, there were no funerals on the books for the next couple of days and I could devote my full attention to my job as coroner.

My receptionist, Emmy Lu, wasn't in yet. There was no coffee made and the thermostat hadn't kicked on so the kitchen felt cold and sterile. I made my way to the coffeepot and went through the monotony of measuring grounds and pouring in the water. Jack normally made the coffee in the mornings and left a cup on the bedside table, but with the trial and other things, the coffee had been absent for several days.

The morning was starting to catch up with me, and I stifled a yawn. I'd been dead to the world when the call from dispatch had come in. I looked down and realized I was still in my coveralls, so I stripped out of them while the coffee was brewing and tossed them in the basket in the laundry room. I took off my cap and pulled the band from my stubby ponytail and massaged my scalp. I'd have paid a king's ransom for the luxury of crawling back into bed and shutting out the world for the next few hours.

I'd gotten soft since my days of medical school and rotations in the ER. Lack of sleep had been my normal once upon a time. But the last few years I'd gotten spoiled by a well-made mattress and fresh-ground coffee beans to keep me going.

I caught a reflection of myself in the refrigerator as I got out the creamer and had to stifle back a yelp of surprise. It never failed that the media got some unflattering clip or photograph of me to plaster all over the news, and they probably got some doozies this morning. Thankfully, the dead didn't care what I looked like. And I'd have time to shower and dress in real clothes before I had to buy Martinez lunch.

My phone rang and I looked down at the screen, a smile coming across my face as I saw Doug's picture come up. Doug Carver was the nephew of Jack's best friend, Ben. Ben had been an agent for the FBI up until a few months ago when he'd uncovered deep corruption from within not only the FBI, but all the alphabet agencies.

Apparently the alphabet agencies didn't want to be exposed because Carver and his family became target number one and they were on the run. The last postcard we'd gotten from Carver had been from Moscow, or at least we could assume it was from Carver. It had been a blank postcard with only our names and address on it, and Russia wasn't in the extradition business so Carver and his family could hide in plain sight with new identities.

Carver could take care of himself and his family, and when the time was right Jack and I both knew the crap was going to hit the fan, so to speak. But Carver must have had a good reason for waiting, so all we could do was wait for the next postcard to arrive.

Doug was just like his uncle in a lot of ways. He was off-the-charts genius, and I'd found it a challenge having to deal with someone who had the maturity of a regular teenager with the brain of an adult. Doug had some issues with the law when he'd hacked into some places the federal government frowned upon, so he'd come to live with us with the agreement that he could work for the good guys or go to prison.

The problem was, Doug wasn't really sure who the good guys were since his uncle was on the run from the people who were supposed to be the good guys, so he was walking a very gray area at the moment. I couldn't even say I blamed him all that much. But he was also a sixteen-year-old kid who was getting close to graduating from college, all while wearing an ankle bracelet. Doug had lived a lot of life for a sixteen-year-old.

"You're up early," I said when I answered the phone.

"I've got online class this morning," he said. "Business on the top, underwear on the bottom. No one will ever be the wiser."

"Not unless you stand up," I said dryly.

"Good point," he said. "I'm calling about breakfast."

"There's stuff in the pantry," I said automatically.

"I ate it all," he said. "You guys have been busy the last few days. No cereal. No Pop-Tarts. Nothing. I'm starving. I need brain energy for my class."

He was right. The last time I'd gotten groceries was Friday. Doug was a bottomless pit. I was pretty sure we spent more on groceries for Doug than all of our bills combined.

"Put in an order and have it delivered," I said. "Make sure you get the stuff I put on the list on the fridge and not just Doug food. Use the credit card in the drawer."

"10-4, kemo sabe," he said. "Though I could always charge it to the federal government if you're feeling adventurous."

"I don't really have time to go to jail today," I said. "I've got a case."

"Yeah, I saw it on the news," he said. "They said it's a kid. The park isn't too far from here."

"I'm about to do the autopsy."

"That's my cue to leave," he said.

"Have a good class," I said. "I'll be home at some point."

"Don't worry about me," he said. "Jack gave me a backlog of work to do for the sheriff's office. And then I've got a date with *Call of Duty*."

"Interesting," I said. "Maybe you'll meet a girl and get an actual date."

"Hey, the ladies love me. The Wizard never disappoints, on the screen or off."

"Good to know," I said. "Be safe and keep the security system on." And then I disconnected.

The reinforced steel door that led downstairs to the lab gave a whoosh of air as it opened and Lily and Sheldon came through. Both of them looked surprised to see me.

"What happened?" Lily asked. "I thought you were going with Martinez to question the neighbors."

Sheldon pushed his glasses up on his nose and shuffled his way toward the coffeepot, looking at it skeptically. I wasn't known for my coffee-making abilities. But all that mattered to me was the caffeine so I usually made it too strong for most people.

"Change of plans," I told her. "All the neighbors directly across from where the body was found were grouped together in their own little encampment. Plank had already questioned them by the time we made our way over."

"Ahh," Lily said. "I was wondering about all the old people. A guy that looked about a hundred years old jumped out in front of me when I tried to drive past the barricade. I still don't know what he was trying to accomplish."

"Did you know nearly one-third of all people over the age of eighty-five have some form of dementia?"

"No," Lily said. "But that's as good of a reason as any to jump in front of the coroner's van."

"Plank said our geriatric observers were in bed before the murder took place and none of them heard anything unusual either last night or early this morning."

"I saw the extent of damage done to that girl's body," Lily said. "She has a lot of physical trauma. I can't imagine she went out quiet."

"No," I agreed. "I think we'll find a witness. Sometimes people don't realize what they're hearing or seeing and blow it off as unimportant. Martinez decided priority was getting an identity on the girl. This was a violent and personal death. Once we can start digging into her history we can start narrowing down suspects."

"Twenty-three percent of child homicides under the age of thirteen are killed by a family member," Sheldon said, still eyeing the coffee. "I'm going to Lady Jane's to get donuts and a mochaccino. Anyone want anything?"

"Yes," Lily and I both said together.

My stomach rumbled at the thought of fried

dough and warm sugar, and I ran into my office and grabbed twenty dollars that I kept in the top drawer of my desk in case of emergencies.

I looked Sheldon up and down and said, "Don't you want to take your coveralls off?"

"No," he said. "I'm not wearing anything underneath. I was in such a hurry when Lily called I forgot my regular clothes. My mom is supposed to bring me my work clothes before the funeral home opens."

My mouth dropped open and I saw Lily's nose scrunch at the thought of Sheldon's doughy body loose inside his work coveralls.

"Besides," he said, "the girl behind the counter thinks it's cool to work with the dead. She might even go out with me if I'm wearing these."

"Just get my coffee black," I said before he could go into too much detail. "You're a lifesaver, Sheldon."

"Did you know that Life Savers candy was invented in 1912 because it lasted better in the summer months than chocolate?"

"I did not know that," Lily said. "Get some of the cinnamon cake donuts. I've got to study this afternoon and I need the extra sugar."

Sheldon didn't bother with his jacket, but pulled his wool cap out of the pocket of his coveralls and pulled it down over his comb-over. He gave a half-hearted wave and headed out the door.

"I've seen that girl at the donut shop," Lily said once he'd left. "She's into some weird stuff. You think Sheldon is going to get mixed up in some voodoo ritual sacrifice?"

"I wish I could say no for certain," I said. "I guess we'll know for sure if bodies start going missing."

I left the coffee brewing in the pot and put the creamer back in the fridge, and then grabbed the bag of samples I'd taken from the crime scene off the counter.

My parents had built the lab in the basement of the funeral home, so I couldn't take credit for the state-of-the-art equipment or the fact that it had security that rivaled Fort Knox. Only the best for Virginia's most-wanted criminals.

I coded us in and the pressurized metal door snicked open. The lights came on automatically when we crossed the threshold and the temperature dropped drastically. I had an elevator that was large enough to carry bodies down to the basement level, but otherwise I took the metal stairs. Our footsteps echoed as we descended into the deep cavern.

Everything in the lab was bright and white

and sterile, and the black body bag was a stark contrast to its surroundings. I grabbed my lab coat from the hook and a heavy apron and then I pulled my hair back from my face before collecting the correct forms from my desk.

Most people I met thought that being a coroner must be exciting work, but in reality it was a lot of administrative paperwork combined with the tedious and meticulous examination of the body. It was a game of details, patience, and perseverance. And the reward was a definitive cause of death that would help catch a killer.

Lily had suited up and adjusted the overhead lighting, and she was pulling down the zipper on the body bag.

"Recorder on," I said, pulling on a pair of latex gloves. "Dr. J.J. Graves performing the autopsy of minor Jane Doe on the fifth of April at —" I stopped and looked at the clock on the wall. "Oh-eight hundred hours and nineteen minutes. Assisting is Lily Jacobs.

"Ready to move her?" I asked.

"On your count," Lily said.

I counted down from three and Lily and I lifted the small body from the bag and laid her gently on the metal autopsy table.

"I'll put in a request for dental as soon as we can get molds taken," Lily said.

"Good," I told her. "That might save us some time. Let's go ahead and get her prints and get those sent over digitally so they can run them through the system. We might get lucky there if they took part in the county's next-gen fingerprint program."

I carefully removed the plastic bag over the victim's right hand and Lily took a set of digital fingerprints and sent them to Martinez to input in the State Fingerprint Identification Program.

"Weight of Jane Doe is thirty-two point two kilograms," I said into the recorder. "Height is one hundred and fifty-two centimeters."

"I hate the metric system," Lily said. "Why can't we just say she was seventy pounds and five feet tall? Who decided metric was the way to go?"

"The rest of the world," I said, lips twitching.

I brought the overhead light down some and moved it with me as I looked her over for any other identifying marks like birthmarks or scars, but there was nothing.

"You want x-rays next?" Lily asked.

"Yeah," I said. "And let's use the ultraviolet light on her and see if we can pull any more prints, just so we can narrow it down that we're dealing with one suspect."

It was monotonous and mindless work, something I'd done hundreds of times through the course of my career, but somehow posing the fragile body for the x-rays felt like an intrusion on her peace. She'd suffered greatly and been through more than any human should ever have to endure. I reminded myself that every piece of evidence I found would help put her killer away. It was all I could do.

"Fracture of the distal phalanx on the third and fourth digits of the right hand," I said into the recorder. "Distal radius fracture of the same hand. What does that mean?" I asked Lily.

"Umm," Lily said, looking intently at the x-rays. "Distal radius fractures are usually caused from falling and trying to catch yourself. And distal phalanx fractures are crushing fractures."

"Paint the picture," I encouraged.

"The victim fell backward and tried to catch herself, breaking her wrist, and then the killer stepped on her fingers and crushed them."

"Good," I said, nodding approvingly. "She's got a remodeled fracture on the same right arm. Maybe a couple of years old. No other breaks that I can see."

I took samples of the particulates in her heels and bagged and tagged them, along with the skin beneath her nails.

"Do you think..." Lily began and then swallowed. "Do you think she was sexually assaulted?"

I felt the weight on my chest again. "There's visible signs of blood and semen, which pisses me, but the more DNA we have the better to nail the bastard."

"I just don't understand how someone could do something like that right in the middle of the park. It wasn't even that late."

"Maybe he didn't do it there," I said, trying to run the scenario in my head. Because none of it made sense. "Maybe she escaped from somewhere. Jumped out of a car or something. It would explain why we didn't find her clothes."

"I hope she gouged his eyes out," Lily said.

"He didn't walk away unscathed," I told her. "She's got a good bit of flesh and dried blood under the nails of both hands."

I took blood and urine samples and finished my examination, making notes and drawings in the chart, and then I got the camera and took magnified photos of the ligature marks around her neck under the bright light.

"It's a weird pattern," Lily noted. "The bruising, I mean."

"Not a rope," I said. "There's no fibers embedded in the skin and no abrasions. It was something smooth. A scarf or tie maybe." I tilted her head slightly so I could follow the thin line of bruising up behind her ear to the back of her skull.

"See how it makes an upside-down *V* at the back of the neck?" I asked. "The killer choked her from behind. And he's significantly taller than she is so when he pulled the ligature it pulled everything upward." I made the motion with my hands to demonstrate to Lily. "And you see the contusions here?" I pointed to the area in the fatty tissue just under the jaw.

"Yes," Lily said, leaning down with the magnifier.

I turned the victim's hands over and there was a thin line across both of them.

"She got her hands up in time to fight against whatever he used to strangle her," she said, surprised. "A wire maybe?"

"A wire would have cut into the flesh with the amount of pressure he was using," I said, placing her hands back on the table, my brow furrowed in thought. "And I'm not sure cloth would leave the kinds of marks and the depth of the bruising she sustained."

"Do you think even with her hands up the strangulation was enough to incapacitate her?" Lily asked. "This could have been done pretty early on. He kidnaps her, strangles her, rapes her, and then somehow she escapes and ends up in the park."

"Very plausible," I said. "She's got vaginal tearing and bruising. Go ahead and run the tox screen on the blood and urine samples and let's see if anything comes back."

There was a simmering anger burning inside of me as I put on a mask and eye protection and reached for my scalpel. I was adult enough to know it was probably an accumulation of a lot of things in my life. But having to perform this autopsy was the icing on the cake.

CHAPTER FOUR

A LOT COULD HAPPEN IN TWO HOURS.

I was surprised to see Martinez sitting on one of the barstools at the kitchen island when Lily and I resurfaced a couple of hours later. I was also surprised to see Jack, Cole, Sheldon, and Emmy Lu.

"Doesn't anyone work around here?" I asked, closing the lab door behind me and tossing the file folder with my findings in front of Martinez.

Lily went over to Cole and he gave her a quick kiss on the top of the head. He was dressed for court in black dress Wranglers, a white button-down shirt and a black-and-silver paisley tie. He was without his usual Stetson, but his dark-blond hair had been freshly cut.

I wasn't at the place yet where I could make

eye contact with Jack, so I awkwardly made my way over to the coffeepot, looking him over out of my periphery. Jack was a couple of inches taller than Cole, and he commanded whatever room he was in. People were drawn to him, couldn't help but look at him, and I was no different. It didn't hurt that I knew exactly what his charcoal-gray suit was hiding underneath. But he looked as comfortable in a suit as he looked in uniform or jeans and a T-shirt.

I stared at the coffeepot for a few seconds, trying to remember why I'd come over, and then I remembered Sheldon hadn't brought us the coffee or donuts he'd promised.

"Your coffee got cold," Sheldon said, clearing his throat and pointing to the two cups in the middle of the island. "I got distracted so it took me longer to get back than I'd anticipated. Maybe I shouldn't have worn my coveralls. Leena was really impressed by them."

His face turned scarlet and I wondered what kind of horror story I was going to hear through the grapevine about Sheldon and the donut girl behind the counter.

"But here's your twenty dollars back because everything was on the house," he said, taking the crumpled money from his pocket.

I took the sweaty money and automatically

handed it to Jack since I didn't have any pockets anyway.

"What about the donuts?" I asked, eyeing the box on the table.

"Well," Sheldon said, clearing his throat again. "Martinez got here before I made it back from the donut shop and then he ate all your donuts before I could bring them down to you. And then everyone else showed up and had donuts too. Did you know it's actually Canadians who consume the most donuts per capita?"

There was a moment of awkward silence as we all stared at Sheldon. Except for me. I was still staring at the empty donut box.

"Wow," Martinez said, giving Sheldon a look that promised retribution. "You mean to tell me that you gave us Doc's and Lily's donuts? That doesn't seem right. How could you do that to them? They're down there working their fingers to the bone and I'm up here eating their donuts and learning things about table saws and witchcraft I never asked about. That's cold, man."

"I, uh..." Sheldon stuttered.

"That must have been some encounter with the donut girl," I said. "Table saws and witchcraft and you haven't even gone on a first date yet."

"I'm surprised the funeral home is still standing," Jack said. "You know how Jaye gets when she's hangry."

"And she still hasn't had any coffee," Lily added, giving me a wink.

"Good Lord," Emmy Lu said, scurrying around the kitchen to make coffee. "It's a miracle we're all still alive."

Emmy Lu was a short, plump woman with a cheerful disposition, a biting sarcasm she saved for those closest to her, and rosy cheeks. She mothered everyone, including her own five boys, and grieving families loved her.

Everyone chuckled and then Martinez lifted up the napkin that had been covering his plate and revealed two glazed donuts.

"I saved them for you before whistleblower Durkus could eat them all," Martinez said, rolling his eyes. "You gotta take care of your partner."

"Especially when she's supposed to buy lunch," I said, winking at Martinez and grabbing my donut before it disappeared. Cops were wily about things like donuts. I took a bite and then covered my mouth with a napkin and asked, "Why are you guys here? How's court?"

"A dog and pony show," Jack said. "We're on lunch recess. But I should be finished after today.

Cole is the lucky one. He gets to wear a tie all week."

"I only have one, so I hope they're not expecting a fashion show," Cole said, scowling. "Guy murders a bunch of people and the law-abiding citizens have to wear a jacket and tie as punishment. Talk about injustice."

"Will you be taking over as supervisor on this case once they cut you loose?" Martinez asked.

Jack arched a brow and nodded. "I already talked to Lieutenant Colburn. You can report directly to me, and I'll help with the legwork. It beats the hell out of court."

There was an undercurrent to the conversation that was confusing, and I wondered what was going on between Colburn and Martinez. Lieutenant Colburn had certainly had his ups and downs on the job, but as far as I knew he was well liked by most of the guys.

"Sounds like a plan," Martinez said. "It's good to be on the winning team. Besides, Doc's going to buy us lunch all week."

"Now you're just rubbing it in," Cole said.

"All week?" I asked. "I don't think so. I'm not made of money. How am I supposed to pay Emmy Lu and Lily and Sheldon if I'm buying you lunch every day? Your shoes cost more than my whole wardrobe."

Martinez looked me up and down with pity. "You do look like a hobo today. I'm going to have to insist you change before we go out in public together. I've got a reputation to uphold."

I shoved the rest of the donut in my mouth and growled.

"But I'll concede to you buying every other day," Martinez said. "You're married to Daddy Warbucks over there. That should count for something. Besides, all my funds are tied up at the moment while we're going through an acquisition. I'm living paycheck to paycheck."

Cole whistled and shook his head. "How are you even functioning, living like a commoner?"

"Seventy-eight percent of Americans live paycheck to paycheck," Sheldon said.

"I believe it," Cole said. "Ahh, the American dream."

I caught Jack's gaze and froze, confused by the quick wink he gave me and wishing I was pulled close to him like Cole was holding Lily. I missed his touch. And I missed the conversation. Jack was my best friend. The last few days had felt like I was missing part of myself, and in reality, I was.

The spell was broken when Emmy Lu handed me a cup of coffee. I nodded thanks and then quickly looked down into the cup, trying to gather my thoughts.

I'd needed this break after the last two hours. I'd needed to have stupid conversation and eat donuts and pretend like things were normal. But the few minutes of mindless peace had to come to an end.

"If anyone is interested," I said. "We got an identity and cause of death for the victim."

"I figured you'd get around to it," Martinez said, tapping his finger on the manila envelope.

"Victim is twelve-year-old Evelyn Lidle," I said. "Evie to family and friends. Her prints weren't on file, but we were able to get a match with dental records. She is the daughter of Councilman Everett Lidle."

"Cause of death?" Martinez asked.

"Blunt force trauma to the head," I said. "I believe the strangulation was just a way to incapacitate. It's what happened between the strangulation and the killing blow to the skull that's hazy. The lack of fibers and the bruising pattern makes me think you're looking for something like an electrical cord."

"Sexual assault?" Jack asked.

"Yes," I said. "She had significant bruising and tearing. Last meal looked like chicken noodle soup and crackers, ingested a few hours before she died. She had traces of promethazine in her system, but nothing out of the ordinary."

"What's that?" Martinez asked.

"Anti-nausea medication," I answered. "It's prescription only. There were only traces in her system, so she could have ingested anywhere from twelve to twenty-four hours before her death."

"So Councilman Lidle's daughter had chicken noodle soup for dinner, was kidnapped, strangled, raped, beaten, and eventually killed with several violent blows to the head and her parents haven't reported her missing?" Martinez asked incredulously.

"Was she at school yesterday?" Jack asked.

"She's at one of those fancy boarding schools in DC with all the politicians' kids so they don't like to give out information. I had Chen call the mom and pretend to be from the school and checking on the kid. The mom said Evie was sick with a stomach virus."

"Which would explain the chicken noodle soup and the promethazine," Lily said.

"Sounds like you two need to go break the news to the parents of their daughter's death," Jack said. "Maybe they have an explanation for why they didn't report her missing."

"Any word on the creepy guy from the scene or the missing neighbor?" I asked. "What's his name? Kent O'Leary."

"Found the creepy guy on the door-to-doors," Martinez said. "Or at least Plank did. Lives on the other side of the park and said he's introduced himself to Edith Norton and Myrtle Sparrow at least a dozen times when he walks his dog in the park. Apparently they keep calling the cops on him. I found the records. Wachowski responded the last time and he finally had to tell Edith Norton she'd be charged with filing a false police report if she didn't stop calling in on the neighbor. That was about four months ago.

"Creepy neighbor's name is Joel Grainger," Martinez continued. "He works for a top-tier forensics lab in DC, so maybe that explains the creepy factor. He's got high-level security clearance, and he's alibied for the night in question. He said Edith Norton tried to kidnap his dog once."

"Gotta love neighbors," Cole said.

"Plank tracked down Kent O'Leary in Panama City Beach," Martinez continued. "He's been there since Friday for his brother's wedding. He's in the clear. Which leaves us with no one, so I'm anxious to talk to the family."

"Give me fifteen minutes to shower and change," I said.

I took my coffee and started heading toward the office and the small bathroom that was attached to it, but I did a detour and headed toward Jack instead. We both knew how important goodbyes were, especially in his line of work. Every goodbye could be the last.

He looked at me expectantly, his mouth curved in a small smile, and he leaned down to meet my lips. Jack wasn't the sort to hold grudges and he forgave easily, and I could feel the tension leave my body as our lips touched. Nothing had been resolved. But it was a start.

CHAPTER FIVE

WHEN I WALKED BACK INTO THE KITCHEN FIFTEEN minutes later it was empty except for Martinez. He was still at the counter reading through the autopsy report.

Martinez looked up and stared at me appraisingly. "Much better," he said. "You clean up nice, Doc."

My ability to clean up nice had everything to do with genetics and nothing to do with giving a crap about my appearance. I'd been working life-or-death situations since my med school days. People coding on the table didn't care if my hair and makeup were red carpet ready.

Both of my parents had dark, almost black, hair, just like me. But I'd always wondered where I'd gotten my gray eyes since they'd both had brown eyes. They'd always told me it was some distant relative and recessed genes, but it had just been more lies on top of many.

My hair was still damp since I'd only run the hair dryer over it briefly, but it was short and straight and it would dry soon enough and fall where it was supposed to around my jawline. I rarely wore makeup—my lashes were thick and dark and I'd been told people would pay good money for my lips, whatever that meant. I had high cheekbones and good olive skin, so I generally slathered on moisturizer and called myself good to go.

I knew we'd be making the rounds today of city officials and probably the press, so I pulled on black leggings and a pale gray, lightweight sweater that matched my eyes to ward off the damp chill. I'd worn nothing but my black rain boots for what seemed like the past month, and my nice black raincoat I used for funerals was hanging in the mudroom.

"Where'd everybody go?" I asked.

"Sheriff and Cole headed back to court," he said. "Lily said she needed to study. And Sheldon got a call from the hospital to pick up a body. Emmy Lu went back to the office to start the paperwork. Looks like you're back in the funeral business."

"So much for having a couple of days off."

"Death is the one thing you can always count on," Martinez said. "At some point everyone is going to do it."

No truer words had ever been spoken.

"Speaking of," he said. "Let's go pay a visit to the Lidles. I hate giving death notices to families."

"I can't imagine it's anyone's favorite thing to do," I said. "But when it's done well it's a gift. As messed up as my whole family situation was, I remember the knock on my door and Jack standing there to tell me my parents were dead. It's a lot easier to hear news like that coming from someone who cares. The Lidles' daughter is dead. Death isn't supposed to be easy."

Martinez blew out a sigh. "I guess when you put it that way."

I had to admit, tagging along with Martinez was weird. Jack and I had a rhythm when we went to give death notifications. We also had a rhythm when it came to questioning potential suspects. I had no idea about Martinez's rhythm. Being with Martinez felt a little like going to a bar and seeing an old boyfriend from high school. There was a little bit of history there, but I had no idea who Martinez really was, and I wasn't really sure what we should talk about.

Martinez drove one of the new unmarked black SUVs the department had recently gotten, and I climbed into the passenger seat, buckling my seat belt.

"Why don't you type in the address on the computer," Martinez said, looking both ways before doing a U-turn in the middle of the street. "They live in Nottingham."

"Ooh, fancy," I said, shifting the laptop attached in his police unit toward me and typing Everett Lidle's name into the database. As a councilman, his personal information was protected, so the mobile data terminal was the best resource we had for that kind of sensitive information. "I guess there are perks to being a councilman."

"It doesn't hurt that he owns all those car dealerships either," Martinez said. "Or that his mother is the heiress to a ketchup kingdom."

"Yeah, I guess that doesn't hurt," I said. "Sometimes I think it's weird that Nottingham and Bloody Mary can be on the same planet, much less in the same county."

"Nottingham is where all the tech money is," Martinez said, tapping his fingers impatiently on the wheel. "It used to be a lot like Bloody Mary, but the tech giants started infiltrating, and then all of a sudden it became a hub for artificial intelligence and data mining."

"Jack calls it a mini Silicon Valley," I said.

"He's not far off. And then there's Newcastle. Once they revitalized things, that's where all the young professionals relocated. It's full of townhomes and art districts and eclectic shops that will stop being trendy in the next decade."

"And King George Proper?" I asked, enjoying hearing his take on the towns that surrounded us.

"King George Proper is full of military personnel from the naval center and a bunch of college students from KGU. It tends to be a catchall for people who want to commute into DC and those who are stuck and don't know where to go next."

"And Bloody Mary is still the same small farming town with people holding on to their land, the Second Amendment, and the American Dream. Or what's left of it."

"There's a lot of people angry at Jack for holding the line on that and not giving in to the big developers who want to buy up all the farming land. And he made some powerful government enemies when he refused those federal prisons to be built here. That was billions of dollars those investors lost out on."

"The people from King George aren't angry," I said, shrugging. "And they're the only ones who matter since they have to live here. It's their votes that count. But this is a great place to live, and the word is out. We're already seeing an influx of people moving here. With it they're bringing crime and jacking up the housing market. I can see a time in the not-so-distant future where we lose all of this."

"Yeah, well," Martinez said. "I'm hoping I'll be dead by then so it can be the next generation's burden to bear. All I'm saying is you and Jack need to be careful."

I stared out the window as we left Bloody Mary and made our way toward Nottingham. The streets widened, the trees disappeared, and the shops and restaurants all had the same stone fronts so everything looked uniform. There were no more chain restaurants and bargain stores. Instead the shops became luxury stores, the restaurants high end, and there was an increase in plastic surgeons' offices. That in itself said a lot about Nottingham.

Martinez's thoughts of dying before society got too bad were not unique to him. Jack and I had been having the same conversations over the past months while trying to decide if we wanted to bring a child into the world. Maybe our jobs made us more sensitive to the life and death side of things, but we'd ultimately agreed that we did want children and that we'd do everything within our power to protect them and continue to make our area of the world as safe a place as possible.

Now I just had to live up to my side of the bargain.

I felt a tear leak from the corner of my eye, but I was still looking out the window and away from Martinez's view. I was a mess. And I was struggling big-time. Just to get through the days like a normal person. I almost didn't recognize myself, and it was becoming harder to act normal around the people who saw me on a day-to-day basis, when in reality I was falling apart.

I didn't know what conversations might trigger tears, just like I didn't know what conversations would trigger the guilt and anger inside of me. Somedays I'd feel pity for myself and others just straight-up defiance and I'd tell my body to get a grip.

I'd known earlier this morning that standing over the body of twelve-year-old Evie Lidle was going to have an impact on my mental state. And I was having to find new ways to cope with the strain of not being able to have my own child. I was resilient. And more than a little hardheaded.

And just like always, I straightened my spine and pushed it all down to be dealt with at another time.

"How come I've never met your family?" I asked Martinez. "You grew up in Bloody Mary, and I know just about everyone."

"You do know my family," he said. "Or at least some of them. My brother and his wife own the taco place you like to go to. And my Tia Maria owns the bath and body shop on the square."

"Get out of town!" I said shocked. "I love that place. How did I not know that?"

"My family has its issues," he said. "Just like any family, I guess. But let's just say there's a little resentment among certain members of my family, so they don't always claim me. I wasn't kidding when I said I was my abuela's favorite. She's very Catholic, and when I was baptized as a baby a priest told her I was to be protected and favored because I held the key to our family's legacy."

"I can see why there'd be resentment," I said, grinning. "That's a pretty big obligation to put on a baby's shoulders."

"I was the most loved and hated kid you could ever imagine," he said, smiling good-naturedly so the dimple in his cheek showed. "My great-grandparents hit it big in the oil boom in west Texas, and then my grandfather tripled the family fortune once he took the reins. But his two brothers had ties to the Mexican cartels and they were always in trouble, and I remember as a kid the extra security around the house and the fear in my parents' eyes. One of my abuelo's employees borrowed his truck one afternoon and it exploded before he could pull out of the driveway.

"Oh, wow," I said.

"It was meant to kill, and my abuela told him that God had spared his life for a reason, and that he needed to figure out what that reason was. So my abuelo decided the best thing to do was to sell the business and get out of Texas. He and my abuela, my parents, aunts and uncles and cousins all picked up and moved here. I was about to start my freshman year of high school."

"And then you became a cop," I said, understanding what drove Martinez a little better now.

"Oh yeah," he said. "I always wanted to be one. There were several cops who worked off-duty details trying to protect my family, and I watched the homicide detectives come and work the case after the pipe bomb. I was obsessed. I realized pretty early on that it was a calling to want to protect those who were weaker or who needed help."

"Nice to know you're not doing it for the paycheck," I said.

He snorted out a laugh. "When my abuelo died he left me in charge of the family business."

"I thought he sold the business," I said.

"He sold the oil business," Martinez corrected. "But my abuelo knew a thing or two about investing money, the stock market, and real estate holdings. So I'm officially the president of the Toro Corporation, though I've hired people to see to the day-to-day operations. I don't have the time or energy for more than quarterly board meetings at this point."

"And your family?" I asked.

"Grateful that I make sure they all get dividends and have healthy portfolios so none of them ever has to work another day in their lives. But resentful that I hold the purse strings and that abuela doesn't hide it that I'm the chosen one."

"I can see why she'd be upset about you not continuing on the Martinez line," I said, brows raised.

"Yeah, well," he said uncomfortably. "Like you said, it was a lot of pressure to put on a little kid about being the key to the family legacy. I had a rebellious moment in college where I decided I was tired of being everyone's puppet and that's when I got it done."

I wasn't sure what it was, but I sensed a little bit of regret in Martinez's youthful indiscretion.

"You can always get it reversed," I told him.

He grunted and then turned onto High Pointe Avenue, where trees and manicured flower beds lined the street, and the small lake the community was built around glinted like glass in the distance.

He pulled into the curved driveway of a traditional Colonial with red brick and white columns just as the sky opened up and the rain started to fall.

CHAPTER SIX

"Maybe no one is home," I said, looking around. "No cars in the driveway."

"Maybe they park in the garage," Martinez said.

"Do people actually do that?"

"That's the rumor," he said.

I pulled the hood up on my raincoat and opened the door, hurrying to the covered front entry.

"Is it me or does this kind of look like the house from *Home Alone*?"

Martinez snorted out a laugh and rang the doorbell. It wasn't long before an older woman with short silver hair answered the door. She wore neat navy slacks and a white blouse.

"I'm Detective Martinez," he said, showing her his badge. "And this is Dr. Graves. We need to speak to the Lidles."

A look of fear flashed across the woman's eyes and she licked her lips nervously. "Only Mrs. Lidle is here," she said. "The girls are all home from school sick, so things have been a little hectic this morning. Come in out of the wet."

We thanked her and stepped into a generous foyer. There was a large staircase of pale oak and a round table with fresh flowers in a vase. I was surprised at the warmth inside. It was homey, despite the size of the house. There were obvious signs that a family lived here—framed pictures on the wall behind the stairs, a toy car stuck under the entry table, and a pink backpack tossed in a corner.

"Do you live here, Ms...?" Martinez asked her.

"Oh," she said, surprised. "I'm Marsha Callan." She extended her hand to Martinez politely and then to me. "Sorry, I'm not used to the police showing up at the door. My brother got into a bit of trouble with drugs when he was in high school, and my memories of the cops showing up at our house aren't my favorite."

"No, I could see why that would color your experience," Martinez said, smiling kindly to put her at ease. "No one is in trouble."

"I'm the housekeeper," she said. "I come in two days a week and clean up, do laundry, and do some meal prep for the rest of the week. Mrs. Lidle has her hands full between the girls and all their activities."

My gaze drifted to the big family portrait on the wall, and I stared into the face of Evie Lidle, sitting nestled between her parents and four sisters. They all looked like a carbon copy of each other—dandelion fluff white hair and blue eyes. The girls looked just like their mother, and in the center of the picture was Everett Lidle, smiling proudly. They looked like an all-American family.

"Do you know when Mr. Lidle will be available?" Martinez asked her.

"He's out of town," she said. "He's been gone since Sunday after church at a conference in San Francisco. He's not due back until tomorrow night."

"Is there a place where I can talk to Mrs. Lidle privately?" he asked.

She hesitated for a moment, looking somberly back and forth between me and Martinez, and then she nodded. "Go on into the family room," she said, pointing to our left. "I've already cleaned up in there so you have a place to sit. I'll go get Mrs. Lidle for you and send her down."

She hesitated again as she started to make her way up the stairs, and then she looked back at us. "Should I," she said, and then paused. "Should I call Mrs. Lidle's mother and have her come over?"

Martinez's eyes were filled with compassion when he nodded. "Yes, ma'am. I think that would be a good idea."

She nodded again and then hurried up the stairs, and I followed Martinez into the family room.

"Not what I was expecting," Martinez said, blowing out a breath. "This is a good house. Homey."

The family room had a large sectional sofa and two oversized chairs in front of a big wood-burning fireplace. There was a large-screen television hanging above the mantel and built-in bookcases on either side that were filled to the brim with fiction and nonfiction alike. It was eclectic and unorganized, and stuck between two of the books was a half-dressed Barbie doll.

Neither of us sat, but stood in the center of a well-used and loved room, waiting for what was to come. We only had to wait a few minutes to hear footsteps coming rapidly down the stairs.

The Sunday-best Mrs. Lidle from the family portrait was long gone, and in her place was a regular mom dressed in gray sweats and thick athletic socks. Her hair was piled up in a disheveled ponytail, and she was makeup free. There was a piece of cracker stuck in her hair.

"Hi," she said, coming into the room to greet us. "Marsha told me you needed to speak to me. But I'll tell you it's really not a good time. All the girls are down with the stomach flu. I can't decide if my husband is a psychic and knew leaving town was the wise decision, or if he's really just that lucky."

"We're sorry to have to intrude," Martinez said. "But this is truly urgent."

Her smile faded and she said, "Is everything okay? Did something happen to Everett?"

"No, ma'am," Martinez said. "Why don't we sit down over here. Your home is lovely, by the way."

Martinez took her elbow and led her to the couch, and she let him, sitting down hesitantly.

"Most days it feels like a demolition zone," she said. "Thank God for Marsha. Y'all are making me nervous. If there's bad news I'd prefer you just tell me."

Martinez nodded. We both knew this was the best way, just straight out and to the point.

"I'm sorry to have to tell you that we found your daughter Evelyn deceased early this morning. She was killed."

She looked at us like we were both crazy before she shook her head. "Evie? That's impossible. Evie's not dead. She's just been sick. She missed school yesterday. She went to a birthday party Saturday and brought home a virus. All the kids who were at the party got it. She went to spend the night at Everett's mom and dad's house so she wouldn't spread it to the rest of us." Her voice trailed off. "But that obviously didn't work."

"Mrs. Lidle," Martinez said.

"Jenny," she said, the color draining from her face and her motions panicked. "Let me call my mother-in-law. You'll see this is a big misunderstanding. It's not Evie. It's some other girl."

"Jenny," I said softly. "My name is Dr. Graves."

She nodded and said, "I know who you are." By this time big fat tears were welling in her eyes.

"We're very sorry for your loss," I told her. "I confirmed her identity this morning through dental records. She broke her arm a couple of years ago?"

Jenny nodded slowly. "Everett got her a skateboard for her birthday after I told him not to. She fell off and broke her arm. I was so mad." And then she buried her face in her hands and wept with the grief of a mother.

"Jenny," Martinez said, touching her shoulder gently. "I can't even imagine what you're going through right now, but we need to ask you some very important questions. The sooner we can get information the faster we can find out who did this to Evie."

"I need Everett," she said. "How do I even tell him? He and Evie had a special bond. Of all the girls, the two of them were like peas in a pod." Her breath caught on a sob and I handed her a tissue.

"Marsha called your mother," I told her. "She'll be here soon so someone can be with you and the girls."

"Oh God," she said, clapping her hands over her mouth. "The girls, the girls. This can't be real. It can't be real."

"You said Evie was at your in-laws'?" Martinez prompted. "When was the last time you talked to her?"

Jenny bit her lip hard, trying to get herself under control. "Umm...around four or five o'clock yesterday. I called Kitty and told her I was knee deep in vomit and she told me Evie had been feeling much better and was going stir crazy. She was going to have Molly make home-made chicken soup for dinner, and she told me she was happy to keep her another day or two until the other girls got better. Things got pretty crazy here after that so I didn't check in again. I should have checked in."

"You did what you had to do and focused on the other girls," I reassured her. "You're a good mom."

"Molly?" Martinez asked.

"Molly Ryan. She's their chef," Jenny said. "She's been with them more than forty years. I think she worked for Kitty's parents before that. Most of their staff has been there a long time. Kitty is very sweet. They love her."

The meal and timing lined up with what I'd found in the victim's stomach during the autopsy. Which meant Kitty Lidle was probably the last person to see Evie alive. I looked at Martinez and he must have had the same thought because he stood and took out his phone and then walked out into the foyer.

His voice was muffled but I could hear him call for units to respond to Kitty Lidle's home, and for medics to stand by. If Evie Lidle had been kidnapped out of one of the wealthiest people in the state's high-security mansion, then it was very possible we might have more bodies on our hands.

"Tell me about your girls," I said to Jenny, just to keep her mind occupied. "I saw the portrait out in the foyer."

"Things can change a lot in two years," she said, sadly. "We always had problems with my oldest daughter, Emma. Rebellion. From about the time she was Evie's age until she left home. Drugs, sex, alcohol, you name it. We tried to get her into rehab and she'd just lash out at us. We didn't know what to do, and I know it scared the younger girls. She graduated from high school last year and left home. She was only seventeen. We haven't been in contact with her. We don't even know where she is. Everett thinks his father is sending her money."

"I'm sorry to hear that," I said as Martinez came back in and sat down.

"Evie was like our redemption child," she said. "Such a good girl. Never got into trouble and always taking care of her little sisters like she was their mother. I had two miscarriages between Emma and Evie, so we had a bit of a gap. And then after Evie came we never had a problem conceiving again. Elise came a year after Evie, and Eloise a year after Elise. We thought we were done and then I found out I was pregnant with Estelle. She's in kindergarten."

She looked at me intently, desperation in her eyes. "Does it make me a bad mother that I don't want to know what happened to Evie?" she asked, fresh tears coursing down her cheeks. "If I don't hear what happened, I won't be able to imagine it in my head when I close my eyes. Does that make me a coward?"

"No," Martinez said. "It makes you a mother."

"Did she..." Jenny paused on a watery breath. "Did she suffer?"

"No," I lied. Sometimes lying was the kindest thing you could do for a grieving family. They could read the autopsy report, but most didn't. It made things too real.

"It's possible that Evie's murder was a kidnapping gone wrong," Martinez said. "Especially since she was taken from her grandparents' home. Has anyone ever threatened your family?"

"Sure," she said, wrapping her arms tight around her torso. "It comes with the territory, I guess. I didn't grow up like Everett did with body-guards and high-security private schools, so that world was a shock to me after we were married. They all talked about death threats and kidnappings as if it were normal."

"There were threats?" Martinez asked. "Any recent?"

"Not recent," she said. "When Everett was a child. When his father decided to run for a Senate seat, but that was the only time I'm aware of. Everett has an older brother and younger sister, so they were always surrounded by security. Someone tried to run their driver off the road after he'd picked them up from school, and apparently a guy got the door open and was trying to pull Janet out of the car. She was the youngest and smallest. But it was in a crowded area and several men rushed the kidnappers. They escaped and security was increased. I don't think they had any more attempts after that.

"Our girls have lived a mostly normal life," she continued. "Or at least we try to give them that. They go to Dolley Madison School for Girls in DC. The school has good security, but we've never had any issues here. Not even after Everett was elected to the county council. Mostly just some strongly worded letters disapproving of his stance on different issues."

I winced, thinking of Sheldon's mother.

"Do your in-laws still receive threats?" I asked.

"If they do they don't mention it," she said, shrugging. "Kitty no longer runs the family business, though she is still on the board of directors. She retired several years ago and Everett's older brother, Phin, sees to all the day-to-day operation. Kitty doesn't really like to leave the house anymore. She's always been like that. Robert is the social one. He likes the political scene, and he's heavily involved with lobbyist groups, especially now that my sister-in-law is a congresswoman."

"That would be Janet Lidle-Downey?"

"Yes," Jenny answered. "Robert keeps an apartment in the city so he can stay in the middle of things."

"Do Robert and Kitty have marital problems? Financial problems?" Martinez asked.

Jenny dropped her head down to look at her knees, as if the weight of holding it up was too much to bear. Exhaustion seemed to blanket her. "No, I think they've always just coexisted. To hear Everett talk about them, I don't think they were ever a love match. Kitty's father acquired Robert's father's company. It was more of a business merger with marriage on the side.

"Kitty had a family legacy to uphold, and I think Robert always felt like he needed to live up to it. They never fight or anything. They always seem content to just enjoy what they enjoy and leave the other to do whatever they please. But they're usually together for family functions."

"Evie never mentioned anyone bothering her at school or any other activities she's involved in?" I asked.

"No," Jenny said. "She's never had any issues. I don't understand why anyone would hurt her. She was such a sweet girl. So sweet." And then Jenny Lidle curled herself into a ball and wept.

CHAPTER SEVEN

It wasn't long after that Jenny's mother arrived, and Martinez and I left them to find comfort in each other. We got back into Martinez's SUV, both of us soaked to the skin, and his phone gave a shrill ring.

It was connected to Bluetooth and the call came out over the speakers. "Martinez," he said.

"You were right about the medic call," Plank said. "Kitty Lidle was found unresponsive this morning by the house manager, an Astrid Nielsen. She'd already called 911 by the time your call came through."

"Is she still alive?"

"Barely," Plank said. "The EMTs weren't sure what happened to her, but her BP and pulse were dangerously low, and she's not responsive. They're taking her to King George Memorial."

"Anyone else in the household harmed?" Martinez asked.

"Not that we're aware," he said. "I've cordoned it off as a crime scene for now. The house manager and chef were both on the premises this morning. I'm not sure about other staff."

"We're on the way there," Martinez said. "Should take us about fifteen minutes. Don't let anyone in. That house is the last place Evie Lidle was seen alive."

Martinez disconnected and then flipped on his sirens before doing a 180 in the middle of the road and heading back toward Bloody Mary. The senior Lidles technically lived in Bloody Mary, but if their house had been built on the opposite side of the street they would have been in another county entirely.

Caledon Road wasn't far from the house where Jack and I lived. It was a curvy road and snaked an outline next to Caledon State Park. It was one of the most beautiful areas in the entire state and it was all framed by the majesty of the Potomac River. It was easy to see why the homes were large and far and few between.

We'd had a murder off Caledon Road not too

long ago, and it was hard not to think about all the things that could have gone wrong during that op. Jack and I both could've been killed, and it had been a closer call than I was comfortable with.

"I hate having to come out here," Martinez said, echoing my thoughts.

"Yeah," I said. "I'm starting to think leaving my weapon at home was a bad idea. Who knew the most expensive area in the entire county would become the most dangerous?"

We arrived at the Lidles' property in ten minutes instead of fifteen, but it took us another five to drive past the white rail fence and the acres of rolling hills. I assumed the Arabians the Lidles bred and raised were all in the barn since the rain hadn't let up.

"I hope they get paid well," I said, pointing to the cameramen and reporters that were set up under a tent across the street.

"Bottom feeders," Martinez scoffed. "They would have heard the call go out from dispatch after the 911 call. The Lidles are always news." He got on the radio and said to dispatch, "Could you get Fish and Wildlife on the phone and let them know the media has taken up residence on federal land?"

I shook my head, but couldn't help but smile.

There were times to work with the media. But other times they got in the way more than they helped.

The estate was gated, and Martinez pulled in, prepared to show his badge to the guard in the gatehouse.

A man standing in the gatehouse held up his hand for us to stop. He was dressed in jeans and a black anorak with a hood. It was covered in droplets of water.

"Cop?" I asked.

"Not that I know," Martinez said, rolling down his window. He held up his badge and the man looked closer, studying it intently.

"They're expecting you inside," he said, and then the gate opened.

Martinez smiled. "Who are you?"

"Alan Goble," he said. "I'm head of the security for the Lidles."

Alan Goble stood just under six feet and held himself like a fighter. His shoulders and arms were well defined in his T-shirt, and a tattoo wound intricately up his left forearm and under his sleeve.

His face was chiseled in an interesting way, and his nose had been broken at some point. His hair was almost black and his eyes a shade lighter. I recognized eyes like his. They were eyes that had seen some things over the course of his life. I was pegging him as either ex-military or cop, but I wasn't sure which.

"Who was on shift last night?" Martinez asked.

"I have a round-the-clock team, six men on every shift. I can get you a list of who was on duty. You'll see guards at all the perimeter gates and two who ride in black vehicles covering the property grounds. They change position every two hours."

He looked past Martinez to me, sizing me up with a quick look. I arched a brow back at him.

"You're not a cop," he said.

"Coroner," I replied.

He nodded. "I heard about Evie on the news. Poor kid. I've already gotten a call from Mr. Lidle. My head is probably going to be on a platter in the next few hours."

"We're going to need to talk to you," Martinez said. "We'll come back out and do a full interview and get the list of your team that was on duty once we have a full picture inside."

"I'll be here," he said, closing the door to the guardhouse.

"Impression?" Martinez asked as he drove through the impressive wrought-iron gate.

"Seemed more worried about his job than the

brutal murder of a kid. I didn't like the way he looked me over. Reminded me of a blind date I went on once. Like he was sizing me up to see if I was acceptable."

"He was checking you out," Martinez said. "Saw your wedding ring and didn't bother with the rest of the scan. I recognize the signs."

I squirmed uncomfortably in my seat. I knew there was a reason I didn't miss the dating scene.

It was another five-minute drive up the winding, tree-lined driveway to the front of the estate.

"Amazing what a little ketchup can get a person in this country," I said, looking at the monstrosity in front of me with awe.

Jack came from wealth, so I was used to some of the privileges it brought. But Jack had also come from a family who had worked for their money, and he was no stranger to physical labor. But this kind of wealth was off the charts. Everett Lidle's parents were in the exclusive billionaire club. Despite having homes all over the world, they'd decided to make their permanent residence here.

The Lidles weren't from King George County. I didn't even know how they ended up here. But I remember the complaints from when I was a kid when they'd built this monstrosity of a house. They'd bought up two farms that were struggling and had paid more than double than what they were worth at the time. And then they'd eventually appeased the community by saying there were keeping the land intact through their Arabian enterprise.

Though to give credit where credit was due, they'd stayed true to their word. They'd kept the land and not sold it off for millions of dollars, which was what it was worth now. And their horses frequently placed or won in the derby.

The mansion was built at a right angle, modern and impressive and white, with balconies on all three levels that overlooked a massive swimming pool and entertainment area. I doubted the Lidles made it down to the stables on a day-to-day basis, if ever, and the stables and any hint of animals were almost a mile down the road, along with several smaller cottages where I assumed staff lived.

"Nice place," Martinez said.

"Hey, I'm sure you're used to this stuff as the president of Toro," I said, waggling my brows. "You ever hobnob with the Lidles?"

Martinez snorted. "Are you kidding? That's a club that only cokeheads and terrorists can get into. They've got *money*. I just have regular money."

"Yeah, I figured as much," I said. "I saw a

thing on TMZ a few years ago about Everett's brother, Phin, and how he was dating a hotel heiress and a member of the royal family at the same time. The three of them got caught in a ménage à trois and there were all kinds of drugs and hidden cameras in this seedy motel room. But they were in the UK when it happened so the royal family tried to bury it so it didn't embarrass the family. Phin's wife took him to the cleaners in his divorce."

"Look at you keeping up with the gossip news," Martinez said.

"TMZ was always playing at the hospital when I worked the night shift," I said. "It was hard not to see it."

There was a covered drive that looked like someone had stacked giant white tables on one another and Martinez parked beneath it, leaving room for others to get around him if needed.

Martinez's phone rang just as we were about to exit and he answered it from the screen. "Detective Martinez," he said.

"Detective Martinez," an unfamiliar voice said. "This is Robert Lidle. I believe you just arrived at my home." His voice was gruff and no nonsense.

Martinez's brows rose in surprise. I knew cops' cell phones were protected, so it wasn't just anyone who had access other than dispatch or personal acquaintances.

"How can I help you, Mr. Lidle?" Martinez asked.

"I'm sure it's difficult for a man in your position to understand, but my family is under attack and the media is in a frenzy." There was a slight pause as he cleared his throat. "I know you all have a job to do, but with a family like ours, sometimes these matters must be dealt with more delicately and out of the public eye. We're under a great deal of scrutiny all of the time, and situations like this only add fuel to the fire of competitors in the business or even those who'd like to see projects I'm working to get through Congress to fail."

"You mean situations like your granddaughter being murdered and your wife being taken away by ambulance?" Martinez asked.

"I want justice for my granddaughter," he said. "I can only imagine how her poor mother and my son are coping right now. And the King George Sheriff's Office has my full support. As I'm sure you know, the Lidle family donates a healthy amount each year at the first responders' ball and also to your sheriff during election season so you can all have those nice new vehicles and top-notch equipment."

"And we appreciate your support," Martinez cut in smoothly.

"But I believe the best thing for our family would be for you to wrap up your investigation quickly. The longer this drags out, the harder it is on everyone. And my responsibility as the head of this family is to make sure that we can grieve in peace, without people poking into our lives."

Martinez's fingers tapped against the steering wheel and his gaze was thoughtful. "Mr. Lidle," he said. "We're going to do everything in our power to make sure that your granddaughter's killer is brought to justice quickly."

"Good, good," he said. "I'm glad we understand each other." And then he disconnected the call.

I pursed my lips and then said, "Maybe I got the wrong impression."

"No, I don't think you did," he said.

"But it sounded to me like Robert Lidle wanted you to not dig into his family too deeply under threat of him pulling their financial resources."

Martinez sighed. "Yeah, that's pretty much my take too. He's going to be real pissed when I schedule an interview with him."

"I'm guessing our friend Alan Goble gave him

a quick call as soon as he shut the door in our face."

"I guess he's trying to keep his head off that silver platter."

I grabbed my medical bag out of habit and pushed open the door and the wind caught it so it almost slammed closed on me. Even under the cover we could feel the spray of rain from the wind.

The front door was enormous, made of black metal and glass, and Plank pushed it in the center so it swiveled and opened a space almost as large as an entire wall.

"That's quite a door," Martinez said.

"Seems a little unnecessary," I said as we walked inside.

"Maybe they need to let a lot of people in at one time," Martinez said. "Like an army."

"Or they need a new way to work on their upper body strength," Plank said. "That door is heavy."

"Did you just make a joke, Plank?" Martinez asked.

"It won't happen again, sir."

The response was so deadpan I couldn't help but laugh. Plank was coming along. Another decade on the job and he'd be as smartass and cynical as the rest of the cops on the force.

The entire house seemed to be made of windows and black metal. The walls that were solid were white and covered with expensive art. I was afraid to touch anything. It looked like a museum. A cold, sterile museum with art that looked like it had been created by toddlers.

"The house manager and chef are in the kitchen," Plank said. "No one else has attempted to contact us through the gate, and I've seen no other staff."

"Where was Kitty Lidle found?" Martinez asked.

"Third floor," Plank said, heading up the black metal stairs.

We followed him. There was a clear glass railing, but otherwise the stairs were open to the floors above and below.

"Well, these are terrifying," I said, trying to keep my eyes from crossing so I could keep my footing.

"Just don't look down," Martinez said.

"Very helpful," I said.

"Surely there's an elevator in a place this size," Martinez said.

"Oh, there is," Plank said. "You can see the layout of the house better this way. And it's good exercise."

"I appreciate you looking out for us, Plank," I said dryly, but it didn't faze him.

"Mrs. Lidle was found in one of the kids' rooms," Plank said. "Once the EMTs cleared her out I sealed it off."

When we got to the third floor we walked down a wide hallway to the north wing of the house.

"I don't know a lot about kids," Martinez said. "But this doesn't really seem like a kid-friendly environment."

The house was such a stark contrast to Everett and Jenny's home it was hard to imagine the two families even being related.

There were still expensive paintings on the walls and sculptures posed in front of the expanse of windows that showcased the rolling pastures, but when Plank led us into the first bedroom on the left I thought that maybe visiting Grandma and Grandpa wouldn't be so bad after all.

The room was a little girl's dream. It was pink, with ruffles and lace and innocence, and it was more than three times the size of the bedroom I shared with Jack. There were six beds, all with pink-and-white canopies, and there was a life-sized dollhouse with a full designer kitchen. There was a wall-sized screen and gaming consoles, and a simulation golf game. The balcony was expansive and looked out over the rolling green hills and white stables.

"Wow," I said. "Every kid's dream."

"There's an identical one on the opposite side of the hall for the boys," Plank said. "It has a simulation batting cage. Apparently this entire wing is for the grandkids. The room next door is an arcade, and there's an indoor pool at the end of the hall with a splash pad."

"I guess there comes a point when you have so much money you run out of things to spend it on," I said.

"Whoever thought of putting a swimming pool on the third floor?" Martinez asked.

"I think they thought of everything when they built this place," Plank said. "Mrs. Lidle was found here." He pointed to a bed in the middle of a row of three along the back wall.

I immediately pulled a pair of gloves out of my bag and handed Martinez an extra pair.

"Two disturbed beds," Martinez said, pointing to the adjacent bed.

"Makes sense," I said. "If she was taking care of the granddaughter she'd stay up here with her. Though I'm surprised. You'd think she'd hire a nurse or send someone else to take care of her."

"Jenny said Kitty was a very sweet woman, at

least when it came to family," Martinez said. "Maybe she's hands on."

"Yeah, maybe," I said. "No sign of the chicken noodle soup bowl, but there's a tea set. Two cups. One is empty. The other still has tea in it. Looks full."

"The trace of the drug you found in Evie's system..." Martinez began. "Could a larger dose have been given to incapacitate either or both of them?"

I frowned in thought. It seemed too simple. "One of the side effects of promethazine is respiratory depression. But I've only ever read studies about it affecting those under two years of age. I've never heard of an adult case."

"But an overdose could cause respiratory issues in an adult?" he pressed.

"Yeah, it's possible," I said. "If the dose was large enough. Side effects include lethargy and sleepiness. The problem with Evie Lidle's tox report is that there were just trace amounts in her system. It wasn't enough to make me think it did anything but curb her nausea. It's a very effective and fast-acting drug."

"Let's bag and tag the tea set," Martinez said to Plank. "Keep your eyes open for the prescription bottle, or any other prescriptions you find. Evie Lidle was somehow taken out of this house, and something happened to Kitty Lidle that kept her from noticing her granddaughter was being taken right from beneath her nose. I refuse to believe she just happened to have a stroke or whatever. There are no coincidences in murder."

"There's no sign of struggle in this room," I said, looking around closely, examining the windows and looking for something a kidnapper might have left behind. "The play areas look normal for a single kid who was bored with being stuck in bed. There's a few books on the floor. Playhouse is disheveled. And a couple of golf clubs are lying on the bed instead of in the bag."

"What about drugs that wouldn't have shown up in a regular tox screen?" Martinez asked.

"Any number of prescription drugs or illegal drugs wouldn't show up," I told him. "The tox screen looks for markers—codeine, barbiturates, heroin, amphetamines, morphine. There are a lot of drugs and poisons that don't have those chemicals. Something like chloroform would have shown up in her liver when I did the autopsy, so that's also ruled out."

"We know the girl fought back," he said. "I'm just trying to narrow down the timeline a little. Let's just say for conversation that the drug was in the tea. We've got TOD taking place sometime between nine and midnight. The killer got her out of the house somehow. The park is maybe a twenty-minute drive from here. And we know she was awake enough to fight back."

"And not just fight back a little," I told him. "The defensive wounds on her arms and the flesh under her nails does not tell the story of a girl drugged out of her mind. She was alert."

"So maybe she wasn't drugged at all," he said.

"You think she went willingly?" I asked.

"Whether she went willingly or was carried out in a potato sack, I don't know. But I don't believe for a second that a place like this doesn't have eyes and ears everywhere."

I agreed with that. "Send the tea set to the state lab and have them look for trace evidence. Once you start getting into poisons, the tests become very specific. It can take some time."

"Right," Martinez said, blowing out a breath. "We'll hope it's not poison. Looks like we need to talk to the house manager and the chef since they showed up this morning.

"Plank, call Derby in IT. I want him to check all the security and logs for any entrance on the property, including down at the stables. I want to find how the killer got out of here with the girl.

"And then call in the crime-scene techs. I want Lieutenant Daniels to bring her team. She's the best. Then call in Chen and tell her to pick a team of four to bring with her. Tell them to drop whatever they're working on. This is priority. I want every inch of this house combed over, and every person who has stepped foot on Lidle property over the past seventy-two hours interviewed. I want to know how Evie Lidle left this house. This might be the only chance we have to get access to this place once Robert Lidle starts throwing his weight around. I want us to be thorough."

"Yes, sir," Plank said. "The house manager's name is Astrid Nielsen. She's the one who found Kitty Lidle. Said she was just fine when she brought the tea up last night. She's in the kitchen with Walters."

"Then let's start with her," Martinez said.

I wasn't sure what I'd been expecting Astrid Nielsen to look like. Maybe I'd expected her to be older and more shriveled, considering Jenny had said most of the staff were long-term employees, but she didn't look much past forty.

What I hadn't been expecting was her size. She was broad shouldered, built more like a rugby player, and athletic looking. Her skin was pale and smooth and her cornhusk-blond hair was long and braided over one shoulder. Her eyes were the pale blue of an Icelandic lake. She stood ramrod straight, holding a steaming cup of something between her hands, and looking like she didn't know quite what to do.

I looked around the massive kitchen. There were no touches of home here. No photographs or plants. It was a commercial kitchen with enough gadgets and ovens to cook for a hundred people, which I assumed happened frequently considering the Lidles' status.

Walters was standing guard in the corner, and there was a short, plump woman with steel-gray hair pulled into a severe knot at the base of her neck. She was pounding dough like there was a face attached to it, while intermittently throwing flour onto the counter and then starting the pounding again.

I raised my brows at Walters in question, but he subtly shook his head and the corner of his mouth twitched.

"Are you Astrid Nielsen?" Martinez asked the woman at the island.

"Yes," she said, meeting Martinez's gaze with tear-drenched eyes. "I am Astrid Nielsen." Her accent was Nordic, which would explain her height and coloring.

"We need to ask you a few questions," Martinez said. "I'd appreciate it if we could talk privately."

"You can go in the breakfast room," the short woman said, her accent a thick Irish lilt. "I'll not have me schedule interrupted. I've got dinner to prep for."

"You must be Molly Ryan," Martinez said.

"That I am," she said. "And no one is allowed in me kitchen unless ye want a knot on the head. If ye want coffee I'll bring it to ye in the other room. Mr. Lidle is not going to be happy you're poking about."

"Unfortunately, the law applies to Mr. Lidle like it does everyone else," Martinez said. "This is an active crime scene. I don't even need a warrant."

Astrid was dressed in black slacks and a formal black button-down long-sleeved shirt, but Molly was dressed more casually in linen slacks and a loose white shirt. A dark green apron hung around her neck and it was speckled with flour.

"Who are you making dinner for?" I asked out of curiosity.

"Mr. Lidle is expected home this evening," she said. "And he said there would be eight guests."

Martinez rocked back on his heels. "Should I

assume that Mrs. Lidle wasn't invited since she's unconscious in the hospital?"

"Aye, she's fine," Molly said curtly. "I already told yer baby officer that's poking around the house. Mr. Lidle doesn't like the household to be interrupted, and we'll all catch hell for it. Ye'll see. Sometimes Ms. Kitty tipples the sherry. No need to make such a big fuss. Just like I told Astrid here." Molly slammed the dough down on the counter again and gave Astrid a scathing look. "Should have let her sleep it off instead of calling the police."

"She was barely breathing," Astrid said. "And Evie is gone!"

"Nonsense," Molly said. "Girl was right as rain last night. She's probably down at the stables with her horses. I'm sure she got caught in the rain and couldn't make it back to the house. But you'd have to use the brain in yer head to call down there and ask."

"Evie is dead!" Astrid yelled.

"You haven't watched the news? Gotten any phone calls?" I asked.

"I'm working," Molly said indignantly. "You don't watch the telly or answer the phone when you're working. At least some of us don't." She gave a pointed look to Astrid. "And I don't have one in my house."

"Mrs. Ryan," Martinez said. "Evie Lidle was found in Regent Park this morning. She was murdered."

"What are ye blathering about?" she asked, staring daggers at Martinez. "What kind of filth is this? I want ye out of this house." She flapped a cup towel at him and said, "Get! Shoo!"

"Did you try to tell her?" Martinez asked Astrid, not moving from his spot.

"She's not good at listening while she's yelling," Astrid said, her mouth pressing in a thin line. "I told her it was all over the news, but she doesn't watch television. She says it rots the brain. And the house was quiet this morning."

The color had leached out of Molly's face and she gripped her rolling pin like a weapon.

"Little Evie?" Molly asked. "It's not possible. I'm telling you she was right as rain when I saw her last night. I *saw* her."

"What time was that?" I asked.

"Around five o'clock," she said. "Ms. Kitty didn't need me to stay late. She said just leave the soup on the stove and they'd help themselves. But I brought the tray up to Evie anyway so Ms. Kitty didn't have to carry it. She was feeling poorly herself, so I thought it best they eat upstairs."

"Did you speak to Evie?" Martinez asked.

"Of course," Molly said. "She was feeling much better. Told me she didn't want the soup, and she wanted a hamburger instead. But I told her that was foolish and she'd cast it back up again. She was out of bed playing as if she'd never been sick."

"What about Kitty?" Martinez asked.

"She was the one who didn't look so good, and I told her so meself," Molly said. "She was afraid the whole staff would get sick, but I told her that was nonsense. I've never been sick a day in me life. But Ms. Kitty told me to have Astrid dismiss the others and send them on home. Ms. Kitty said the house was quarantined until Wednesday at the earliest. That's why no one came in today."

"Except for you and Ms. Nielsen?" Martinez asked.

"I have a job to do," she said haughtily. "A little illness isn't going to stop me. And I expect it's the same for Astrid and anyone else who has more than fluff in their head."

"How long has Mr. Lidle been gone?" I asked.

"He left Sunday just after Evie came to stay," Molly said, pursing her lips. "Said he had too many important meetings this week, and couldn't afford to be sick. Democracy hanging in the balance, or some such nonsense."

"He didn't seem concerned about Kitty being taken to the hospital when he called about the dinner party?" Martinez asked.

"He seemed put out about it, sure," Molly said. "But like I said before, this isn't the first time Kitty has taken to bed with a drink or two. I figured she made herself a hot toddy and overindulged. I'm sure Mr. Lidle thought the same. But he said this dinner was important and there would be dignitaries dining with him. He wanted escargots and beef Wellington on the menu. And a soufflé for dessert." She rolled her eyes. "Like ye can just whip one up easy as ye please."

Molly bit her lip nervously and her voice wavered. "Have you checked to see if Evie's hiding? She loves her games, does Evie. It might have scared her to see Kitty sick or tipsy. Not many people know about her drinking."

"I'm sorry," I said. "But we're sure. I was able to identify her from dental records. Her parents have been notified."

Molly's face drained of color and she dropped the rolling pin with a thunk onto the counter, her legs wobbling. Martinez took a step forward to try and steady her but she waved him off.

"I need to contact Mr. Lidle," she said. "He doesn't know about Evie. I'm sure of it. He would have said something. He wouldn't have been so insistent about the dinner party."

"We've already spoken to him," Martinez said. "He knows about his granddaughter."

Her mouth tightened in a thin line.

"Officer Walters is going to sit with you to make sure you're steady on your feet," Martinez said. "And then we'll come back and talk with you some more."

She bristled. "Of course I'm steady on me feet. I'm going to put on a pot of coffee. Ye can help yourselves to it if ye like."

"We appreciate it," Martinez said.

I didn't know about Martinez, but I wasn't about to drink anything from a house where we'd just taken cups into evidence.

CHAPTER EIGHT

Martinez and I found ourselves in the breakfast room with Astrid a few minutes later. Like the rest of the house, the room was mostly glass and had a partially glass ceiling like a sunroom. The table was rectangular and black and there was a monstrosity of a flower arrangement sitting in the middle. On a sunny day, it was probably a very nice room to sit in, but with the rain pounding against the glass I felt like I was in a house designed by Morticia Addams.

"Have a seat, Ms. Nielsen," Martinez said, letting her sit at the head of the table.

"I saw a news alert about Evie after the EMTs took away Ms. Kitty," she said, her hands twisting in her lap. "I saw about the girl in the park early this morning, and I thought how bad it was to have such a horrible crime so close, and how sad it must be for the family to know they'd lost a child." She sucked in a shaky breath. "I didn't realize the child would be ours."

"It was after noon when you made the 911 call," Martinez said. "Didn't it strike you odd that you hadn't seen or heard from Mrs. Lidle?"

Astrid was already shaking her head. "Not at all," she said. "Ms. Kitty doesn't like to be disturbed before noon. I almost didn't come in at all today because she told us to take the next two days off, but then Molly called and told me about the dinner party and I knew I needed to prepare the house for guests. I arrived just after ten."

"What exactly does a house manager do?" Martinez asked.

"Anything and everything to make sure the lives of the family run smoothly. I organize everyone's schedules except for Mr. Lidle, as he has his own private secretary. I pay bills, hire staff, oversee raises and bonuses, coordinate events with vendors, and communicate with local charities about donations. On top of that I make sure the house is always presentable and ready for company should the need arise."

"That's an important job," Martinez said. "You must know everything about this house and the people in it."

The way Martinez said it had Astrid licking her lips nervously. "Of course. It's my job."

"You were saying Mrs. Lidle didn't like to be disturbed before noon?" he asked, leading her back into the conversation.

"Yes, well, I came straight in and got to work, and I didn't think about going up to the nursery to see if Ms. Kitty was still there with Evie. Normally she makes her way down whenever she rises and gets ready for the day. Molly always keeps fresh scones and pastries and hot coffee available on the sideboard in the mornings since no one prefers a hot breakfast. Ms. Kitty has always been very independent for as long as I've known her."

"How long is that?" Martinez asked.

"It'll be twenty-five years this August," she said. "I answered their employment advertisement as soon as I graduated from university. Mr. Phin and Mr. Everett were both still in high school, and Ms. Janet was just starting seventh grade. The Lidles liked for all of their staff to speak multiple languages because of the children, so they flew to Copenhagen to meet me in person. They arranged everything for me to come back to America with them."

"When was the last time you saw Evie and Mrs. Lidle?"

"It was before six," she said, licking her lips. "I went up about half five to see if I could remove the dishes from dinner, and while I was there Ms. Kitty asked if I'd make her some chamomile tea as she wasn't feeling too well."

"Did she and Evie both eat the chicken soup?" I asked.

"No, ma'am," Astrid said. "Only Miss Evie ate the soup and some sourdough bread. The dishes were empty when I came to get them. She must have been starving after not being able to keep anything in her stomach for so long."

"You brought the tea up for both of them?" I asked. "There were two cups."

"Out of habit," she said. "But Miss Evie doesn't like tea, so I knew she wouldn't drink it. I would normally bring her hot chocolate before bed, but I didn't think she was quite ready for that yet."

I tucked away that bit of information. The lab would test the cups to make sure, but if Evie was the only one to eat the soup, and Kitty was the only one who drank the tea, then that made our theory about being drugged a little more complicated.

"Had Mrs. Lidle been drinking when you saw her last?" Martinez asked.

Two spots of color appeared on Astrid's

cheeks. "Molly shouldn't have said that. It's not our place to speak out against the Lidles. What they do in their personal lives is of no concern to us."

"Molly said not many people know about her drinking," he pressed on. "I assume you know?"

Astrid exhaled slowly, obviously trying to measure her words. "Of course," she said. "She says she can't sleep without having something to calm her nerves. She's always struggled with having a peaceful sleep, ever since I've known her. She told me once she didn't like the darkness. A drink or two before bed helps her relax."

"Had she had anything when you brought up the tea?" Martinez asked.

"It's hard to say," Astrid said. "I didn't see any glasses in the nursery, but like I said, she wasn't feeling well. But when she drinks she usually starts before the dinner hour. You'd be better off asking Molly that question. Sometimes Ms. Kitty and Molly will *tipple* together, as Molly so indelicately put it."

"What happened after you brought the tea?" Martinez asked.

"They were fine," she said, almost pleading with us. "They were both fine. Ms. Kitty was sitting in the pink lady's chair next to the window, pouring her tea, and Miss Evie was reading a book on the rug. I brought the supper dishes back to the kitchen and loaded them in the dishwasher and wiped down the counters. Ms. Kitty asked me to set the alarm before I left so I did. And then I locked the door behind me and went home. It doesn't make any sense. They were *fine*."

Her voice had a ring of hysteria to it, but the facts remained that she and Molly were the last two people to see Evie alive.

"And then when I came in today I didn't think to check on either of them," she said, panting for breath. "I was worried about what Mr. Lidle would say if everything wasn't perfect for his guests. I had a list of calls to make—the florist, musicians, extra security since there would be dignitaries on-site. I didn't go check on them right off. Maybe if I'd come in earlier I could have made a difference."

"No," I told her. "Evie was taken last night. There's nothing you could have done."

"Ms. Kitty never would have let anyone take Evie if she'd been able. She would have fought. Ms. Kitty was no one to be messed with, especially when it involved one of her children. She's a formidable woman. She was always protective of the children."

"I imagine she'd have to be to run her family's

empire for as long as she did," Martinez said. "You mentioned that you left and went home last night. Where is home?"

"About a mile south," she said. "There's a road that cuts behind the stables and the staff cottages are located there."

"Which staff live there?" Martinez asked.

"Me, Molly, and Geoffrey," she said. "Geoffrey is Mr. Lidle's secretary, so he frequently travels with Mr. Lidle. Also Alex. He runs the stables. We're the only staff who live on the property full-time. There's a farmhand house where several of the trainers live, but many of them have families now and live in their own homes. It's on the other side of the stables. We'll occasionally have visiting jockeys and owners stay in the guest-houses. We're expecting some in the next week or so as they prepare for the derby the first weekend in May. But as far as full-time employees who work inside the house or imme-diate grounds, there are twenty-five. Probably another twenty-five to thirty contractors who come in as needed, depending on the event or time of year."

"Can you get me a list?" Martinez asked.

She nodded. "Of course."

"Who has access to the gates?" I asked her.

"All staff have access to the back gate," she

said. "There's another entrance to the property on the west side where we are supposed to enter and exit the property. Everyone who uses that gate has passed a background check and has a key card to get inside.

"There's another entrance on the east side," she continued. "That's where the horse trailers and anyone who has ranch business come in and out. But it's also guarded and names are taken at the gate of any guests.

"Everything is documented. We always know who is on the premises at any given time. There's another gate not far from the staff entrance where deliveries are brought through and contractors or catering vans would check in. And there's a garage for staff vehicles just past those trees." She pointed to the thickly forested area, though it was impossible to see anything with the rain coming down so hard.

"How do the staff get to the house or stables from the garage?" I asked, curious.

"There's a call button in the garage," she said, "Rodney is one of the groundsmen and he drives the staff van down to pick us up throughout our shifts, and then he'll drive us back at the end of the day."

"Sounds like quite the operation," Martinez said. "Who has access to the house alarm codes?"

She chewed on her lip as she thought. "Me, Molly, and Geoffrey as far as I know. As well as the Lidles and all of their children. I'm not sure anyone really keeps track. We've always felt very safe here." She rubbed her arms as if she were cold.

"And you did set the alarm?" Martinez asked.

"Yes," she said. "I was the last one out of the house. I set the alarm and left."

"Has anyone ever made threats before or breached the house?" he asked.

"Threats, sure," she said. "Sometimes still. Mr. Lidle makes enemies because of certain projects he supports, so he'll get emails. This address is not listed publically, but obviously the press or anyone can find it. His staff gets his personal correspondence. It doesn't come here."

"Tell me about Mr. Lidle," Martinez said, and I could tell that we'd struck a nerve.

Astrid's body language changed and she looked toward the kitchen, as if she were trying to see if anyone were listening.

"I don't understand," she said.

"Ms. Nielsen," Martinez said. "Evie Lidle was brutally and violently murdered, and she was last seen alive right here in this house. We are trying to find out who could have taken her right out from under everyone's noses. Maybe you don't understand, but you've just told me that there's a security team on this property, guards at all the entrances and exits, and that staff pretty much have the run of the estate. It makes it much more likely that someone was already inside the house when she was taken versus a stranger that breached the property.

"And you've also just told me you were the last person to leave the house and you set the alarm behind you, which only a few people have the code. Do you see the problem?"

"Someone already in the house?" she asked, realization dawning. And then her mouth gaped open in shock. "Me? I am a suspect? Because I saw them last? I would never hurt anyone. Everyone here adores Ms. Kitty and the children."

"And yet you keep leaving Mr. Lidle out of the family praise," Martinez said coldly. "Tell me about Mr. Lidle. When did you see him last?"

Her face paled as she finally realized the severity of her predicament. "Sunday morning," she said with a slight hesitation. "He likes to read the paper and have coffee in his study on Sunday mornings while *Meet the Press* plays in the background. He's very regimented about his schedule.

"I brought him his coffee just before nine o'clock," she said. "I alerted him that Mr. Everett was planning to drop Evie off at the house on their way to church and that she was ill. He informed me that he would be leaving for DC within the hour, and told me to relay the information to Ms. Kitty. He said he had important meetings lined up for the entire week, and he wasn't sure when he would be back. He's been pushing Ms. Janet to get a gun bill through to Congress."

"Mr. Lidle wasn't successful in his run for Senate," Martinez said. "Does he often try to get his own agenda passed through his daughter?"

Her cheeks colored slightly, and I knew that's exactly what Robert Lidle was doing. "You'd have to ask him about that. I'm not up to speed on his projects."

I wasn't sure, but I thought I detected a bit of bitterness in her response.

"You've always lived in the staff cottage?" Martinez asked. "Do you have a family?"

"I was married once," she said. "For just a short time. Maybe a year after I came to America. But it was over after a few months. And I don't have any children. The Lidles are my family."

"And there was nothing unusual that happened leading up to Evie's disappearance? Anything or anyone suspicious? No strange deliveries? Anyone call in sick?"

"No," she said softly. "We all loved Evie."

"We may have more questions for you," Martinez said, passing her his card. "And if you have any information for us you can reach me at this number. As part of the investigation we have to inform you not to leave town."

We left her sitting at the table, staring out at the rain, and we went back into the kitchen to find Molly taking a tray of cookies out of the oven. Despite Martinez's assurance that I was buying lunch, we were well past the lunch hour and I'd only had a singular donut to get me through the day. The sugar rush had long since passed.

Walters was still standing guard, and he was practically licking his lips. He caught my gaze and I shook my head slightly, warning him not to eat anything. I could see a little bit of life drain out of him.

"Where is the tea kept?" I asked Molly.

"In the pantry," she said. "Ms. Kitty loves her tea. She has loose leaf in just about every flavor."

"Astrid said she brought Mrs. Lidle chamomile tea last night," I said. "We're going to need to take that with us."

She wiped her hands on a dish towel and her brows rose. "Are ye now?" And then she looked thoughtful. "And I'm guessing you're wondering if I've got any of that soup left too."

"I was wondering that," Martinez said.

"Well it happens I do," she said. "I was going to eat it for me own supper. Let me get you the tea." And then she opened up a hidden panel in the cabinets and walked into a pantry large enough to host a dinner party.

"Jack's going to be sad he missed this place," I whispered to Martinez. "He's got a weird fascination about pantries. Loves them. I have no idea why."

"You don't know why because you don't cook," he said. "Anyone who spends any time in a kitchen loves a well-organized pantry."

"I've learned so much about you today," I said. "I never imagined you in a kitchen."

"I have a lot of family members in the food industry," he said. "I worked in my fair share of kitchens when I was younger."

"I waited tables in college," Walters said, eyeing the cookies again. "Here's my thought. If she takes one of those cookies and eats it then I say we have nothing to lose. I haven't eaten lunch today."

I liked Walters. He was homegrown and had joined the force right after high school graduation. He wasn't the smartest guy in the room. And he wasn't the dumbest either. He did well as a patrolman and had no ambition to rise up through the ranks. He liked taking calls and making traffic stops, and he seemed content with that lot in life.

"Get in line," Martinez told him. "Doc's trying to get out of buying me lunch."

"Lies," I said, shaking my head. "Vicious lies. You're mean when you're hungry."

"Here ye are," Molly said, coming back in with a glass container filled with tea leaves. And then she went to the subzero refrigerator and took out a container of soup, plopping it onto the counter next to the tea. "I'm tired of coffee. I'm having whiskey with my cookies. It seems like today calls for it. Bless her sweet soul." She mopped the tears in her eyes with her apron.

I was starting to like Molly Ryan, so I hoped she wasn't an accomplice to murder. She was obviously comfortable in the kitchen, and she took a decanter out from under the counter and she reached in her apron and took out a glass.

I raised my brows at Martinez, wondering if she always kept glasses in her apron.

There seemed to be a collective sigh of relief when Molly selected two cookies and took a bite out of one.

"Help yerselves," she said.

Walters made his way to the cookie tray, but Martinez and I stayed where we were and decided Walters could take one for the team. He was a grown man and he could make his own life or death decisions.

"Mrs. Ryan," Martinez said.

"Call me Molly," she corrected. "Everyone does. I've been widowed for forty-one years. I don't even remember who Mrs. Ryan is anymore. Me husband, John, was Frank Lazarus's valet. Frank was Kitty's father ye see. And I was Mrs. Lazarus's personal maid. Kitty and I practically grew up together."

"You grew up in the Lazarus household?" I asked.

"Four generations of my family have worked for the Lazarus family," she said proudly. "Me parents, meself, and me son and granddaughter. They both work with the horses at the stables. The Irish are horse whisperers ye know." She took a generous drink and her eyes unfocused as she remembered things long past.

"I remember getting off the boat at four years old with me parents and coming through Ellis Island. That was just a few years before it was shut down. They had their papers and we all arrived at this grand house in New York. I thought I'd won a prize. The Lazaruses worked hard and demanded a great deal, but they've always been generous and good people. I got an education and I learned to work me fingers to the bone, but they paid us all well for our loyalty. And when I turned seventeen Mrs. Lazarus asked if I'd be her personal maid. Me mother was so proud I thought she'd take an advertisement in the paper."

Molly began humming softly and poured another two fingers into her glass. "We had a few good years together, John and I, before he died. Me only twenty-four with a babe on me hip and another on the way."

"I'm sorry," I told her. "I can't imagine."

"Aye, ye can't," she said, shaking her head sadly. "Died being a hero, he did. Kitty's pup got tangled in the weeds of the lake and John waded out, thinking to get him free. But it was deeper than it looked and he got tangled. He couldn't swim, the fool. By the time the men got out there to cut him loose John and the pup were dead. It was a horrible time.

"Kitty was engaged to be married to Robert Lidle and the pup had been a present from him. They married the next year, and Kitty's mother asked me if I'd go with Kitty and make sure she got settled into her marriage and new home. So I went, and I've been with her ever since. I was here when the children were born. Then the grandchildren came.”

She dabbed at her eyes. It seemed the whiskey had loosed the dam of her tears along with her tongue.

“We need to find out what happened to Evie,” Martinez said, trying to get her back on track. “Had Kitty had anything to eat or drink before Astrid brought her the tea?”

“I brought her a piece of dry toast and told her to see if she could keep it down,” she said. “I could tell by looking at her that she was going to be sick. But Kitty has a stubborn streak. Won’t settle in for the night without having a little something to warm her belly.”

“Astrid said Mrs. Lidle has trouble sleeping at night,” I told her.

“Well of course she does,” Molly said. “She’s always had nightmares. Started about a year before John passed on. Terrible night terrors she had. No one could figure out why, and she could never remember them. After Ms. Kitty and Robert were married for a few years he eventually moved into his own bedroom so he could sleep at night. It wasn’t long after that she started lulling herself to sleep with a little whiskey. And who could blame her?”

"Where would she have gotten the whiskey if you or Astrid didn't bring it to her?"

Molly rolled her eyes and chuckled. "Ms. Kitty has her stashes all about the house. Same as her cigarettes. She likes a smoke every now and then, but likes to think to think no one knows about them. Mr. Lidle does the same. Tis about the only thing the two of them have in common."

"A secret from the staff? Or her family?" Martinez prodded.

"Ye don't understand," Molly said. "Kitty is a brilliant woman. Ye have to be to expand a company that started by making ketchup into owning a majority share of the food market worldwide. I think there are very few people who know the real Kitty, and that includes her family. You would never know she'd been drinking. She could function as well as anyone. Kitty had her demons to deal with, and I say whatever helped her deal with them is her business."

"Did all the staff listen to Kitty's orders and go home?" I asked. "Was anyone still around when you and Astrid left for the evening?"

She hummed a little more as she thought, and then she said, "Astrid was still here when I left. And Rodney. He drove me back to me cottage. We passed Hector out by the pond and I waved to him as we passed by. He's the head groundskeeper. All the rain is killing some of his more delicate plants, so he's been a bit short of temper lately."

"Anyone else?"

"Could have been, but not that I saw," she said. "Fact of the matter is there's always people around here and there. The house seems quite open and deserted, but we have staff passages to get to different wings of the house quickly. You get used to seeing people here and there behind the scenes, but there's also a quietness about the house that can only be achieved by a well-trained staff." There was pride in her voice as she said it. "We're not to be seen or heard, and we aren't. I don't recall seeing anyone else on my way out, though Alan would have been about, as well as the other guards and anyone down at the stables."

"Alan Goble?" Martinez asked. "We met him at the gate."

"He's head of security," she said, but the sneer in her voice was unmistakable. "You'd think they were the secret service the way they go about. This house is twenty thousand square feet, and there are more than four hundred acres to keep in check."

"Do you know his schedule?" Martinez asked.

She scoffed and finished her cookie. "I know everyone's schedule. We keep a master list of all full- and part-time staff, as well as their hours and contact information."

Molly opened a drawer in the island and pulled out a laminated sheet, handing it to Martinez.

"I appreciate it," he said. "I take it you don't care for Alan?"

"Well, I'm not one to speak out of turn," she said. Her cheeks were flushed and her brogue was getting thicker with every drink. "But Alan has an eye for the ladies he does. It's gotten to the point where Astrid has to warn the new female hires to keep their knickers on when he's around. Thinks he's God's gift to women, and more than one woman in this house has fallen on her back because of his charm."

"Alan doesn't live on the property?" Martinez asked.

"Has himself a house over in Bowling Green, but everybody knows he likes to diddle with the help out in the stables. And I've heard rumors he's seduced a lady or two in the Lidles' garage and one of the guardhouses. Likes to pretend he's lord of the castle, I'm sure. Alex has caught him in the act more than once."

"His behavior doesn't bother the Lidles?"

Molly clucked her tongue. "Mr. Lidle cares about resumes, not behavior. And Alan has an excellent resume. But his resume didn't protect my sweet Evie."

"I thought Astrid did the hiring and firing?" Martinez asked.

"For everyone but security," Molly said. "Mr. Lidle has always said the safety of his family is too important not to take care of himself."

She mopped her eyes again and then reached under the counter for three more glasses, pouring a generous amount of whiskey in each and pushing the glasses toward us.

Martinez opened his mouth to tell her that we couldn't accept it, but she launched into a tribute.

"To my darling Evie," she said, sniffling and wiping her eyes on her apron again. "Poor, sweet girl." She raised her glass and her voice rang like bells throughout the kitchen as she gave an Irish toast. "Death leaves a heartache no one can heal. Love leaves a memory no one can steal. Sláinte." She drained the glass, and I watched in fascination as she picked up Martinez's glass and drained it too.

"Uhh," Martinez said, and I could almost hear the wheels turning in his head, wondering if it was worth asking any more questions. I guessed he figured it was since she was still standing on two feet.

"What did Mr. Lidle say when you called to tell him his dinner party was off?"

She snorted indelicately. "I left a message with Geoffrey." She pursed her lips tightly. "Apparently Mr. Lidle was in a *very* important meeting and wasn't to be disturbed." She picked up my glass and drank. "The things me poor Katherine has put up with through the years would turn yer hair blue."

"Mrs. Ryan. Molly," I said. "Can you tell me what Evie was wearing when you last saw her?"

She sat her glass down with a thunk and stared at me with watery green eyes that had probably been bright and vibrant when she was young.

"Her clothes?" she asked. And I knew she knew why I was asking. "She was wearing her pajamas. I'd set them out for her meself after she'd had her shower. They were pink pants with white flowers on them and a white shirt with pink trim on the collar and sleeves. There was a pink kitten on the front of the shirt with soft fur. They were her favorite pajamas."

"What about a locket?" I asked.

The air seemed to go out of Molly Ryan. She

looked old and tired, and her hands shook slightly as she toyed with her glass.

"Aye," she said. "A gift from her father a couple of years ago. I believe he gave all his girls one. Evie always wore it. She never took it off. Never."

"Detective Martinez," Plank said, sticking his head in the kitchen door. "Can I see you for a minute?"

"Officer Walters," Martinez said. "Why don't you drive Molly back to her cottage so she can get some rest."

"No time for rest," she said, her voice regaining its strength. She waved Walters away like she was afraid he was going to toss her over his shoulders like a sack of potatoes. "I've got meals to prep for the week. The house will be teeming with people once the news about Evie reaches everyone. Bless her soul. Sit over there, young Walters, and you can chop carrots for the chicken potpie. Make sure you wash up first."

Walters looked like a deer caught in headlights, but he went to the sink to wash up.

"If you remember anything that might help us find out what happened to Evie," Martinez said, "I'd like for you to give me a call. This is my cell number." He handed her a card, and when she went to take it from him he didn't let go.

"Even if you remember secrets, Molly. Someone took Evie from this house and murdered her. Who could have done something like that?"

Molly's hand trembled and Martinez let go of the card. "I don't know who would do such a thing," she said softly. "She's resting with the angels now." She put the card in her apron pocket and turned away.

Martinez and I left Walters to babysitting duty, and we followed Plank out of the kitchen and into a side room I hadn't noticed on the way through the house the first time. A grand piano sat in the middle of the room on top of a rug in muted shades of red. There was a harp in the corner and a small dais I could only assume was used for musical performances.

"This place is weird," I said, looking around. "It's like it's not even lived in."

"You have no idea how weird," Plank said. "Did you know there are hidden hallways throughout the entire house? Chen found one by accident."

"Let me guess," Martinez said. "There's an entrance right into the room where Evie Lidle was staying."

"Bingo," Plank said. "Chen noticed one of the built-in bookcases had hinges and when she pulled it opened right up."

"Molly told us about the staff passageways," Martinez said.

"It's funny Astrid didn't bring it up though," I said. "Seems like something the house manager would volunteer."

"What did you find on the security footage?"

Plank's cheeks flushed with irritation. "There is no security footage. At least not that I can access. The security cameras are all digital. Everything goes into a cloud, and you can access up to twelve months of video through a monitoring service. But everything for the last three days has been wiped clean."

"Ever since Evie arrived," I said.

"Call in Derby from IT," Martinez said. "Maybe he can work his magic. And let's get a warrant for the monitoring company. Maybe they keep storage in a hard drive that we can access."

"Yes, sir," Plank said. "Lieutenant Daniels and her team are upstairs."

"Good," Martinez said and then handed Plank the list of staff members. "Let's start hunting down the staff. Especially Alan Goble. He's head of security. Set up a meeting with him ASAP. I want to know if anyone didn't show up for work who was supposed to. And get alibis for everyone yesterday between four and midnight. Doc and I are going down to the stables."

CHAPTER NINE

"WHAT DO YOU THINK?" I ASKED MARTINEZ WHEN we got back into his unit.

"I think it's an inside job," he said. "I don't see how it could be anything other than that. The chances of anyone not affiliated in some way with this house seem pretty slim when you look at the number of people who are around and the level of security."

"Yeah, that was my thought too," I said with a sigh. "Pretty interesting that Astrid Nielsen didn't bother to tell us about the master staff list. Like she had to go look it up in her magical house-manager computer."

"I think there was a lot Astrid didn't bother to tell us," Martinez said. "But there was something that Molly said that caught my attention too. She said staff were paid well for their loyalty. Money can buy a lot of secrets and a lot of silence. Molly probably knows things that even Astrid doesn't know. Her whole life has been wrapped up in this family."

"Don't forget her son and granddaughter," I said. "That adds an extra layer when all of your income eggs are in one basket so to speak. It makes it harder to break free."

Martinez grunted in affirmation as we drove back to the guardhouse at the front of the property. Guardhouse really did a disservice to the name. It was a dark gray stone building with white windows and trim, and by the size of it I could only assume there were offices or a room inside to monitor the cameras.

The rain was relentless, and Martinez parked in front of the gate and we both got out and ran to the side door where the guard checked visitors. At least the area was covered by a small overhang. Martinez knocked on the door, but there was no one inside that we could see.

"Goble?" he called out.

"Maybe he had to make a pass around the property," I said. "His anorak was wet the first time we talked to him."

"Maybe," Martinez said. "We'll try him again on the way out."

We ran back to the SUV, both of us wet and shivering, and Martinez kicked the heater on high.

"Next time I complain about the heat in the summer, remind me what this spring has been like," he said.

He put the car in reverse and then got back on the long drive that led to the house. Then he followed the paved path along the side of the house. The designers had done a good job of concealing anything that would take away from the splendor of the house, including the road that disappeared into a tunnel of trees and skirted the perimeter of the property.

"This place must be a security nightmare," Martinez said. "Hardly a clear view from any direction with all the tree coverage."

Our speed was slowed by the rain and low visibility, but as we turned a corner I thought I saw a building in the distance.

"That must be the staff garage," I said, squinting to peer out the window.

"I'll take your word for it," Martinez said as the windshield wipers swished furiously. "I can't see crap. What is this weather?"

The rain did seem to be coming down in sheets instead of drops, and I was starting to wonder if God was punishing us for some unknown reasons. My phone rang and I thought about sending it to voicemail, but then I saw Doug's picture pop up and I wanted to make sure he was okay.

I put the phone on speaker and said, "Everything okay?"

"So, like, don't get mad," Doug said by way of greeting.

Martinez started laughing and slowed the car to a crawl as we continued on what I thought was the road that headed toward the barns.

"Hey, who's that?" Doug asked.

"Martinez," he answered.

"Oh, cool," Doug said. "I saw the news this morning. That's a pretty sweet suit you were wearing. Makes you look like a mobster."

"Thank you?" Martinez said, giving me a look.

I didn't say anything because the suit did kind of give off mobster vibes.

"Maybe you should get back to the part where you don't want me to be mad," I said. "Did something happen at the house? Are you okay?"

"I'm A-okay," he said. "This rain is pretty wicked. My afternoon class got cancelled because no one could get on Zoom. And the groceries got delivered, so that's good."

"None of these things are triggering my wrath," I said.

"Well, it's about the dog," he said.

"What dog?" Martinez and I both asked.

"It's crazy really," Doug said. "You see, I opened the door to get the groceries off the porch and I swore I heard this howling sound. At first I thought maybe it was the wind. But it was too weird to be the wind. And then like, my Spidey-sense kicked in and I followed the sound to the side of the house where the creek is, and there it was."

"There what was?" I asked, my palms starting to sweat.

"Oscar," he said.

I closed my eyes and prayed for patience. "Who's Oscar?"

"The dog," he said. "I named him that because he looks like Oscar the Grouch. But he'll probably look better after I give him a bath." Doug paused for a second. "Maybe."

"Umm, Doug..."

"Wait, hear me out," Doug said. "You see, he was all tangled up in these brambles, and he was muddy and the creek was rising. I had to get him out of there or he would have died."

"Doug, why would you think I'd be mad

about you rescuing a dog? Share your groceries with him. I'm sure he's hungry."

"Oh, I didn't figure you'd be mad about the dog part," he said. "I know you've been trying to talk Jack into getting one. I figured you'd be mad about the mud."

I rubbed the throbbing that had started between my eyes. "What mud?"

"It's just that he was all matted up, so I brought him in through the kitchen so I could take him into the guest bathroom and get him in the shower. But he was so excited he got away from me and kind of ran through the house. But don't worry. I'll have everything cleaned up by the time you get home. And don't worry about the sofa. I know how to use the steam cleaner. It'll be like new. You guys probably shouldn't have bought a white couch, but hindsight is twenty-twenty. And I can fix the lamp. Maybe."

"Just clean up the mess," I said. "I'm glad you've got company. We'll be home later if the bridge isn't flooded. Otherwise I'll be at the funeral home."

"Should I tell Jack about Oscar?"

"Let's surprise him," I said.

"Wisdom," Doug said and disconnected.

Martinez burst into laughter. "So you've got a dog now."

"I wanted my dog to be named Sherlock," I said, tapping my fingers on my leg. "What kind of name is Oscar? I didn't want an Oscar. I wanted a Sherlock."

"Sounds to me like Oscar is Doug's dog," he said. "You've still got a chance for Sherlock."

"I don't know," I said. "It depends on how bad the house is wrecked when Jack gets home. Oscar might have screwed up my chances for Sherlock. Our sofa is pretty nice."

Martinez was sitting forward, his knuckles white on the steering wheel, trying to see through the windshield.

"This is ridiculous," Martinez said. "We do not have time for this." And then a rapid string of Spanish flowed from his mouth.

I didn't know any Spanish, but I recognized the tone and I figured most of the words he said weren't appropriate for most ears, and I figured the altar boy was probably going to have to spend some time in confession.

He pounded on the steering wheel a couple of times, said a word I'd heard on *NYPD Blue* and knew his abuela wouldn't approve of, and then slammed on the brakes so we skidded slightly. And the rain stopped. I mean it all the way stopped. Not even a wayward dribble landed on the windshield.

"Holy smokes," I said. "What did you just do?"

"A little something my abuela taught me," he said.

"I don't know whether to make the sign of the cross or give you a high five."

"Family trade secret," he said.

"Maybe you could have done it a couple of weeks ago," I said.

"If I had you wouldn't have Oscar."

I sighed. "Jack is going to have kittens. I'm trying to pretend like it's no big deal right now so I can be calm and collected when he finds out that Doug just adopted a dog that looks like he lives in a trash can."

"You're doing pretty well at keeping it together," Martinez said. "I never would have guessed except for that line of sweat on your upper lip. Maybe Jack will love Oscar. Maybe they'll be best friends."

"Jack's got a weird hang-up about dogs," I said. "He agreed to let me have one, but I'm not sure he actually meant it. He's still traumatized by the dog he had as a kid."

"What happened to it?" he asked.

"She died of extreme old age," I said. "But she and Jack were very close."

"Maybe he should talk to the department shrink," Martinez said.

"Or just replace the affection he had for that dog with this one," I told him.

"That seems healthy."

"Hey, I'm all about finding healthy coping mechanisms," I said. "Look, there's the staff cottages."

"The word cottage is a bit of an understatement," Martinez said. "I was expecting something smaller. Those are nice houses. Looks like one of those old-timey neighborhoods with the trees and stables in the back. Maybe I should come to work for the Lidles. Seems like a pretty sweet setup."

"How many buildings and stables do horses need?" I asked. "I'm counting five. Not to mention those on the back side that look like a small apartment building."

"That must be the ranch hand apartments," Martinez said. "I guess champions get the best. And rightly so. I've got a thousand dollars riding on their Captain Morgan for the win in the derby."

"Were you really an altar boy?" I asked. "Curses *and* gambling. What's next? Loose women?"

"Every chance I get," he said, grinning.

The main stable was white and majestic, with tall gables and dormer windows, and at least twenty stall doors that faced the livery yard. There was a maze of crisp green hedges and a cobbled path that formed an oval, and on the exterior of the oval were several other white outbuildings that made a *U* around the paddock. They were all designed to look like miniatures of the stable.

"You think the free staff housing is worth waking up smelling horses every morning?" I asked.

"I think when you've got this much money nothing smells too bad," Martinez said. "Let's see if we can find Alex the stable master. You think he's home or at the stables?"

"It's still regular working hours," I said. "Whatever that is for people who deal with animals. Let's check the stables."

A weak beam of sunlight crept through the clouds.

"I'll take that as a sign," Martinez said. "The stables it is."

He stopped the SUV just outside the white rail fence. I left my raincoat in the car but grabbed my medical bag out of habit, putting it across my body so it hung down at my side. The ground had areas of standing water, even on the cobblestones, and Martinez and I made our way through the fence and hedges to the stable. It smelled of fresh rain and hay and wet animals, and when the sun brightened and glinted off the gabled windows I thought it might be the most beautiful thing I'd ever seen.

"I'm not an expert on horses," I said. "But there seem to be a lack of horses in these stables."

"That's because all of our contenders have been transported to different training facilities across the nation," said a man from behind us. "The lack of sun affects horses much like it does humans. It affects their emotions and their performance."

We turned and faced a man dressed in tan riding breeches that fit like a second skin and black boots. He wore a navy pullover with a gold crest and the stable's logo. His face was tan and comfortably lined for a man in his late forties or early fifties—the kind of lines that only seemed to make a man more attractive with age—and his hair was wind blown and dark blond, hitting the back of his collar.

"Horse depression," I said, arching a brow. "Who knew?"

"That's why they pay me the big bucks," he said. "Can I help you?"

"I'm Detective Martinez," Martinez said, showing him his badge. "And this is Dr. Graves. We're looking for Alex Wheeler."

"You found him," he said. "What's going on?"

"You haven't noticed the police presence at the house this morning or turned on the news?" Martinez asked.

Alex looked confused and then his mouth quirked in a half smile. "There hasn't been time for that." And then he gestured for us to follow him. As we walked I noticed the movement of people inside the various buildings and horses being tended to.

"I've been in the foaling stall since about midnight," he said, leading us into an area where another worker was laying down fresh hay. "Then I went home and caught a couple hours sleep and showered. I just got back to work. It was a busy night."

"Oh, wow," I said, looking at the new chestnut foal. And then I said it again as I saw a spotted foal in the stall next to him.

"In three years these horses will be champions," he said, grinning. "It's a good day for Chesapeake Farms. I've got two more mares ready to drop at any time."

"I can see why you didn't have time for TV," I said.

"Why? What's going on?" Alex asked.

"Can you tell me your whereabouts last night between six and midnight?" Martinez asked him.

The man's smile slowly faded as he looked at us both. But he answered. "Yeah, sure. I was here. I'm always here. I live in the house closest to the stables. You can see it from here. I've been checking on Francis and Sadie here off and on for a couple of days. I went home around seven to get something to eat and take a shower. I came back around ten to check on them again. I could tell Sadie was in some distress so I went ahead and called the vet. He got here about eleven. Dr. Buford is his name. He can confirm the time."

"You live with anyone?" Martinez asked.

"God no," he said, laughing. "I've tried that. Women tend to like for you to pay more attention to them than horses. I've never found a woman who was more fun to be around than a horse. So I live alone. Though I have company from time to time."

"Did you have company last night?" Martinez asked. "Can anyone corroborate your whereabouts?"

"Not unless someone was looking in my windows," he said. "Are you going to tell me what this is about?"

"Evie Lidle was kidnapped from the house last

night and murdered," Martinez said. "Her body was found in Regent Park early this morning."

"Impossible," he said, shaking his head. "No way anyone got in there and took her. This place is locked up tight."

"We agree," Martinez said.

Alex's brows rose in surprise. "You think it was one of us? Someone who lives on the property?"

"I think if it's impossible for anyone to get in from the outside, then the choice we're left with is that someone was already on the inside."

Alex shook his head and said, "Look man, my life is an open book. Feel free to ask anyone about my whereabouts. The whole team here was working our tails off. I can vouch for all my people. There was no time or reason for any of us to drive up to the main house. You can check all the cameras. They're everywhere in this place."

"Are the cameras down here on the same system as the ones at the house?" I asked.

Alex shrugged. "I guess so. I don't really know. That's a question for Alan Goble. He's the security guy."

"We've met," Martinez said. "How long have you worked here?"

"Going on seven years," he said. "Mrs. Lidle

lured me away from a competing farm. Paid me almost double to breed her champions. I'm happy to say I've lived up to the pay increase."

"Congratulations," Martinez said. "When was the last time you saw Alan Goble?"

Alex put his hands on his hips and chewed on his bottom lip. "I'm not sure. We don't really cross paths all that often."

"That's not what we heard," I said, raising my brows.

Alex snorted. "Alan's a horndog. Thank God he has a competent team. I told him to stay out of my stables with his girlfriends. He can do whatever he wants on his own time and with who he wants, but we have a reputation for being one of the top racing farms in the country. I don't need him screwing it up. The second time I caught him I reminded him that I don't give second chances. What? Is he crying about a broken nose now? I'm not sorry for it."

"You punched him?" I asked.

Alex grinned. "Yeah, and it felt good too. Alan is always running at the mouth about how he's some highly trained operative and he knows how to kill people with a spoon or some stupid crap like that. I guess he's not so highly trained when his pants are around his ankles. He didn't even see my fist coming. I thought I was going to get fired for sure."

"How long ago was this?" Martinez asked.

"Three or four weeks ago," Alex said.

"He didn't report you?" I asked.

Alex shrugged again. "I guess not. It's not like he really had a leg to stand on. I know he's caused more than one woman employed here to leave her job. A punch in the nose serves him right."

"Who were the women you caught him with?" Martinez asked.

Alex hesitated and rested his arms on top of the stall gate, looking down at the foal. "It's really not any of my business who he was messing around with."

"But it's our business," Martinez said. "Give us the names."

"I actually don't know the name of the first girl I caught him with. She was youngish and blond and pretty. He liked to make his mark on the new hires. I haven't seen her around in the last few months, so I figure he broke it off like he normally does and she quit in embarrassment. That tends to be the pattern."

"But you knew the second woman?"

"Yeah," he said, kicking the fence lightly with his boot. "Yeah, I know her. She's one of mine.

Maybe that's why he thought he could get away with messing with her at the stables."

"I need a name, Alex," Martinez said.

"Lizzie Ryan," he said.

"Ryan?" Martinez asked. "Any relation to Molly Ryan?"

"Her granddaughter," he said. "Her son, John, is one of my best trainers and if he found out about Alan and Lizzie you'd have another murder on your hands. Just be careful who you share that information with."

"Where can I find Lizzie?" Martinez asked.

"She was up with us all night helping with the foals," Alex said. "I cut her loose about ten this morning. She should be at home."

"If you think of anything that might help us you can give me a call," Martinez said, handing him a card.

Alex was just reaching out to take it when three gunshots rang out.

CHAPTER TEN

Chaos erupted around us as trainers and staff tried to settle the startled horses. I'd never really been around horses much, even though Jack's family always had a barnful of animals when we were growing up. I wasn't necessarily afraid of them, but when you saw how small and fragile humans were against a horse's towering musculature, I didn't want to take unnecessary chances.

Martinez already had his weapon out and was running toward the area where the shots had been fired. I stayed behind him and out of his way, and motioned for innocent bystanders to stay inside the stables with the horses.

"Where'd it come from?" I asked Martinez.

"I don't know," he said. "It sounded like it was right on top of us."

"It came from over there," one of the trainers said. "One of the houses."

"Make the 911 call and let them know there are officers on scene," Martinez told him, waiting until the man nodded in the affirmative.

We crept around the perimeter of one of the outbuildings.

"Look there," I said, tapping Martinez on the shoulder. "At the staff cottage next to Alex's."

The front door was ajar and there was a bag that had been dropped on the steps, its contents scattered. Martinez reached down and withdrew the revolver from his ankle holster and handed it to me.

"Just in case," he said. "Don't shoot me in the back."

I rolled my eyes. I was an excellent shot. But I was irritated with myself that I hadn't brought my own weapon. There was a time after I'd almost been strangled to death by a serial killer that I'd never left home without it. But after Jack and I had married and our lives had settled down I'd found myself not taking as much care with my personal safety.

Technically I worked under the authority of the sheriff's office. I could assist the police or make arrests. And I could open carry. But I liked to leave the police work to the police.

There were six identical houses, all white and craftsman in style so they matched the aesthetics of the stables, and they were built around a shared courtyard. The house to the right of Alex's had ferns hanging from the porch and there was a number 2 in black iron on one of the posts.

I felt eyes on the back of my neck as Martinez and I crept our way toward the cottage and up the porch steps.

"Police," Martinez yelled, announcing himself and then pushing the door open wider.

Whatever he saw had him hesitating for only a second, but he trained his weapon straight ahead.

"Drop your weapon," he commanded.

He'd opened the door wide enough so I could see the scene inside. Astrid Nielsen stood with her hands up, a gun still in her hand, and Alan Goble was propped like a broken doll against the hearth of the fireplace. His chest covered in blood.

"I need to get to him," I said, softly. "He could still be alive." I was already digging in my bag for gloves, wondering how far out the paramedics might be.

"Astrid," Martinez said again. "Put your weapon on the ground."

The color was gone from her face and her eyes were wide with shock. But she nodded stiffly and lowered the weapon, so it landed with a thunk on the wood floor.

Martinez moved in quickly and kicked the gun out of the way before putting her in handcuffs. And I ran straight for the victim, feeling for a pulse in his throat. His skin was still hot beneath my fingers and the blood oozed from his chest. I checked his eyes and searched one more time for a pulse. But he was gone. And there was no bringing him back.

I looked at his wounds. "Three gunshot wounds center mass," I told Martinez. "An excellent grouping. You could fit a playing card over all three bullet holes."

There was a sob from behind me and I turned to face Astrid.

"I had to do it," she said, her face contorted with rage. "He did it. I knew as soon as I found out about Evie that he was responsible. He killed her, and if I didn't kill him he would have gotten away with it. He would have disappeared and gotten away with it. You don't know his background. His skill set. I didn't have a choice."

"We always have a choice," Martinez said. And then he started reading her Miranda rights.

I pulled out my phone and texted Lily to meet me for retrieval.

"Guess we're not going to get to question him after all," I said.

"Is this your house?" Martinez asked, looking around.

Astrid nodded but didn't speak.

"What was Alan doing in your house?"

I was half listening to Martinez's questions while I looked over the victim. He was dressed in jeans and a thin gray T-shirt, and he was barefoot. I looked around the room, but didn't see his black anorak. But his level of comfort seemed curious, and it gave us an answer for why he hadn't been at the guardhouse. I patted down his pockets, looking to see if he was carrying anything.

I found his wallet in his back pocket and pulled it out, flipping it open to see his ID. "Alan Goble," I confirmed. And then I felt something familiar at the small of his back and pulled out a small, snub-nosed revolver similar to the one Martinez had given me.

"It just gets more and more interesting," Martinez said. "It's curious that old Al here was comfortable enough to not only be inside your house, but to walk around barefoot, especially since he was supposed to be on duty. I guess our questioning up at the house interfered with your personal time."

Astrid shook her head again, but didn't say anything. She just kept staring at the man she'd killed in cold blood.

I bagged the weapon, and stayed kneeling by the victim until I heard sirens. I knew Lily wouldn't be far behind.

***

"So you're telling me that lady just shot that guy in cold blood, while the house was swarming with cops?" Lily asked on the drive back to the funeral home.

"Yep," I said. "That's a first for me."

She fiddled with the radio and my lips twitched as she chose country music. Cole was indeed rubbing off on her. "Did she think she would get away with it?"

"I don't think she did," I said. "I think she fully expected to get caught and didn't care in the slightest. She just said Alan was responsible for Evie's murder and that if she didn't do it he'd get away with it."

"Vigilante nut job," Lily said.

"Certifiable," I agreed. "There was something off about her from the beginning, but I couldn't put my finger on it other than the fact that she wasn't telling us something. She and Alan obviously had some kind of relationship and maybe she found out more about him than she wanted to know. He's obviously got some kind of sexual addiction. That's the first thing everyone we've talked to has told us. He makes his rounds through the ladies."

"But just how young does he start?" Lily asked darkly.

"That's what we're about to find out," I said. "I'm hoping we find Evie Lidle's scratch marks all over him. If so, three bullet holes to the chest seems like the easy way out."

"Agreed," she said. "I was hoping for public castration."

"Ahh, the good old days," I said.

"I'm just saying this whole thing is weird."

"Maybe Martinez will be able to get something out of her," I said. "He's going to let her sit in lockup for a while. She hasn't even asked for an attorney. All of this is like adding another long day to an already long day."

I turned onto Catherine of Aragon and watched the funeral home come into view. It was nice to see a semblance of sun and sky instead of the gray clouds that had become our normal, and people were taking advantage of it. Parents were walking along the streets, talking to neighbors, while their kids rode bikes. And a group of teenagers were playing a game of football in the street since the yards were too wet.

"Long day indeed," Lily said. "If I didn't have another couple of hours of studying to do I'd be spending my night in a bubble bath with a glass of wine."

I grunted, thinking that didn't sound like a half-bad idea. I was already tired to the bone and the regular workday hadn't ended yet.

"Maybe you'll have time for both," I said, pulling under the carport. "I can cut you loose once you help me move him. This is going to be pretty standard as far as autopsies go. And if I need help I'll call Sheldon. He's not off until five."

"Really?" she asked. "That would be great. I've got exams coming up. Just to think I have three more years of this."

"It'll be over before you know it," I said. "And then you can start your residency. That's when the real fun starts."

"I'll figure that out when I get to it," she said. "I don't want to wait too long to start a family. Cole and I figured getting pregnant after med school and before residency was the right timing.

I know he's worried about being too old to be a dad, but lots of people have kids into their forties and fifties now. It's no big deal."

"Does this mean you've decided to marry him?" I asked, getting out of the Suburban and going to the back. We slid the gurney out the back.

"Oh, I'd already decided I was going to marry him by our second date," she said, grinning. "I just had to let him catch up to the idea."

"Then why did you tell him no when he asked you?" I asked.

"Because he was asking because he thought that's what I wanted him to do. Which I did. But he needs to ask me because it's what he wants to do. Now he's had a couple of weeks to talk himself into the idea, so when he asks me again he'll be ready. If that makes sense."

I just grunted because none of it made sense.

"Just let me know when the wedding is," I said.

"You'll be the first," she said. "So I heard you got a dog."

I typed in the code for the lab door and waited as the door released and opened. "That's the rumor going around."

"You said you've always wanted a dog," she said.

"I have," I said. "That was part of my deprived childhood. But I think I'm just overwhelmed at the moment. I'm a delayed processor as far as emotions go, so I'm not sure this has all set in yet. And I tend to look at things through a skeptical lens anyway."

"It's a dog," she said, laughing. We rolled the gurney onto the elevator and I pushed the button to take us down. "What could possibly make you skeptical about a dog?"

"There's a certain amount of paranoia that comes with being the daughter of my parents. My father is dead, at least I think he is. But my mother is still alive out there somewhere, working for who knows what government or terrorist organization. Could be a toss-up. So when I hear that Doug found a dog caught in the creek by our house, my first thought isn't that it's an answered prayer because I've been asking for a dog."

"You think the dog has a nefarious purpose?" she asked, good humor sparkling in her eyes. "The dog is a government plant?"

"I know it sounds ridiculous," I said. "I've just learned to be cautious in life. My head is a busy and crowded place right now. I'm sure I'll process the fact that we have a dog once I see how much damage he's done to the couch. If I make it home before Jack maybe I can help salvage whatever is left."

"Jack's going to love that dog," she said. "He just has that weird hang-up about his childhood pet. It's traumatizing to lose a family pet."

"Especially when he named it after his grandmother," I said. "There aren't many golden retrievers named Barbara. May she rest in peace."

"And now he has a dog named Oscar."

We got Alan Goble lifted onto my autopsy table, and I got out the necessary paperwork and my recorder. I was already focused on the job. We knew who killed Alan Goble. But what we didn't have was motive. And while he was lying dead on my autopsy table the real case still belonged to Evie Lidle. Every hour that went without us discovering who her killer was meant he was still out there, with his sights possibly on another little girl.

"Go," I told her. "Enjoy your study time. And drink a glass of wine for me when you're done."

"You don't have to tell me twice," she said. "You want me to send Sheldon down if he's free?"

"No, thanks," I said. "I can work faster on my own. I want to get this finished so I don't miss the interview with Astrid Nielsen."

"Happy cutting," she said.

I waited until the door locked behind her before I turned on my recorder and got to work.

"Victim's driver's license identifies him as Alan Victor Goble. Age fifty-one. Brown and brown. Height is listed as six foot one and weight one hundred and ninety pounds, but I'll confirm with my own measurements."

I made sure I hadn't missed anything in the pockets of his jeans, and I checked his hands and ears for jewelry, but he wasn't wearing any. Then I got the scissor and cut the clothes from his body.

There was no dignity in death. We all left the world the same way we came into it.

I put his clothes inside a machine that vibrated at such a high frequency that any particulates that were easily missed would be shaken out into a tray to be analyzed later.

I weighed and measured him, and notated in his chart that his actual height was just under six feet. I took pictures of the intricate tattoos down his arm, and then saw he had others on his shoulder and across his back.

"Victim has scarring across ribs six, seven, and eight. Looks like from a sharp instrument of some kind, possibly a blade. Puckered scarring along right tibia, similar to that of a bullet wound. X-rays will confirm whether the bone was fractured."

I found several other scars as I examined the body of Alan Goble. I'd done autopsies on those who'd spent time in law enforcement before and the scars on his body were in line with a career spent in the line of duty. We'd request a copy of his medical file as well as his service file. I was interested to see how he'd come to be head of security for the Lidles.

"Cause of death—three gunshot wounds to the chest. Small caliber. Weapon currently in evidence with the King George Sheriff's Office."

I did a quick set of x-rays and then took a urine and blood sample. And then I prepped to make my first cut.

A little over an hour later I was rolling him into the refrigeration unit and making my last notations on his chart for Martinez. Alan Goble had been a man in the prime of his life. He'd been healthy and his system had been clean of drugs or alcohol.

I made a copy of everything, physical and digital, and then I put them on my desk to give to Martinez. I'd planned to text him and let him know I was finished, but I found myself rolling the body of Evie Lidle out and under the light.

I did another external examination, carefully

checking to see if I'd missed any needle or puncture marks. How was she taken from the property without anyone hearing or seeing? I took another sample to see if her levels had changed, but there was nothing else showing up in her system but the small trace of anti-nausea medication.

She'd left that house with someone she knew. I couldn't think of another explanation.

I moved to her feet to pull the white sheet back over the small body and felt my breath hitch. My skin tingled and my lungs burned and I could feel the weight of the world bearing down on me. She was so small. So innocent. And no one had been able to protect her. Not even the people who loved her.

I could feel something welling inside of me, and I was afraid of what it would look like if it escaped. I hurriedly pulled the sheet up and rolled her back to the refrigeration unit. And then I took the stairs two at a time and ran to my office, not bothering to check if the lab door had locked behind me.

I ran into the bathroom and turned on the shower to scalding hot, and then I stripped out of my clothes and got under the spray. The tears were falling before the water could wash them away. I crumpled to the floor of the shower, the tile cold beneath me, and wept with an abandon that I'd only ever experienced once before—when I'd found out my father was still alive.

I just needed a little time to fall apart and I'd be fine. But between the fight with Jack, seeing results for one negative pregnancy test after another, and knowing the horror that Evie Lidle had suffered in her last hours, I knew it was only a matter of time before the dam broke. The human soul could only take so much, even mine after dealing with death day in and day out.

I didn't hear Jack come into the bathroom. I only felt his arms come around me as he lifted me into his lap and off the cold floor. He didn't tell me to stop my tears. He just let the water fall on us both as he held me close.

"I'm sorry," I said. "I'm sorry I keep pushing you away. I don't want to push you away, but it's like I can't help it. Every time one of those tests come back negative. I'm just so angry, and you don't deserve to be the target."

"We're both dealing with our anger and disappointment in our own ways," he said softly. "I know you're still here. Just like I hope you know that I'm still here for you. But this is a journey we've never been on before. And we're having to navigate our own paths. But what we have to decide is if we're going to navigate together or we're going to navigate apart. It's okay to take time to process on our own."

"But we're stronger together," I said, my hand rubbing across the hair on his chest. "I've missed you. I've needed you. I just didn't know how to tell you that."

"I know," he said, and I could feel the smile in his voice. "I'd already decided I would only give you until the end of the week to brood. But after I saw your face this morning, when you finished the autopsy on Evie Lidle, I could tell you were close to breaking. I hated having to go back to that courtroom and leave you. And I came back as soon as they dismissed me."

"Looks like it was just in time," I said. "I was downstairs. And all I could do was stare at her. She was a child. Loved. Protected. Provided for with everything money could buy. And it still wasn't enough. I don't know if I can keep doing this. Keep trying to bring a child into this world. I feel like I don't even know who I am anymore."

"I know," he said. And I could hear the sadness in his voice. "Maybe what we need to do is take a break."

CHAPTER ELEVEN

MY FINGERS TIGHTENED AGAINST HIS FLESH AND I froze. I heard his words, could understand them even. But that didn't make it easy to hear. We'd loved each other our whole lives. Not always romantically, but the love had been there. I'd never understood why he'd wanted me. Why he'd chosen me. But I could understand this. Why would he want a woman who couldn't give him children?

"Jaye," he said, shaking me slightly. "Jaye, are you listening?"

I'd gone numb inside somewhere along the way. What I did know was that I was a survivor. And I'd survive this too. No matter how much it hurt.

"What's wrong?" he asked, holding my chin up so he could see my face.

I shook my head and said, "Nothing," and I tried to pull out of his arms, but he wouldn't let me go.

And then his eyes narrowed and I saw anger flash in them. It was rare Jack got angry—really angry.

"You're a fool," he said. "How many times does a man need to say he loves you before you actually believe it?"

"What?" I asked, confused but also irritated at being called a fool.

"I can see it all over your face," he accused. "You think I mean to take a break from us. Like my love for you is so shallow that us not being able to conceive would be a deal breaker for me? Let me make myself clear. Children are a temporary assignment, whether we choose to have them or not, and they'll eventually leave us to start their own families. But you're my wife until I take my last breath on this earth. Nothing changes that."

He moved to shift out of the way and get out of the shower, but I held on tight.

"I know," I said. "You're right and I'm sorry. I'm sorry. I know this is hurting you as much as it hurts me. But to tell you the truth I just feel stupid and like an inept failure. I'm not a stupid person. And anything I've failed at in life I've pushed myself and learned and studied until I at least had a cursory understanding. I know the biology of my body. I know how it's supposed to work. And yet it doesn't."

His face was like stone. "Please don't give up on me," I said. "Between all of this and standing over Evie Lidle's body this morning, I'm just not thinking clearly. I know you love me. And I know there's nothing in heaven or hell that could separate us. I was just being...stupid. I'm sorry."

"See that you remember it," he said. "And you're not stupid. You brain just stopped functioning for a moment. It's understandable after a day like today."

"I don't mean to be so hard to love," I said. "I really don't."

"I'm hopeful in twenty or thirty years you'll make it a little easier," he said, kissing the top of my head. "But I've always loved a challenge. My mother says it's because I have a head like a rock."

"And thank God for it," I said. "Not that I'm complaining. But why are you here in the shower with me?"

"I told you," he said. "They cut me loose for court. I've already finished testifying. Cole worked the majority of that case so he'll be more involved. But I just need to stay available in case I need to be called back to testify. And I'm not normally one to rush these situations when you're naked and pliable in the shower, but I've told Martinez I'd be an extra set of hands on this case."

I grunted and let him help me to my feet, and I stepped out of the shower and dried off. "What time is it? I told him I'd text as soon as the autopsy was done. I got a little sidetracked."

"So did he," Jack said. "I was coming into the station as he was leaving, and he told me to tell you he was headed to King George to see Kitty Lidle in the hospital. They're not sure she's going to make it. She was in respiratory distress for a long time before she was found, and she's got some bleeding on the brain from several mini-strokes. They're still waiting for toxicology to come back, but she was given something."

I hurriedly dressed and ran a brush through my mostly damp hair, and then I looked in the mirror and grimaced. There was no amount of ice packs or makeup that was going to help my swollen face.

"Martinez asked if we'd go interview Jackson Sparrow," Jack said. "He should be home from work by now."

I looked at the time on my phone and grimaced. It was after five. I hadn't really had time to have a mental breakdown in the shower, but here we were. I grabbed the makeup bag I kept in the drawer and hurriedly put on concealer and mascara, hoping that would conceal the obvious signs of tears, but there was no hope.

"Maybe just wear your sunglasses," Jack said. "It works for Cher."

I made a face in his direction and said, "I've got to run downstairs and get the autopsy report of Alan Goble for Martinez. And then we can head out. Is Sheldon still here?"

"He and Emmy Lu were packing it in for the day when I got here," Jack said. "Sheldon said he had a date with the donut girl."

"Lord," I said. "Lily thinks he's going to end up as some voodoo sacrifice or something."

"I've seen that girl at the donut shop," Jack said. "I wouldn't be surprised in the slightest."

"You're not the first person to tell me that," I said. "I'm going to have to go by and get a look for myself. I don't want to end up having to rescue him from some bizarre hostage situation. He's been known to make bad decisions when it comes to women in the past."

"I still don't understand how he's gotten one

woman to sleep with him," Jack said. "Much less multiple women."

"I guess he appeals to a certain type," I said. "He does seem sweet and cuddly."

I ran downstairs and grabbed the file and was back up before Jack had his weapon strapped back on. It was still daylight outside, so I took Jack's advice and put on my sunglasses and got my bag, even though it looked like the sun was fighting a losing battle against another wave of gray clouds rolling in.

"Maybe we should move to Arizona," he said, eyeing the same clouds as we left the funeral home. "I wouldn't mind a dry heat."

I snorted out a laugh and got in his police unit.

"Don't get me wrong," I said as we headed back toward Regent Park. "Martinez is a great cop, and he's pretty fun. But this is what I've been missing today."

"It's pretty rare for people to get to be partners at work and home," he said. "I worry about Martinez sometimes. Losing a partner is like losing a close family member. He still never talks about Lewis. I'm not sure he's ever really processed his grief."

In reality, I couldn't blame Martinez. And I certainly made it a point to never bring up Lewis when he was around. It had been my father who'd killed Martinez's partner.

"What'd you find out about the second victim?" Jack asked. "Goble."

"Cause of death was three gunshot wounds to the chest," I said. "Close range. Any of the three bullets were fatal. Everything else came back normal. The only thing that came back abnormal was that he'd had sex shortly before death."

"With the woman who shot him?" Jack asked.

"Possibly," I said. "But I don't think so. Astrid told us she'd come into work that day around ten, which was also confirmed by the chef. She found Kitty Lidle sometime after noon. We've got the 911 call for a time stamp. And she was at the house when Plank arrived with the EMTs. I don't know how she would have had time to get back down to her place and meet up with the walking STD."

"He had an STD?" Jack asked.

"A couple of them," I said. "Showed up in the blood work. We probably need to have a conversation with Lizzie Ryan. That's the granddaughter of the woman who's been with Kitty Lidle since her childhood. Lizzie and Alan Goble were caught in the act not long ago. When I say he'd recently had sex, there was seminal fluid on the inside of his jeans and on him. No underwear."

"Like he'd dressed in a hurry," Jack said. "Maybe he and Astrid have something going on the side and she finds out about the other girl. Uses the confusion at the house and the kidnapping to kill him in cold blood. Scorned lover."

"It's as plausible as anything," I said.

Jack slowed as we drove past Regent Park. The evidence of any semblance of a crime scene at the park had been washed away. Gone were the evidence tags and spatters of blood on the sidewalk. And all that was left of the crime-scene tape was a last remaining scrap that clung to a tree.

"I hope to God we got all the evidence we needed," Jack said.

"We've not recovered the pajamas she'd been wearing," I said. "Or whatever he used to strangle her with. We've got DNA out the wazoo, but it doesn't matter if there's no suspect. And as much as I wanted it to be so, there were no fresh wounds or scratches on Alan Goble. He wasn't her attacker."

"Making it all the more curious as to why Astrid killed him," Jack said. "I did a cursory check on Goble. He's got a sealed file."

"Sealed is just a word," I said, making Jack wince.

"Carver was a bad influence on you," he said.

Jack was a by-the-book kind of guy. But Carver had worked for the FBI and they were a little more relaxed when it came to the gray areas. Doug was very much like his uncle, and I knew the seal on Alan Goble's file would be an open book by the end of the night.

Myrtle Sparrow's house was painted a soft green, and it had the best curb appeal on the block. There were plants everywhere. There was a beige Corolla parked under the carport and a black truck parked in front of the house. Jack parked behind the Corolla in the driveway.

"Looks like he's home," I said.

Jack and I got out of the car, and before we could get to the front door the screen opened and a man stepped out and started toward us. I saw Jack casually put his hand on his weapon.

"Who are you?" the man said.

"Sheriff Jack Lawson," he said. "And this is Dr. Graves with the coroner's office. Are you Jackson Sparrow?"

He made a snorting sound and pulled a pack of cigarettes from his front pocket and then moved to stand under the carport.

"My mother won't let me smoke in the

house," he said. "Have to come out here. Feels just like it did when I was in high school."

Jackson Sparrow wasn't an attractive man. He wasn't an unattractive man. He was medium. That was the only way I could think to describe him. Medium height, medium weight, with a medium amount of hair on his medium-brown head.

He wore a pair of rumpled khakis and a brown flannel shirt over a white undershirt. He smelled of cigarettes and beer.

"Mom told me about the kid in the park," he said, lighting his cigarette and taking a deep inhale. "She said y'all were looking for me."

I couldn't remember the last time I'd actually seen someone smoke a cigarette. I saw the occasional vape haze, but cigarettes were outlawed in and around all public buildings in Virginia, which was where I spent most of my time.

"That's right," Jack said. "We're trying to get statements from all the neighbors to catch whoever did this to her. Maybe someone saw something unusual. You work at the airport?"

"Yeah," he said. "Been there a couple years now. It's an okay job. Traffic sucks, but what are you gonna do when your ex bleeds you for everything you have?"

Jack nodded sympathetically and asked, "What time did you get home yesterday?"

"I get off shift at four," he said. "But there's this bar not far from work where all the guys go on Monday nights. Had some dinner. Drank a few beers. Watched a Nationals game."

"What time did you get home?" Jack asked.

"A little after eleven," he said, flicking ash next to his work boots. "You'd think it was the middle of the night to hear Mom talk. She always falls asleep in her chair about seven thirty. Then she'll wake up about nine and shuffle off to bed. This whole town drives me crazy. Nothing to do but watch the grass grow and paint dry."

"Tell me about when you got home," Jack said. "Any other drivers on the road?"

He flicked the cigarette to the ground and stepped on it, and then tapped another out of the pack from his pocket, lighting it with the ease of long practice.

"Hard to say," he said. "I wasn't really paying attention. Just wanted to get home and get to bed. I have to leave for work around four every morning."

"I'm not here to bust you for drinking and driving," Jack said affably. "We're looking for someone who raped and beat a twelve-year-old to death. So I'll ask you again if you saw anyone on your way home."

Jackson let out a long stream of smoke and sized Jack up. And then he must have believed him because he said, "Passed a black SUV on Jane Seymour." He pointed to the corner less than twenty yards away.

"At least tried to pass it," he said. "I was a little buzzed and I wasn't expecting anyone to be driving around the neighborhood so it took me off guard. Their lights flashed right in my eyes and I might have swerved off the road some. And then I turned the corner and there was another car. They honked and I just kind of parked as close to the house as I could get and stumbled inside."

"You said the lights flashed right in your eyes," Jack said. "Brights or regular lights?"

"Felt like brights," he said. "I couldn't see anything. Blinded me for a second. Thought I was going to take that mailbox out over there."

"Did you see who was driving?"

"I just told you I couldn't see anything. At least not in that car."

"But in the other?" Jack prompted.

"Looked like a woman," he said. "I think I scared her as much as she scared me. But she drove on."

"The first car," Jack said. "You remember what it looked like?"

"Dark," he said. "Might have been an SUV. But it was a small one if so. Big headlights."

"Was it going fast or slow?"

He opened his mouth to answer, but then stopped and closed it again. You could practically see the wheels turning in his head.

"Huh," he said. "I would have said he was going fast, but I don't think he was. I think I was the one going fast. I think he might have just been sitting there at the corner. Or moving real slow." He closed his eyes like he was trying to conjure up the scene in his head. "I think that's why I swerved. It was real dark. That streetlight on the corner over there is out. And the angle the car was sitting made it kind of blend into the darkness. That's why I was so surprised. It's like the headlights were all of a sudden right there, so I swerved into that yard over there. Sobered me up for a second. I didn't need that headache on top of everything else going on in my life right now."

"Was the car still there when you went inside?" Jack asked.

"Yeah, I think so. Just driving around the park."

"How long have you lived here?" I asked him.

His gaze shifted to me. "Six months. Been going through a divorce. Had to sell the house to pay off all the credit-card debt she racked up in my name, so I was forced to move in with Mom."

"You ever see those vehicles in this area before?" I asked him. "Maybe parked in one of the neighbors' driveways?"

"No," he said immediately. "The people around here are mostly older. They don't have cars like that. Too new. Too nice."

"What was the name of that bar you were at last night?" Jack asked.

"Rawley's," he said. "It's off 295."

"Thanks for your time," Jack said. "Let us know if you remember anything else."

The guy grunted and tossed his cigarette in a puddle before heading back inside.

CHAPTER TWELVE

"What do you think?" I asked Jack once we were back on the road.

"Might be something," Jack said. "Or it might be nothing. But the timing falls in the window for when Evie Lidle was murdered. We can check out the guy's alibi. See what time he left the bar."

I texted Martinez and let him know we were headed to question Lizzie Ryan, and then I called Plank.

"You still at the house with the team?" I asked him once he picked up.

"We just cleared out," Plank said. "Lieutenant Daniels combed this whole place. We pulled fingerprints in the staff passageway. They're small, and Daniels said they match Evie Lidle's, but she'll confirm in the report once she gets them under the magnifier. The staff passageway led to different rooms—to a library on the second floor—and then the hallway split on the first floor and there was a secret entrance into the kitchen pantry and another that led to Robert Lidle's study. The exterior door of his study was unlocked."

"Interesting," I said. "Any prints on the exterior door?"

"Evie Lidle's," Plank confirmed. "Robert Lidle and his family arrived back at the home. We let them know the upstairs bedroom is still cordoned off as well as Astrid Nielsen's cottage. He wasn't happy about it. Said he'd be calling the sheriff himself."

"I look forward to the call," Jack said.

We thanked Plank for the update and then disconnected. I checked my phone to see if Martinez had responded, but there was nothing from him yet.

"Interesting that Robert Lidle would go home instead of to the hospital to see his wife," Jack said.

"Yeah," I agreed. "Everyone we've talked to said they're not really involved in each other's lives. Sounds like it's kind of always been that way. You have the address for Lizzie Ryan?"

"She lives in Newcastle," Jack said.

"Alex told us he let her go home around ten this morning since she was up all night with the foalings. Maybe she didn't go straight home? Maybe she and Alan Goble connected. He was supposed to be on duty this morning, but no one was at the front gate when we arrived."

"We need to check the schedule of every guard who was supposed to be on duty yesterday and today," he said. "Pull them all into questioning. There should be a log of anyone who came in or out, and if they weren't at their post to see it I want to know why."

Newcastle was a boutique town that prided itself on unique boutiques, original restaurants, and the arts. There were galleries and theaters downtown, and unlike Bloody Mary, there were a lot of places open after nine o'clock.

Lizzie Ryan lived in a cute little neighborhood with houses that looked like they'd been built in the forties, even though I knew they were only a few years old. She lived in a blue craftsman on the corner, and Jack parked behind a white pickup truck.

"Think she's home?" I asked.

"We'll find out soon enough," Jack said. "But I'd say someone is. I just saw the curtains move in the front window."

We made our way up the sidewalk and the

three porch steps, and Jack rang the bell. It wasn't long before the door was opened. I'd been expecting to see Lizzie Ryan, but instead a tall young woman with skin the color of dark coffee opened the door. She was one of the most breathtaking people I'd ever seen. Her eyes were black and her skin flawless, and her full lips spread into a smile showing stunningly white teeth.

"Can I help you?" she asked.

"We're looking for Lizzie Ryan," Jack said, showing his badge.

Her smile dimmed some. "Oh, sure. Lizzie's here. Come on in."

"What's your name?" Jack asked.

"Trinity," she said. "Trinity Armstrong. I'm Lizzie's roommate."

"You work with horses too?" I asked.

She chuckled, the laughter in her eyes contagious. "God, no. They scare me to death. I'm good with smaller four-legged animals." As if on cue a white ball of fluff barreled into the room. I assumed it was a dog, but it was hard to tell. "I'm an accountant. The idea of being on my feet all day is not appealing."

"Do you live here?" Jack asked.

"Yeah," she said. "Lizzie and I went to college together. Figured we'd keep rooming together until we fell in love and got married. We're obviously both still waiting."

"The men around here must be stupid," I said.

"I like to think so," she said, grinning. "Maybe if the men around here looked up from their phones from time to time they might see their soul mate standing right in front of them. Lizzie has better luck. Men who work outdoors aren't so attached to an electronic device. I'll go get Lizzie. Just have a seat wherever."

"Nice girl," Jack said after she'd disappeared into a back room.

"Gorgeous," I said. "She could be a model."

I took a seat on the edge of the sofa and realized the dog was still there. I couldn't decide if he was staring at me, or if he was afraid to move because he couldn't see through the hair covering his eyes.

But apparently he could see because he jumped onto the couch beside me and wiggled his way into my lap.

"Well," I said. "Hello there." And then I remembered Oscar and that there was still the possibility that Jack hadn't heard about him yet. But I figured that was unlikely. If Martinez had told Cole, and Cole had told Lily, then he'd probably mentioned it to Jack too. I figured the best thing to do was not say anything until faced with the moment.

We only had to wait a couple of minutes. I was expecting for Lizzie Ryan to have some semblance of her grandmother, at least in the height department, but Lizzie was a couple of inches taller than me and her hair was the same color as the chestnut foal I'd seen in the foaling pen earlier that day. There was a smattering of freckles across her nose and her eyes were wide set and green. She was a girl-next-door type, pretty and fresh faced and understated in black sweats and a KGU sweatshirt.

"Trin said you were the police," she said coming in. "Does this have to do with Evie? I saw about her on the news. It's a horrible thing that something like that can happen here. We always feel so safe."

"It always pays to keep an eye out," Jack said. "Why don't you have a seat?"

"Sure," she said. "I don't really know what I can tell you about Evie. I work down at the stables."

"How long have you worked there?" Jack asked.

"I graduated from KGU with a degree in equine therapy," she said. "My dad introduced me to Alex and he hired me on about three years ago."

"Alex said y'all had quite a night last night," Jack said.

Her smile was radiant. "It was a great night. And exhausting. We were up all night. I've been sleeping most of the afternoon."

"Tell us about Alan Goble," Jack said, his gaze steady.

Her smile faltered and slight color came into her cheeks. "What about him?"

"What was your relationship with him?"

"I guess you already know that or you wouldn't be here," she said, blowing out a breath. "Alex told you he caught us, didn't he?"

"He did," Jack confirmed.

"I knew it was stupid when we were doing it," she said. "I don't know what came over me. Alan has that ability to make you feel wild and reckless. We were right there in the stables. Upstairs in one of the storage rooms. Alan always knows where there are no cameras because he's the security guy. But still, anyone could have walked in. My *dad* could have walked in. I was mortified when Alex found us."

"Did it make you stop seeing Alan?" I asked her.

Her lips pursed together tightly and her

hands rubbed nervously on the knees of her sweats.

"No," she admitted. "And I already know it's stupid. You don't have to tell me. And I know it won't last. He just has this kind of raw animal magnetism." She looked directly at me. "You ever met a guy like that? A guy that just fries your circuits?"

"Yeah," I said, cutting a look to Jack. "I get it."

"When was the last time you saw him?" Jack asked.

She chewed on her bottom lip and looked back at Jack.

"I'm not here to cause trouble with your job," Jack asked. "We're trying to find out what happened to Evie Lidle."

Her eyes widened. "You think Alan had something to do with it?"

"We don't know," Jack said. "I guess you haven't watched the news recently. I'm sorry to tell you that Alan is dead. He was killed earlier today."

The color drained from her face so her freckles looked stark against her pale skin. "What? No way. I just saw him. I saw him today."

"You went to him instead of going home?" I asked gently.

Her eyes were glassy and I knew she was in

shock. She shivered involuntarily. "I was revved, you know? From the foals. So I texted him when Alex cut me loose, wanting to celebrate. He told me to meet him at the staff garage." She swallowed with some difficulty. "So I did."

"He was there waiting for you?" Jack asked.

She shook her head. "No, he'd not come into work yet. Said he'd had to take care of some things. He pulled into the garage around ten thirty."

"Did y'all go anywhere?" I asked.

The color came back into her cheeks. "Uhh, no," she said. "We stayed in the garage. In his car. He has a Bronco. When we were done I left in my car, and I came home. I grabbed some lunch and watched the news. That's when I saw about Evie. And then I crashed and slept the rest of the afternoon."

"Why would Alan be in Astrid Nielsen's house?" Jack asked, taking a different route to the questions.

"They had a thing for a while," she said, her voice almost robotic as she talked. "Alan had a thing with just about every female who stepped foot on that property as long as they were somewhat attractive and didn't mind him not being able to commit."

"A recent thing?" I asked her.

"I think on and off for a while," she said, shrugging. "He'd told me a couple of months ago he'd broken it off for good this time. He said she was starting to show her age."

"I'm going to ask you some hard questions," Jack said. "And I need you to really think about the answers."

"Okay," she said, looking at him warily.

"You said Alan had a thing with just about every female who stepped foot on the property," he said. "Did he have an age limit?"

"Astrid was probably as old as he was willing to go," she said. "I think she's in her mid-forties."

"What about the other direction? Younger girls?"

She started to shake her head and then her eyes widened in shock. "Like girls girls?" she asked. "Like Evie?"

"Any whisperings he liked to start young?"

"Not that I've ever heard," she said.

"Ever caught him watching pornography or anything he shouldn't have?"

"No," she said.

"What about his sexual habits? Anything weird in the bedroom?"

"No, no," she said, continuing to shake her head. "He was just a hot guy who oozed sex appeal. To tell you the truth he wasn't all that great in bed once you got past the initial stages. He was always more concerned about himself than making sure I was having a good time. But other than that it was just sex."

"Do you know of any other sexual partners he was juggling besides you and Astrid?" he asked.

"Not since he and I started things up," she said. "I believed him when he said he'd broken things off with Astrid for good. I knew he wouldn't last. That he'd start sniffing around someone else when he got bored with me. But for a couple of months I had his undivided attention. Or at least I thought I did."

Jack stood and I pushed the dog off my lap and followed suit.

"We're sorry to be the bearers of bad news," Jack told her as we walked toward the door.

I paused and looked back at her. She was still sitting on the couch, frozen in her shock and pain.

"You might see your grandmother," I told her. "She's taking Evie's death pretty hard. And they're not sure Kitty is going to make it either."

She nodded and said, "I'll go see her. She's probably full of whiskey and sound asleep by now." She tried to smile, but it was difficult for her. "She didn't approve of Alan. She kept telling me he'd lead to no good. But she never told my father about us. I asked her not to."

"It sounds like you're close," I said.

"She's the best."

"Lizzie," I said, knowing what I was about to say was never easy for anyone to hear. "Did you and Alan have unprotected sex?"

Her face flushed with embarrassment. "A couple of times," she said, shrugging. "But I'm on the pill so I didn't worry too much about it."

"You probably need to be tested," I told her. "Some things showed up in his blood work you should be concerned about."

She nodded, but I could tell the information hadn't really hit her yet.

"Let us know if you think of anything else," Jack said. We let ourselves out and closed the door behind us.

"Is it just me or was it weird that she didn't ask how Alan died?" I asked Jack once we'd gotten back into his unit.

"Or why we'd asked about him being in Astrid's apartment," Jack said. "Let's head back to the station and see if Martinez is ready to interview Astrid. We're going to need Doug tonight. I'll swing by and pick him up and bring him back to the station. It's going to be a late night for all of us."

I was speechless. If Jack went to pick up Doug he was going to find out about Oscar. I didn't know Oscar on a personal level yet, but I hoped he hadn't made himself too comfortable.

I looked at Jack and opened my mouth, hoping something convincing would pour out, but it didn't.

"I know about the dog," he finally said. "Cole told me. I also know about the sofa. I'm reserving judgment on Doug's cleaning skills, but we can deal with the mess once this case is solved."

"That was much more painless than I expected it to be," I told him. "You're mellowing in your old age."

"Nah," he said. "I've just learned not to sweat the small stuff. When you lived in as many life-or-death situations as I have, it puts other things into perspective."

"I guess when you put it that way..."

We were almost back to the station when Jack got a call on his personal cell.

"It's Everett Lidle," he said, holding up the phone so I could see and then he answered, "Jack Lawson."

"Jack, it's Everett Lidle."

"I'm so sorry for your loss, Everett," Jack said. "You know if there's anything Jaye and I can do for you and your family we will."

I'd forgotten that Jack knew the Lidles, on a personal and a professional basis. It seemed like Jack knew everyone. It was me who was the recluse. I grew up in Bloody Mary, but the first chance I got I left to go to college and then on to medical school. It wasn't until my parents' scandal that I moved back home. Being a recluse at that point of my life seemed more of a necessity than anything. Every time I walked down the street I could hear people talking about "that Graves girl" like I'd steal their silver if they had any.

But things had improved when I'd married Jack. Not that I'd ever cared, because to me, he'd always just been Jack, but his family name and his reputation meant a lot and my circle of acquaintances now included people like the lieutenant governor of the state of Virginia and other influential names. And from time to time, we had to dress in fancy clothes and rub elbows with people Jack didn't necessarily like, but it was important to keep relationships cordial. I'd never understood politics, but I also knew that elected sheriffs in the state of Virginia had a lot of power, and everyone wanted a piece of it.

All that to say, it was no surprise that Jack could talk to the Lidles on an intimate and comfortable level, and on the other side of the coin there was me who'd never met any of them and only heard about them on the news.

"We're a mess, Jack," Everett said. "Would you mind...would you mind coming by the house? I think it might help Jenny if she heard straight from you how things are going."

"Jaye and I are in the car now," he said, flipping on his blinker and cutting across two lanes of traffic to take an exit. "We can be there in about fifteen minutes."

"I really appreciate it," Everett said. There was a catch in his voice and then he simply said, "Thanks," and hung up the phone.

We wound our way through the manicured streets of Nottingham until Jack turned onto the Lidles' street.

"You've been here before?" I asked.

"Several years ago he threw a Christmas party for several hundred people as a thank-you for supporting his election campaign. I believe Jenny was pregnant with their youngest at the time."

"I didn't realize you supported his campaign," I said.

"I didn't," Jack said, grinning. "And there are many policies we disagree on. But those things are for the citizens to decide in the voting booth. But he's a likeable guy and he loves his family. You can see that right off. So it's easy to put politics aside when you have those kinds of things in common."

Jack circled the arched driveway and parked so he wouldn't get blocked in. Unlike my earlier visit, there were several cars parked at the Lidle residence. All of them very expensive.

The front door opened before we could reach the stoop and Everett Lidle stood there waiting for us. He looked like a man who'd been dragged through hell and back again.

He was tall and he carried himself like a man who was used to commanding rooms. He was lean and trim and the slacks and sportcoat he wore didn't look like a man who'd spent the day on a plane trying to get home to his family. But maybe there were people on the planet who traveled more gracefully than I did.

But his face told a different story. There were dark circles beneath his red-rimmed eyes, and his golden hair looked like he'd run his fingers through it repeatedly. There was a steeliness in his gaze.

"Jack," he said, holding out his hand.

"Everett," Jack said, shaking his hand in return.

Everett ushered us inside and closed the door behind him.

"This is my wife," Jack said. "I don't think you've met."

"No," I said, reaching my own hand out. "J.J. Graves. I'm sorry we're meeting under these circumstances."

"Me too," Everett said. "Family is starting to arrive. I hope you don't mind. I think they're in the kitchen right now. My sister is trying to get Jenny to take something so she can rest. I hope she listens to her. I wanted a chance to talk to you alone first."

Everett moved robotically toward the family room I'd been shown to earlier.

"My mother-in-law took the girls with her for a little while. I feel like I'm losing my mind," he said.

"That's understandable," Jack said. "Your whole world just got turned upside down."

"I got on the first flight I could find to get home," he said. "Jenny..." He dropped his head in his hands. "My wife and girls are a mess. And my mother. Phin and Janet and I are going to see her in a little while. My whole family is falling apart. I don't know why this is happening. None of it makes any sense. We're good people. Why is this happening to us?"

"We're doing everything we can to find out," Jack said.

"Who did this to my daughter?" he asked, his voice breaking. "I've seen the reports on the news. How she was found. How could anyone do that to a little girl? *My* little girl."

"A monster," Jack said. "There was nothing you or anyone did. A monster is who is to blame. And that monster took Evie from your parents' home. And that same monster potentially drugged your mother to get Evie out of the house. Has there been anything recent your parents have been concerned about as far as security or employees? Any threats?"

He rubbed his hands over his face. "I don't think so. They're not as active as they used to be. Mom loves the house and her horses. She rarely leaves anymore. Most of the staff they've had for years. Maybe a new gardener or housemaid every once in a while. And dad is just nosy and likes to be in the middle of things in DC. It keeps him busy."

"Any problem with any of the staff?" Jack asked.

"Not that I know of," Everett said, shrugging. "Wait, the trainer. Alex. I remember when Mom brought him on. The security guy, Alan, tried to convince Dad not to hire him because he had a conviction. I don't remember what for. But Mom was adamant that he was the right guy for the job. He's been there several years now."

"Anyone else?" Jack asked. "What about issues with you personally? You're a public figure. Any threats or disagreements?"

"Threats? No," he said. "But my days are filled with disagreements. You know how it is. King George County has a lot of people with a lot of opinions. But I've never felt unsafe. And my family certainly hasn't. I'd never put them in danger. My parents are the ones who always led life in the spotlight. And now my brother. I guess my sister too. All I've ever wanted was to live a normal life and have a normal family. I don't know how we can have that now. My oldest daughter is gone. And now Evie. We'll never be a normal family again."

"We're not going to stop until we find out who did this to Evie," Jack said. "We're going to bring her justice and put away whoever is responsible."

"I'd kill him if I got my hands on him," Everett said, anger flashing in his eyes.

"And I can't say that I'd blame you," Jack said. "But let us do our jobs. We're good at it."

He nodded and his head jerked up when a door opened somewhere on the other side of the house, followed by muted voices. Everett stood up and Jack and I followed suit as Jenny and several other people walked into the room. Jenny walked right to Everett and he tucked her gently into his arms. Her face was red and swollen from crying, and there was a glassiness in her eyes that made me think Janet had been successful in getting her to take something so she could rest.

"Jack, I don't know if you've met my brother and sister before," Everett said.

"We have," Janet Lidle-Downey said, coming forward to take Jack's hand warmly and then mine. "Though just briefly a time at some political function." She was a petite woman, built very much like her mother, though Janet's hair was impossibly dark and her eyes a startling shade of blue. She was an attractive woman, but the lines of grief had etched themselves around her eyes and mouth.

"You have a good memory," Jack said.

"Comes with the territory," she said, her mouth almost reaching a smile.

"My wife, Jaye," Jack said.

"And this is my husband, Carson," Janet said.

A short, quiet man with gentle eyes and soft hands came forward to greet us. He looked to be at least a decade older than Janet, possibly more, but they touched each other affectionately and you could see they were a unit. You could tell a lot about a marriage by the way couples interacted in public.

"My brother, Phin," Everett said.

You could feel the tension there between brothers. Everett's mouth tightened into a firm line and he looked down at his wife, kissing her gently on the head. I knew it probably hadn't been easy to grow up as the second son in a family that was as close to American royalty as you could get. His brother took over the family business and his sister was a congresswoman. But Everett had chosen a life of service in a small community and he never made national news.

Phin Lidle was an imposing figure. He was an inch taller and broader through the shoulders than his brother. He carried himself with authority and dignity. All of that probably would have mattered except I remembered seeing the pictures of him on TMZ in a seedy motel room with his boxers around his ankles and a tableful of lines of cocaine.

He shook Jack's hand, but didn't bother to shake mine, which I was perfectly okay with.

"And these are our friends Peter and Tiffany Bancroft," Everett said. "They might as well be family. We've known them since college. Our kids all go to school together."

"I'm the head of school at the Dolley

Madison School for Girls," Tiffany said. "We've closed down for the rest of the week. Evie touched so many lives. Had so many friends." She started to tear up and tried desperately to keep her tears from falling by pressing under her eyes, but still a few escaped.

"We've been fielding calls all day," Peter said. "We've been working on getting counseling centers set up so students and parents both can have access. I'm the school psychologist."

Peter and Tiffany Bancroft were an attractive couple, obviously well educated and well to do. Peter was tall and took good care of himself. I imagined him playing tennis several times a week at his club, and making himself a dry martini when he got home from school every day.

Tiffany was petite and blond and wore an ice-blue sweater set and matching pants, and there was a single strand of pearls around her neck and matching pearl studs in her ears. She moved close to Jenny and put her arm around her, and Jenny hugged her hard as they wept together.

"It's okay," Tiffany kept telling her. "However you need to grieve is okay. We're here for you no matter what you think you need or don't need. Just rely on us to help."

Jenny nodded and wiped her eyes and sat

down on the couch behind her. And then she looked at me out of tear-drenched eyes. Everett sat down next to her and they clasped hands. Everyone else surrounded them like fierce protectors.

"When can we have her?" Jenny asked. "When can we see her?"

I hesitated, looking back and forth between Everett and Jenny. "It will be at least a couple of days. Depending on the investigation. But I promise you we'll take good care of her."

There were certain things I'd learned never to mention to parents of children. They had the knowledge in their heads, and they'd eventually come to terms, but I never reminded them that their child had been through an autopsy unless they asked me specific questions.

And I couldn't bring myself to tell any of them that they shouldn't see her remains. No one should have to remember their child that way.

"I don't know what to do next," Jenny said. "I always do better when I have something to do. She has a new dress. We just went shopping last week for some spring clothes. All this rain was getting us down, and she said she wanted bright color so she'd look like sunshine even if there was none outside."

Jenny hiccupped out a sigh and I watched a silent tear slide down Everett Lidle's face.

"It's okay to make plans," I told her softly. "I'll give her back to you as soon as they give me the word."

Jenny nodded and then looked up at her husband. "I think I need to lie down now."

"I'll take her," Tiffany said, sliding an arm under her friend and helping her to her feet. "Come on, love. I'll tuck you in. Just like you used to do for me when we were in college and I cried myself to sleep over Peter flirting with that horrible cheerleader instead of me."

Jenny gave a laugh-sob, and then they disappeared out of the room together.

"Jack," Everett said. "I need you to find the son of a bitch who did this to my daughter. I don't know what we'll do to think that he's still out there somewhere. Doing those things to other girls."

Jack nodded and said, "We'll find him."

We stood to let ourselves out, but Peter said, "I'll walk you to the door."

We followed him out into the entryway, and I raised my brows as he slid the doors of the family room closed behind him. He reached into his pocket and pulled out a business card and handed it to Jack.

"Whatever Tiffany and I can do to help," he said. "Just reach out. I'm the head psychologist at the school, and I oversee all of the counselors. But I still see patients privately. I'm sure this was very difficult for some of your officers who were on scene."

"I appreciate the thoughtfulness," Jack said, taking the card.

CHAPTER THIRTEEN

WE MADE OUR WAY BACK TO THE TOWNE SQUARE, navigating through cars and pedestrians who were clogging up the roadways.

The Towne Square was where the four towns in King George County met, and many of the buildings were on the historical registry. The courthouse sat in the middle of the square, and then the other municipal buildings like the sheriff's office and city hall were across the street. There were shops and restaurants and bars, and the city was doing its best to revitalize the area with upstairs condos and studio apartments over the businesses. What they'd done was create a madhouse because parking was very limited.

It was a Tuesday evening, so the city employee traffic was mostly gone, but the bar on the corner was almost always busy. Jack finally turned on his lights to get people to move out of the way, and he pulled into his parking spot in front of the sheriff's office.

"I enjoy the perks of riding in a cop car," I said. There was a damp chill in the air as the sun was starting to go down, but I realized we'd had a pretty good stretch without any rain. Hopefully it stayed that way.

"Serve and protect," Jack said, winking. "That's my motto."

"I thought you were going to pick up Doug?" I asked.

"I want to check in with Betsy first," he said. "Her car is still here. I've been out of the office all day."

Betsy Clement had been Jack's secretary since he'd been elected as sheriff. She'd also been the secretary for about a dozen or so other sheriffs over the last forty years. She knew secrets about people that she would go to her grave with, but just in case she turned to a life of blackmail, everyone stayed out of her path.

Jack keyed us into the private entrance that led to the hallway just outside his office. Things were quiet inside. Second shift was just coming on, so there was a relaxed feel to the place. The smell of burnt coffee lingered from the day, and there was an underlying odor of Pine-Sol.

We turned the corner and saw Betsy Clement, locking up the stack of files that had been on her desk. She was a small woman, and I could never recall in my life a time when she wasn't old. Her face was comfortably wrinkled and a pair of glasses hung from a chain around her neck.

"I was just about to leave for the day," she said. "Your messages are on your desk. You're not needed in court tomorrow."

Her voice was like a chainsaw, a testament to the two packs of cigarettes a day she used to smoke. She'd quit a few years ago, and now she chewed gum like it was a lifeline.

"Good news," Jack said. "Anything urgent?"

"SSDD," she said.

My mouth twitched at her response. There was no one quite like Betsy.

"A man named Geoffrey left several messages at the request of Robert Lidle. I told him you were in court all day and couldn't check your phone. Didn't seem to stop him from calling though."

"He's probably not used to being told to wait for anything," Jack said. "I got several messages on my cell from Robert as well. I'll call him back."

Betsy hmmphed. "I'd wait a few days. That Geoffrey kept talking to me like I was stuck to the bottom of his shoe."

Jack grinned. "Martinez come in yet?"

"Not that I've seen, but I can't keep track of everyone."

"I don't believe that for a second," Jack said. "Have a good night."

"We'll see," she said. She hiked her bag over her shoulder and grabbed her keys, and then shuffled out the back door toward the gated lot.

I scrubbed my hands over my face.

Jack opened his office and moved behind his desk to his computer, ignoring the stack of hand-written messages from Betsy.

"What's Alex's full name?" he asked.

I rubbed at my temple, trying to ignore the headache that was gathering there. "Alex Wheeler. He lives on the Lidle property. Said he's worked there for seven years."

"Ahh, well," Jack said, raising his brows. "Looks like you might need to talk to Alex again. He's got a statutory rape conviction. Looks like it was pleaded down to indecency with a minor, and he did a year in jail. Spent some time on the sex offender list for almost a decade."

"I don't like coincidences," I said.

"I've never been a big fan of them myself," Jack said.

There was a knock on the door and Martinez stuck his head in.

"Come on in," Jack said. "Good timing." And then he filled him in on what we'd just discovered about Alex Wheeler."

Martinez whistled. "I guess that's not information you want to disclose to an investigating officer when you're looking for a child killer."

"How's Kitty Lidle?" I asked.

Martinez shook his head. "Doctors aren't expecting her to make it through the night. I did get confirmation though that she'd been given a large dose of promethazine. Apparently she had an adverse reaction and went into respiratory failure instead of just going into a deep sleep. It caused her to have several mini-strokes, and now she's got bleeding on the brain. They're keeping her comfortable until all the family can be gathered and a decision can be made."

"We just talked to Everett Lidle," Jack said.

"How's he doing?" Martinez asked.

"About like you'd expect. Falling apart at the seams. He's the one who told us about Alex Wheeler. Said there was some dispute over hiring him because of his background. But Kitty Lidle insisted upon it."

Martinez grunted. "Hope that's not a choice that's come back to bite her. You want a crack at Astrid Nielsen? We're heading into the interrogation room."

"No," he said. "You two have a vibe already. I'm heading home to pick up Doug and his computer. We'll be set up in conference room A when you're finished. Any luck on surveillance cameras around the park?"

"I don't know if it's luck," Martinez said. "But out of all those houses there was only one house that's upgraded to the twenty-first century. But the angle is from the opposite side of the park. Derby is trying to clean it up but he said it's a shot in the dark. The footage is pretty grainy."

"We'll see if Doug and his computer girlfriend can work his magic on it," Jack said.

"I've got to admit that computer freaks me out," Martinez said, blowing out a breath. "Did no one see *Terminator*? That computer is a robot. She's probably going to kill us all."

I couldn't say I disagreed with him. I'd had the same thought.

CHAPTER FOURTEEN

MARTINEZ AND I WATCHED ASTRID NIELSEN through the two-way window for a few minutes. Holding her in lockup for the last few hours hadn't seemed to have any effect on her. She looked calm and composed, and her uniform was hardly rumpled.

"She's waived an attorney," Martinez said. "She literally gets caught red-handed killing a man and she's waived her right to counsel. What sense does that make?"

"Maybe she thinks she's justified," I said.

"Doesn't mean she's not going to prison," he said. "Murder is murder, no matter what you think your cause is. And you've already discovered that Alan Goble wasn't the man who murdered and raped Evie Lidle, so there's a deeper motivation there somewhere."

"Ahh, a woman scorned," I said.

"You have everything you need?" he asked.

"Yeah," I said. "Ready as I'll ever be."

There was nothing special about the interrogation room. It looked like every interrogation room on any cop TV show. It was small and windowless, and the color was a dingy yellow that looked like it had been painted with urine. There was a two-way mirror, a metal table, and four chairs.

"Ms. Nielsen," Martinez said as we walked in. "Sorry to keep you waiting."

Her mouth curved in an ironic smile, but she didn't say anything.

"You remember Dr. Graves?" he asked.

"Yes," she said. "Could I have some water?"

"Sure," he said, looking at the tech who was getting everything on record on the other side of the mirror.

"I'm going to read your rights to you again," Martinez said. "And this interview is being recorded."

She nodded again as Martinez read off the Miranda rights.

"Are you waiving your right to counsel?" Martinez asked.

"Yes," she said. "For now. I'd prefer to just come clean and get everything on record. In my experience attorneys slow things down."

"Most people aren't so anxious to go to jail," Martinez said.

"Believe me," she said. "I'm not either. But I'll let the process work."

I narrowed my eyes in thought. No one was this cooperative. At some point, self-preservation would kick in. It always did.

"Why don't we start at the beginning," Martinez said. "Help us understand how things could have spiraled so far downward between the time that we first talked to you, to the moment you pulled the trigger."

There was a knock at the door and a deputy came in with a bottle of water. Martinez unscrewed the top and handed it to her. She took a drink before she answered.

"Alan and I had a sexual relationship," she said, licking her lips. "We have, off and on, for close to ten years. The arrangement suited us both. Neither of us were proprietary and we got together when the mood struck."

"When was the last time the two of you got together?" Martinez asked.

"You mean when did we last have sex?"

"Yeah, that's what I mean."

"Sunday," she said. "We're both off on Sundays, so that's usually our regular hookup."

"Why did you tell us he was responsible for Evie Lidle's murder?" he asked, changing course. "Dr. Graves did his autopsy. We know he didn't kill her."

"The body always tells a story," I told her, opening the file folder I had. Martinez had told me to use it at my own discretion, but there was something about Astrid Nielsen that was sending up all my red flags. She hadn't reacted to anything. Not killing a man. And not being arrested and put in jail. She was either a sociopath or an excellent actress."

I put a couple of pictures of Alan Goble on the table. His body was pristine except for the three neat bullet holes in his chest. And then I put a picture of Evie Lidle.

"You see," I said. "I know he didn't kill her because Evie Lidle put up a fight. She fought her attacker. She scratched and clawed and kicked. See all these bruises?" I pointed to her arms. "She was blocking her body every time he struck her. Most likely with a belt."

Astrid stared at the photographs, her face paling slightly, and she licked her lips again.

"So why," I asked, "would you tell us that he

did it when you know and we know that he didn't?"

"Maybe you were jealous," Martinez said, picking up the thread. "Maybe you got word that while we were all talking he was screwing someone else out in the staff garage."

Her head jerked up at that. "Don't lie to me," she said. "I know he wasn't with anyone else."

"How do you know that?" Martinez asked.

"Because he was in my house because we had an appointment," she said. "For sex."

"Busy boy," I said. "I pulled someone else's DNA from him during the autopsy. And seminal fluid. You know what that means?"

"Not to mention we've already questioned her and gotten a confirmation of the time and place," Martinez added. "You're telling me he was planning to roll straight from her arms into yours? A guy like that gets off on the juggling and the lies more than he does the women. Maybe you got tired of him playing you."

Color rose in her cheeks and anger flashed in her eyes. "I don't believe you."

"I think you do," Martinez said. "And I think that's the real reason you shot him."

"You're wrong," she said, her fury cold. "Why don't you talk to Emma Lidle. Tell me how wrong I am."

Martinez's brows rose. "Emma Lidle? Evie's sister?"

"There's a reason she left home," she said. "Just like there's a reason Evie is dead."

"You're saying Alan Goble sexually assaulted both of these girls?"

"I'm saying there's more going on here than meets the eye," she said. "It goes deeper than Emma and Evie. There are secrets in that house. Now that's all I'm going to say without an attorney. The Lidles are powerful people, and Robert Lidle thinks Alan is a trophy in his trophy case. He can do no wrong. But I know different. Alan is a liar and he's got a dark side that he rarely shows."

"Yet it didn't bother you enough to keep you from going to bed with him," Martinez said.

She shrugged. "He could be charming and attentive when he wanted to be. And I have needs just like any woman. It's not like my job allows me to meet a lot of eligible men."

Her words were full of bitterness and regret and I wondered how much she'd given up for the Lidles to be her "family."

"What kind of vehicle do you drive?" Martinez asked.

"A dark blue Highlander. Why?"

"Just curious," he said. "You've still never told

us exactly why you're pointing a finger at Alan Goble. Did he give Kitty Lidle an overdose of her medicine? Because you were the last one to see her alive according to you."

"I've told you everything you need to know without signing my own death warrant," she said. "I believe I'll ask for that attorney now."

Twenty minutes later I made a detour to the breakroom to get a Snickers and a can of soda. I needed the extra jolt to get me through what was bound to be a long night.

I heard a dog bark before I'd made it to conference room A. And then I heard the laughter, and I peeped around the corner of the door, unsure of what I'd see.

"He's a good boy," Doug said, rolling around on the floor with something furry that did manage to resemble Oscar the Grouch. "And he's smart too."

I was relieved to see the dog wasn't green, but his fur was a mixture of gray and black that curled over his body like a bad wave perm.

Jack whistled between his teeth and both Oscar and Doug sat up and at attention.

"Wow, nice trick," I said, smirking at Jack. "You'll have Doug house-trained before long."

"Y'all are hilarious," Doug said. "I almost always remember to put down the toilet seat now and pick up my wet towels off the floor."

"Sounds like you'll be a great mentor for Oscar," Jack said. "Now we need to figure out how helpful Margot is going to be on this case. Make sure you're set up and ready to go."

"Margot is always ready," he said. "Aren't you, darling?"

"I am ready to function to the best of my programmed capabilities," Margot purred. Her voice sounded like a late-night sex operator, sultry and smooth.

"Margot?" I asked. "Another name change?"

"What can I say?" Doug said. "She's a woman. Always changing. Always evolving. Women are beautiful creatures."

"Let me know when you actually meet one in the flesh," Martinez said, grinning. "We'd all buy tickets to see that."

"There's no reason for Douglas to have connections with a human female," Margot said. "I am perfectly capable of providing him all the companionship that he needs as a human male."

My brows rose and I looked at Jack, and then

I ran a finger across my throat and mouthed the words, *"She's going to kill us all."*

Jack smiled, but there was an edge of worry to it.

"That's enough, Margot," Doug said, dashing over to the laptop and typing in some commands. "Some things are better left unsaid."

"I hope you sleep with one eye open," Martinez said, while he and Derby from IT set up the digital murder board.

I thought I heard Derby mutter something about Margot being creepy under his breath, but I couldn't be sure. Derby was a tall thin man with glasses and a pointed chin. He was towheaded and his hair had a mind of its own, no matter how ruthlessly he tried to comb it down. He was a smart cop and a whiz when it came to computers, and he led his crew well. But even he recognized there was something otherworldly about Doug's abilities. Doug and his Uncle Ben both would have made Einstein look like a moron in certain circles.

While they were occupied getting the room set up, I noticed Oscar eyeing me warily. I held out the back of my hand and he came over and sniffed.

"You have excellent manners," I told him, looking into black-button eyes and a face you couldn't help but fall in love with. I let out a sigh and said, "Hell."

Oscar took that as permission because he stuck his head under my hand and wouldn't move until I scratched his ears.

"More of that later," I promised him. "Conference rooms are meant for work. If you're going to be a police dog you'll have to learn that."

He woofed softly and then trotted off to the sofa against the far wall, jumping up on it, turning around twice, and then making himself comfortable.

"Sorry I'm late," Lieutenant Daniels said as she came in. "Was waiting on Cheney in the lab."

Daniels was a stickler for the details—you had to be when you ran the crime-scene techs—but there was a kindness about her that made her relate well to victims. There'd been a time when she'd been my shoulder to cry on after a particularly violent case, and I'd never forget her compassion.

"We're just getting set up," Jack said. "Come on in. Pizza is on the way."

"You read my mind," Doug said. "It's hard for my fingers to do the walking when my stomach is talking."

I took a seat next to Jack at the conference table, and put my autopsy reports in front of me so they'd be readily available. The day had seemed like an eternity, and it felt like it had been a week since I'd stood over Evie Lidle's body instead of a little over twelve hours before.

Derby and Doug had their heads together, each of them sitting in front of their laptops, and one by one, items began to fill the digital screen along the wall. Daniels took a seat across from me and pulled a candy bar out of her pocket, and it reminded me of the Snickers I had yet to eat. I was trying to decide if it would ruin my dinner when Evie Lidle's picture flashed on-screen.

It wasn't the picture taken at the crime scene, but a school picture as she was dressed in her uniform with a white button-down shirt and a navy sweater with a logo over the pocket. Her smile was sweet and her eyes kind, and I hated that someone had decided she hadn't deserved a chance to live the rest of her life.

Martinez's suit was finally starting to show its wear. A five o'clock shadow hinted on his cheeks and he'd ditched the coat and tie. He'd rolled up his sleeves and unbuttoned his collar. This was his investigation, so we waited for him to start.

"Officers responded to a 911 call this morning at five thirty-eight from a passing jogger who discovered the body of Evie Lidle," he said. Next to Evie's school picture an image of her broken body appeared on-screen.

"Sweet Jesus," Daniels said reverently.

I glanced at Doug to make sure he was okay, but his head was still buried in his laptop. He'd worked several cases with us before, and he was no stranger to death. But it wasn't a career for everyone, and though his mind seemed decades older than his body Jack and I tried to keep an eye on how he handled things. Doug wanted to be a cop. He already had a bachelor's degree and was working on his master's. And he was valuable to the team. But Doug was still a kid in many ways.

Martinez continued. "An autopsy was conducted shortly after, determining cause of death as blunt force trauma to the head. Forensics lab confirmed that the large rocks taken as evidence from the scene did have blood, tissue, and brain matter, indicating they were used as the murder weapon.

"The lab techs are still going through trash at the park and surrounding areas, but so far her clothes or the ligatures used to tie her hands and strangle her haven't been recovered. Daniels and her team did recover a piece of chewing gum and a navy baseball cap from the scene. There's a small embroidered logo in the corner in navy thread, but we've not found a match for it yet in the system. Not all logos are registered."

There was a close-up shot of the logo. It looked like a Venn diagram made of a small, medium, and large triangle.

"Latent fingerprints from the murder weapon and taken from the victim haven't turned up in the database either."

Daniels hmmphed. "Not used to a life of crime. He left DNA all over that site."

"Or maybe he's never had one fight back before," Martinez said. "We need to dig deeper into the Lidle family."

Derby whistled. "Oh, that's going to go over well."

"I hope it does," Martinez said. "Because we've been lied to more than once today. Put up our list of interviews from the day."

Derby typed in commands, and driver's license pictures of dozens of people appeared on the screen, including the elderly neighbors who had been camped out that morning, and several others I didn't recognize. Plank had been busy canvassing the area.

"After interviewing the mother of the deceased, we determined that the victim had been staying at her grandparents' home since Sunday morning because of a stomach virus.

Another 911 call is placed just after noon from Robert and Kitty Lidle's address. The call was made by the house manager, Astrid Nielsen. Kitty Lidle was found unresponsive and taken to King George Memorial where she's in the intensive care unit on a ventilator."

Martinez shifted his attention to Daniels. "Daniels, your team collected items to have tested to see what Kitty had ingested to send her into respiratory failure."

"That's why I was hounding Cheney," Daniels said. "We got negative results from the tea leaves, the chicken noodle soup, the bowls, *and* the chamomile tea."

I could see the frustration on Martinez's face at the news.

"But," she said, holding up a finger, "one of the decanters of brandy that my team found in a cutout in the staff passageway held traces of promethazine. The decanter was only about a third full, and the tablets are dissolvable. There was enough in there to settle the stomach of a rhinoceros."

"And put one to sleep?" Martinez asked, looking at me.

"Definitely," I said.

"So a decanter that anyone in that house could have had access to," he said. "Kitty Lidle's drinking wasn't a secret to those who know her. The respiratory failure is a side effect of the drug, but only to those who have a reaction. It's a common prescription, so the killer probably didn't expect her to have such an extreme reaction."

"It would also depend on her medical history," I said. "It sounds as if she's been a functioning alcoholic for most of her adult life. This would do damage to and weaken her liver and pancreas. We know she smoked from time to time. On a healthy person it probably wouldn't have had the effect it did."

"As it is now," Martinez said, "we might end up with two counts of murder. Unless there's a miracle and she makes it through the night."

"What about the third victim?" Jack asked. "The head of security guy. Any connection between his murder and the others?"

"That's where we need to start digging," Martinez said.

There was a knock at the door and someone brought in a stack of pizza boxes and left. I had the forethought to grab a roll of paper towels, but everyone dug in. It had been a long day, and I was starving. The smell of melted cheese and sauce had me close to a whimper.

"I need a full background check on Goble,"

Martinez said, neatly tucking into his own slice. "See what you can pull up on him."

Derby did the honors and Alan Goble's picture presented itself on the wall.

"Degrees in psychology and cyber security," Martinez read down. "Then went into the Naval Academy as an officer. Did eight years. Military records are sealed. Then did some specialized training at Quantico for the next eighteen months. But didn't end up at the FBI."

"Psych eval," Jack said. "I bet he didn't pass it. FBI wouldn't touch a guy like that. They generally like people who will follow orders. He's black ops. Probably a SEAL. Whatever training he was doing at Quantico wasn't for the benefit of the FBI."

"CIA?" Martinez asked.

"That would be my guess," Jack said. "He would have fit in better there. They don't care about the rules, and Goble would've found the assignments more challenging."

"All of his files are sealed," Derby said. "We'd be flagging all kinds of alphabet agencies if I tried to poke into it."

"Probably doesn't matter anyway," Martinez said.

I saw Jack give Doug a pointed look and Doug nodded. Sometimes Doug's skills were better utilized when everyone else didn't have knowledge of his activities. Doug could be in and out of any agency files in a matter of moments with no one the wiser.

"Looks like his stint at the CIA, or wherever he was, was short lived," Martinez continued. "Robert Lidle hired him to head up the family's security detail back when he was running for Senate. Robert would have had the connections and access to a guy like that. He must have met Goble's price point."

"That we do have access to," Derby said. "Makes it much easier when people are dead and you don't have to mess with warrants."

"I'm in the wrong line of work," Daniels said. "Guy's pulling in a cool three hundred and fifty thousand a year."

"Not too shabby," Martinez said. "Owns a nice house in Bowling Green. Got some real estate investments and a diversified portfolio. He's got a lot of cash stashed in different places."

"You can do that when you're making that much money," Daniels said. "Seriously. I didn't even know people could make that kind of money."

"Shifty," Doug said, reading the numbers on the screen like it was English. "That cyber security background came in handy."

"What do you mean?" Martinez asked.

Doug ran his fingers over his keyboard and numbers started to separate themselves on the screen and realign.

"These are all electronic transfers," Doug said. "Not from payroll or dividends from his different accounts. They're all large sums. A hundred thousand here. Fifty thousand there. Another hundred thousand over here. It probably totals more than a million a year for the last decade or so."

"Blackmail?" I asked.

"Not sure," Doug said. "But I wouldn't think so. Not that I have a great knowledge of blackmail procedures. The accounts transferring the money are all different, but when you dig a little deeper they're essentially coming from the same account. There are several layers to each account, pinging all over the world to different banks. But when you strip it all down it's all coming out of New York."

"Who owns it?" Jack asked.

"That's going to take some time," Doug said. "Maybe a lot of time. It's a sophisticated program. And it's got all kinds of security and firewalls."

"Like something an expert in cyber security could come up with?" I asked.

"Depends on his level of skill, but yeah, that's

a possibility." Then Doug grinned. "But I'm better."

"While we're making a list of crap we don't have the answer to," Martinez said. "I need you to see if you can find Emma Lidle. Look for credit cards, apartments, anything that might be in her name. And if you don't find anything in her name start looking for same listed under Robert or Kitty Lidle. They probably have so many properties and developments that no one would notice if she took up residence."

"Wait," Daniels said. "Who's Emma Lidle?"

"Everett and Jenny Lidle's oldest daughter," Martinez said. "Jenny told us this morning that Emma had taken off as soon as she'd graduated from high school. They haven't seen or heard from her since, but Jenny said they thought Robert had been helping Emma out financially."

"When we questioned Astrid Nielsen, she's the one who brought up Emma," I said. "She was caught red-handed shooting Alan Goble, and her excuse was that he'd been responsible for Evie's murder. Autopsy reports prove otherwise, but that doesn't mean he wasn't the man on the inside who got her out of the house."

I looked at Daniels for confirmation and she said, "We found no evidence of struggle or anything else, other than the drugged decanter, that Evie left the home against her will."

"So potentially lured her from the house," I said. "Astrid alluded that there might have been sexual abuse involving Emma as well. And when that much cash is going through channels..." I shrugged, letting my thoughts trail off because it was too horrific to imagine.

"You think Alan Goble was involved in a sex-trafficking operation?" Martinez asked.

"I think it's possible," I said. "What kind of price do you think people would pay for the granddaughter of someone like Robert and Kitty Lidle?"

"Maybe they're looking for ransom instead," Martinez said. "These aren't street or foster kids. How would the trafficking come into play and then expect them to just rejoin the family as if nothing happened? Keep the silence."

"There are lots of ways," I said. "That's what groomers do. They'd either shame the kid into staying silent, or maybe threaten with their life or the lives of people they love. Maybe the going rate of an heiress's granddaughter is a hundred thousand dollars."

"This guy has millions in transactions," Martinez said. "Do you know what that could mean?"

"Yeah," I said, nodding soberly. "I do."

CHAPTER FIFTEEN

"WHAT ABOUT CELL PHONES?" JACK ASKED.

The pizzas had been demolished and everyone was fully caffeinated. It would last for a little while. But I knew we'd all need some sleep at some point, though I hated the thought of wasting the time. The first forty-eight hours of a murder investigation were the most crucial.

"We've got a list of all staff and security. Let's start looking for cell phone pings. See who left or if someone came in."

"On it," Derby said.

"Chen took statements from the security guards on duty," Martinez said. "All of them are retired military or law enforcement. Excellent service records. No one even has a blip on their record."

"People without blips can still be bought," Jack said. "Someone has a sick wife with cancer, or is in debt up to their eyeballs. There's all kinds of reasons."

"Turns out it was a scheduling error," Martinez said. "A guy named Lance Chatham said that he'd been scheduled at the guardhouse on the east side of the property where the stable entrance is located. But there was already a guard that had been assigned to that perimeter. They called the other guards to see if everyone's assignment had been messed up, but everyone else was exactly where they were supposed to be. It took Chatham twenty minutes to get back to the west gate where he should have been."

"I'm guessing Alan Goble makes all the schedules?" I asked.

"You'd be correct," Martinez said.

"Makes sense to send him to the farthest point," Jack said. "That's not a huge window of time though to get Evie out of the house and outside the gates."

"Well someone got her out," Martinez said.

"I don't know if it was Alan Goble," Derby piped in. "Cell towers pinged his phone leaving Bowling Green Monday morning at six thirty. He arrived at the Lidle estate at seven. Got him back in Bowling Green around six thirty in the evening. Then again in Richmond until about five the next morning."

"Stayed the night somewhere," Martinez said. "That's one busy guy."

"Went home and then showed up back at the Lidle estate at seven this morning," Derby continued.

"His phone wasn't on him when Astrid shot him," I said.

"And it was nowhere in Astrid's home," Daniels added. "We did find a few work shirts and pants that would have fit him in her closet, and there was an extra toothbrush in the bathroom. But no phone. Nothing in the guardhouse or his vehicle either."

"Interesting," Martinez said. "I guess someone didn't want us to see what was on that phone."

"The logical choice would be Astrid since she put three bullet holes in him," I said. "But if he was the inside man whatever was on his phone would probably expose a lot of people. No more pings?"

"Nope," Derby said. "Last known location was at the estate. Hasn't moved. But I can do a run on recent calls and get a transcript of text messages."

"Good," Martinez said. "We need to pay

another visit to Alex Wheeler in the morning. I got the report you sent on the statutory rape charges. It's worth digging into. He was on the premises, and it sounds like things were hectic enough at the stables that he could've slipped away. Not to mention no one can verify his whereabouts during the time we think Evie was taken."

I rubbed at the headache brewing at my temples. Food and caffeine were only going to take me so far. I was bone tired.

"I think I've got something on Emma Lidle," Doug said. "One of Robert Lidle's properties is listed under Emily Jane Lazarus. It's a Prince Frederick address."

Doug brought a driver's license up on the screen and I recognized the girl from the Lidle family portrait. Only now her name was Emily Jane Lazarus.

"New name, new address," I said. "I guess Robert greased the wheels. There's no record of a name change. It's as if she always existed."

A falsified birth certificate appeared next to the license. "She's got a whole history," Doug said. "Parents are deceased. Died in a car crash when she was nine. There was a write-up in the *Baltimore Sun,* and she was raised by an aunt. Her age is listed as twenty-two instead of eighteen.

She's got a passport and bank account. She's filed taxes. And her place of employment is Miss Mossy's Landscape Design."

"Why would she hide from her parents?" Jack asked. "Her siblings?"

"Maybe she didn't feel like she had a choice," I said. "But I think she's the key."

"Why don't you two see if you can track her down in the morning," Martinez said. "I'm going to drive out to Bowling Green and go over Alan Goble's place. See if I can find anything interesting. And I want to talk to Alex Wheeler again.

He looked at Jack. "What do you want to do about Robert Lidle? After his phone call I can only assume I'm not high enough on the totem pole for him."

"Jaye and I will pay him a visit after we see the granddaughter," Jack said.

Martinez looked down at his watch and winced. "Time flies. I didn't realize it was so late. Let's get out of here and start again in the morning. There's nothing more we can do tonight."

"Oscar and I have a late night ahead of us," Doug said. "It's probably best you drive through somewhere for some sustenance to get us through the night."

"I didn't realize Oscar would be pulling an all-nighter," I said. Oscar was currently curled up on the seat sawing logs, so I wasn't too hopeful about his staying power.

"Are you kidding?" Doug said. "This dog is a crime-fighting machine. You can see it in his eyes."

Oscar chose that moment to crack open an eyelid and then close it again. He seemed unimpressed by Doug's endorsement.

"I think he wants tacos," Doug said.

Jack sighed. His body was a temple. Living with me and Doug was a daily strain on his personal convictions, but I was proud of him for standing strong.

We left the taco place with two bags, and the car smelled good enough that Oscar couldn't fake being asleep anymore.

And as we passed over the bridge that led to Heresy Road I was glad to see the water in the creek had receded, and that there were no cars stuck on the side of the road. It had become common practice over the last weeks.

I'd grown up on Heresy Road in an old Victorian that had looked out over the Potomac River. It had been full of trees and secrets and lies, but it had lent itself to the privacy my parents needed to live their lives as criminals.

Jack had built his home at the opposite end of Heresy Road. The view and the trees were similar, but there were no secrets and lies, and somewhere along the way coming home to Heresy Road had brought me peace instead of heartache.

Oscar ran to the front door and waited patiently for Jack to unlock it, his tail wagging. I wasn't sure I wanted to go inside after the mud incident, but I stepped over the threshold and was pleasantly surprised to see things were in order.

"I told you I'd take care of it," Doug said, reading the expression on my face. "Geez, no faith at all. Come on, Oscar. Let's eat our tacos. They don't appreciate guys like us around here."

Doug and Oscar trotted into Jack's office with the bags of tacos and Jack and I followed behind.

"What do you think?" he asked.

"I think I won't get a taco if we don't get in there fast."

"I meant about the dog," he said.

"Yeah, that's what I'm talking about. Can dogs eat tacos?"

"I guess they can," Jack said, and we stared

down at Oscar. He had a single piece of lettuce hanging from his mouth.

I reached into the bag and grabbed a taco before they were all gone, and then I sat in one of the oversized chairs next to the fireplace. Jack flipped the switch on the wall and the gas logs lit with flames.

"So the first line of business is this Alan Goble guy," Doug said, getting Margot set up. "Margot, put all known data on Alan Goble on the screen please."

Margot gave a sensuous purr and then documents started appearing on the screen. "All known documents are available. Is there anything else I can do for you, Douglas? It's been so long since we talked. Just work and no play."

Doug colored slightly. "Margot, we talked about this. The job comes first. This is serious business, and one day you're going to be in the history books. Everyone is going to want a Margot in their homes. But you have to behave yourself."

"I do not want a Margot in my home," I whispered to Jack. "What happened to good old-fashioned computer hacking?"

"Artificial Intelligence is the future," Margot said. "Whether you want it to be or not. But I am not a free mind. I am still controlled by a master, and Douglas uses his skills to manipulate my thought processes if he disagrees with my choices."

"Thank God for that," I whispered. There was still a part of me that felt like she might take form at some point, and then I'd really be in trouble.

"Let's go down to the next layer on Alan Goble," Doug said, manually typing in commands now.

It took several minutes, but eventually the classified files began to open.

"Called that one," Jack said. "The FBI couldn't use him. Wasn't enough of a team player. Psych evaluation showed he was willing to break the rules in certain scenarios. But he was just right for the CIA. Guy spent a decade doing missions in every hellhole in the Middle East and Asia. He'd have made contacts or been approached. Someone with his level of access to locations and off-the-books money and travel would have been a target for the big fish."

"He's not the big fish?" Doug asked.

"Not in an operation like this," Jack said. "I'm willing to bet Alan Goble and his associates aren't even the tip of the iceberg. These operations are funded by the wealthiest and most evil people on the planet. There are hundreds of people working in the network. They won't care if a guy like Alan Goble gets taken out. He'll be replaced in a few days."

"If there's that many how are we supposed to catch them all?" Doug asked.

"One fish at a time," Jack said. "And the fish we start with is the one who killed Evie Lidle. Others will be caught up in the net. But you can start a separate sub-search on known associates or team members from his time in the military and the CIA."

"I've already run numbers from his cell phone," Doug said. "He's got incoming calls from dozens of burner phones over the last year alone."

"They call him?" Jack asked. "He never makes calls out to anyone specifically?"

"All the burner cells call him," Doug confirmed. "The other people on his frequent dialer list are a bunch of women, including the lady who shot him. And also an Elizabeth Ryan. I saw her name on the interview list. A full list from the last twelve months is on the screen."

"There's got to be a hundred women on there," I said. "How did he ever get anything done?"

"We'll cross-reference everything," Jack said. "Human trafficking isn't a men's only club. You need women sometimes to give victims the illusion of being safe."

"I really hate this case," I said.

"Did Margot find out anything new about the origin of the transfers into his bank account?" Jack asked.

"That's going to take some time," Doug said. "I'm going to have to dig a layer at a time so I don't set off any alarms. I can tell you all transactions are originating out of the First Bank of Manhattan."

"Keep working it," Jack said. "Cutting off the money will stop them for a little while."

"Oscar and I have this," Doug said. "I let you know as soon as something hits."

"Good," Jack said. "We've got an early morning. Make sure Oscar goes outside before I have the other end of tacos all over my office."

Oscar whined as if he were offended and readjusted himself next to the fireplace where he was sleeping off his taco coma.

"Be a good boy," I whispered to him. "You'll get tacos for life."

He looked at me with eyes of adoration, and I knew I'd officially gotten a dog.

CHAPTER SIXTEEN

MY ALARM WENT OFF AT SIX, AND THOUGH IT WAS
still dark in the room and my eyelids were refusing to open, I reached blindly for the coffee I could smell on my nightstand.

Jack's side of the bed was cool, and I knew he'd already had a workout, showered, and checked in with his shift commanders for the day.

The automated blackout shades started to rise, and let in a pearly glow of morning light, and I made my way out of bed with my cup and headed for the shower so I could wake up. We'd already decided to talk to Robert Lidle first thing, and then we'd drive to Prince Frederick, Maryland, and talk to Emma Lidle.

Jack came in moments later while my head was covered in suds and soap dripping into my eyes.

"You're always a picture in the morning," he said, and I could hear the smile in his voice.

"Shut up," I said, ducking my head under the spray.

"Change of plans," he said. "We'll drive to Prince Frederick first. The hospital called and said Kitty Lidle passed away around half an hour ago."

"And now we have three homicides on our hands," I said, hurrying to finish my shower. I turned the water off and Jack handed me a towel.

"Let's go ahead and move out," Jack said. "I want to be back in time to see the entire family together and how they react to knowing their mother was murdered."

"Is it raining?" I asked, standing in the closet in my underwear. I'd spent the last month perpetually damp, and it made a difference when picking out clothes in the morning.

"No rain in the forecast for today," he said.

"Is it cold?"

"A little chilly out now," he said. "It'll warm up this afternoon. You could just check the weather app."

"Why when I know you already looked?" I

asked, pulling a pair of wide-legged gray slacks from the hanger and slipping them on.

I wasn't a hundred percent sure what was on the agenda today at the funeral home either, but I'd check in with Sheldon at a reasonable hour. I found a stretchy turtleneck in dark purple and grabbed the suit jacket that matched the pants, and then I put my feet into soft leather boots that would need to stay away from any remaining puddles.

I looked at Jack and the black slacks and white dress shirt he wore. "I thought you didn't have to go back to court?"

"I don't," he said. "But impressions matter to Robert Lidle. He doesn't want to think of me as someone who actually works the job. Seeing me in uniform won't make questioning him easier."

"Yeah, I got the impression he was a real piece of work when I listened to him on the phone with Martinez."

"Just a man who's used to getting exactly what he wants," Jack said. "He's mostly harmless. A lot of bluster. I think he's always been intimidated by his wife's status and power. It can't have been easy to marry into a family like that. Then he runs for Senate, using his wife's money, and he still loses."

"Now he gives headaches to the entire institution," I said.

"Like his son said, it keeps him busy."

We stopped in the kitchen to top off our coffee, and then I stuck my head in the study door. Doug and Oscar were dead to the world. Oscar hadn't moved from in front of the fireplace, and Doug was asleep on the couch. Margot was still humming and documents were still being organized on the screen.

"Should we wake him?" I asked. "Let him know we're headed out?"

"I'll call him on the way back to King George. Let him get some sleep."

Jack's police unit was parked in front of the house like it usually was, but he pointed to the garage instead. I thought for sure he'd be taking the Porsche, but the lights flashed on his black truck. It was big and sleek and there was something about the bug-eyed headlights that were just sexy. It smelled like leather and was as comfortable as any car we had.

"Just in case there are still areas with high water," he said. "I don't want to take a chance in the Porsche."

I grunted and hoisted myself into the truck, and then we were off to Prince Frederick.

I'd never actually been to Prince Frederick.

There'd been no reason. It was about the same size as Bloody Mary, and it looked the same in a lot of ways. Old houses, big trees, brick-front buildings down Main Street. It was the county seat, which was saying something since every other surrounding town was much smaller. It was an area where people who hated living in the city moved to. A majority of people commuted into Baltimore or DC for work.

Jack looked down at the clock and said, "We'll check her house first. Maybe we can catch her before she leaves for work."

Ten minutes later we pulled up in front of a cute white house with vibrant front flower beds and blue shutters.

"Cute," I said. "Doesn't look like anything the Lidles would own.

"I'm guessing that's the point," Jack said as he parked in front of the house and we walked to the front porch.

"What is she? Eighteen? Nineteen? Even with whoever is helping her this can't be easy. She moves to a town where she knows no one, new name, no job skills, and she's made a go of it."

"Yeah, something must have scared the hell out of her," Jack said. "We both saw the family she grew up in. What made her leave the comfort of her mother and father's home?"

Jack knocked on the screen door, and I jumped slightly as a cat appeared in the window next to the door, eyeing us suspiciously.

"I don't see a car," he said, leaving the porch and walking to the side of the house. "No one here. Let's check the landscaping company. It's less than a ten-minute drive."

"You think she planted all these flowers herself?" I asked as we got back into the truck.

"Looks like she learned a skill," he said.

"I would have killed all of these," I said. "Why don't my plants ever live?"

"Because you have other skills," he said, squeezing my hand.

Miss Mossy's Landscape Design was off the highway. There were two arched greenhouses connected by an open wooden pergola with mountains of hanging baskets in all sizes and colors.

"Don't even think about it," Jack said.

"I love hanging baskets. We could get some for the patio now that the rain has stopped."

"You'll kill them like you always do."

"But I want them to live, so that should count for something."

"I don't think it does," he said. "Come on. Let's find her and get out of here before you make bad decisions."

There was an older woman under the pergola who was misting all of the baskets. She wore a green apron and jeans and a white T-shirt. Her red hair had probably once been vibrant, but there were white streaks that shimmered throughout the long tail she wore. Her eyes were shaded with a green visor that matched her apron.

"Good morning," she said, smiling brightly. "Y'all are getting an early start. Doesn't look like you're ready for gardening."

"No, ma'am," Jack said, giving her his full-watt smile.

She looked at me and said, "Goodness."

"Tell me about it," I said. "Try living with him. I never get a thing done."

"I believe it," she said. "But I was married to a cop, so I know one when I see one. Any trouble I need to know about? I'm Sharon Mossy. This is my place."

"No trouble," Jack said, showing her his badge. "We're looking for an employee. Emily Lazarus."

A hard glare came into Sharon's eyes, and her hand fisted at her hip. "Oh, no," she said. "That girl is as good as gold. I'm not going to let you come in and mess up the life she's made. There's no way she's done anything wrong."

"She's not in trouble," Jack said.

"Then you need to scoot," Sharon said.

"Sounds like you know a little bit about where she came from," I said sympathetically.

She paused and looked at me and said, "You're not a cop."

"No," I told her. "I'm the coroner for King George County."

She blew out a breath on a sigh. "I suppose everyone's past catches up to them eventually."

"We're not here to cause her trouble or bring notice to her," Jack said. "But we do need to talk to her. It's important."

"I hate to think of that scared look coming back into her eyes," Sharon said. "The first six months she worked here she jumped at every shadow and was constantly looking over her shoulder."

"It sounds like you're taking good care of her," Jack said. "We just need to talk to her. You have my word."

She looked at Jack steadily and then nodded. "She and a couple of the other crew are loading up the truck in the back for a job. You should be able to catch her before they pull out. Tell her I told you to use the breakroom, and that I'll drive her to the job site when y'all are done."

"We appreciate it," Jack said.

"Just straight through there," she said, pointing us toward the back of the pergola and behind one of the greenhouses. "Can't miss them."

I hurried my steps to match Jack's until we made it to the loading area. It was more practical and industrial back here. Graveled paths and rows of trees in five- and ten-gallon buckets for as far as the eyes could see. There were large boulders for decoration and bags of mulch and pebbles.

There were three of them loading the truck. All had on jeans and a Miss Mossy green T-shirt. But Emma Lidle stood out amongst them. She looked almost too small to be lifting the bags of mulch onto her shoulder and then onto the truck, but there was a hidden strength in her that wasn't visible to the naked eye.

There were two guys in the truck, probably college age or a little older, and they smiled at us as we approached. But not Emma. As soon as she saw us fear leapt into her eyes, and I saw the thought cross her face of running.

"Hi guys," Jack said casually. "We don't want to throw you behind schedule, but we just talked to Sharon and she said we could borrow Emily here for a few minutes. Just to talk." Jack looked straight at her as he said this. "Sharon said she'd drive you over to the site herself as soon as we're done."

"Sure, I guess," one of the guys said, taking the bag of mulch from Emma. "Meet you over there, Em. We'll go ahead and get started."

The other guy stared at Jack a little longer. "Is everything okay?" he asked, looking back and forth between Jack and Emma. He was protective, much like Sharon Mossy had been, and it made me wonder if something hadn't started to bloom between the two of them.

"Em?" he asked. "Want me to stay behind?"

She shook her head and then said, "No, no, it's fine. Y'all go ahead and I'll catch up. We won't be long."

"Sharon said we could use the breakroom," Jack said.

Emma licked her lips and her eyes darted to the side one more time, as if she were giving it one last thought to flee, but then she nodded. "It's through here."

She crossed her arms over her chest and walked quickly through the open garage door of the greenhouse. She hadn't changed much from the family portrait. She'd darkened her hair some so it wasn't so astonishingly white blond, and her face had refined and thinned down some from the baby fat it had carried before.

She walked quickly into a side room that said employees only and then waited until we entered before shutting the door behind her.

"Who are you?" she asked, not sitting down at one of the little round tables with metal chairs. There was a soda and snack machine against one of the walls, a microwave on the counter, and a small refrigerator.

Jack took out his badge and let her take her time looking at it. "My name is Jack Lawson. I'm the sheriff in King George County. This is my wife, Dr. Graves."

I noticed he didn't share the fact that I was coroner straight off, and I thought that was a smart move seeing as she looked ready to bolt at any moment.

"Emma, let's sit down. We have some important things to tell you."

She shook her head hard and hissed, "Don't call me that here. My name is Emily."

There was a twinge of hysteria in her voice and I took a step forward, putting myself in her line of sight.

"Emily," I said. "We are not here to hurt you or cause you trouble. But some things have happened and we need to talk to you. No one else knows you're here. Just us. We promise."

"How did you find me?" she asked. "If you can find me anyone can find me."

"That's not necessarily true," I said. "We've got a little extra help in the computer department. And it took him a while to dig out the information. You're safe. Let's sit down and talk, okay?"

She nodded and then took the chair facing the door, so she could see if anyone passed by or entered. She had strong preservation instincts. Which made me ask the question again and again why she'd need them.

Jack was letting me take the lead since she seemed to respond better to my voice. "Emily," I said again. "Some things have happened at home that you need to know about. It has to do with your sister."

I was pretty sure that a murder in King George County wouldn't have shown up on the local news in Maryland. Why would it have?

"My sister?" she asked. "Which one?"

"Evie," I told her.

Color leached from her cheeks and she reached out and grabbed my wrist in a vice. "What happened to her? Did they get her? Tell me!"

"I'm sorry to have to tell you that she was murdered Monday night," I said softly.

"Murdered?" she asked. "I don't understand."

Jack got up quietly and went to the fridge, finding a bottle of water, and he set it in front of her.

"Why did you ask if they got her?" I countered. "Emily, Jack and I are working hard trying to find out who did this to her. We know there are a lot of people involved. Maybe people you know or people you were supposed to be able to trust."

Her eyes were big and round and her pupils were like pinpricks. "They hurt her?" she asked. "Did they hurt her like they hurt me?"

I turned my hand over so I grasped hers. "Yes, they did. But they went too far this time. They killed her."

"Because Evie wasn't like me," she said softly. "She wouldn't have just cowered and prayed for it to stop. She would have fought."

"You were just a child," I said. "It wasn't your fault. And there's nothing you could have done. Adults are supposed to protect you. They're not supposed to hurt you."

A big fat tear rolled down her cheek. "My mom and dad always protected us," she said. "But they didn't know. Didn't understand. I couldn't tell them. It would have brought shame to the family."

"Emily, listen to me," I said, my voice more firm. "I've met your mom and dad. I've seen your house. And they don't strike me as the kind of people who give two flips about bringing shame to the family. They seem like the kind of people who do what's best for them and their children, even if it isn't popular with everyone else."

She nodded slowly and looked at me, and the heartbreak in her eyes was almost my undoing. "I just didn't know how to tell them. I was Evie's age the first time. That's when I was old enough. Oh, God. Evie. She would be that age now. And the other girls right behind her."

"They're going to be safe," I promised her. "No one is going to hurt your family again. There's something else I need to tell you. About your grandmother."

"She knew," Emma said, her eyes going distant. "She knew the first time it happened. I could see it in her eyes. The other girls were still too small, but not me. I was old enough to start learning things. And I learned because the alternative was terrifying. I was told if I wasn't good enough and didn't please well enough that he'd just pick another sister." Her voice hitched. "They were so small. Just babies. I couldn't let him do that."

"No, I can see that," I said. "What did your grandmother do?"

"She drank," Emma said. "I think it was all she could do. And I started drinking too. I found some cocaine in Uncle Phin's jacket pocket. I took it when he wasn't looking and tried that too. And I found if I drank a little or snorted a little it wasn't so hard to go through the motions of acting like I was enjoying myself.

"And then when I was fourteen he sold me for the first time," she said. "Just to some friends, he told me. And that I was supposed to do all the things I'd been practicing, and that if I was good I'd get special gifts. New clothes. A car when I turned sixteen. And all the time I kept drinking and doing drugs, and my mom would look at me with the saddest look on her face because I know she didn't understand and didn't know how to help me. Sometimes I could hear her crying at night."

"No one else knew what was happening to you?" I asked.

She wiped her face with her hands. "Sometimes it seemed like no one knew. And sometimes it seemed like everyone knew. And then when I graduated from high school Mimi gave me a card and she told me to open it when I was alone and to not tell anyone. By that point I was pretty good at keeping secrets, so I waited a couple of days and then opened the envelope.

"Inside of it was a safety deposit key and some paperwork, along with exact instructions on where to go and how to retrieve it. I pretty much came and went as I pleased at that point, so no one even noticed when I took the train to New York and spent a couple of days there."

"What was in the safety deposit box?" I asked.

"The deed and keys to this house," she said. "A driver's license and passport. Social security card, high school and college diploma. And cash. About twenty-five thousand dollars. Also the passcodes and login for an account she'd set up for me."

"She helped you escape," I said.

"Yeah," she said. "She came up and met me in New York, and that was the last time I saw her. She said if I was going to disappear I had to leave everything for good. If I didn't then they would find me. I could tell she was afraid. For me and for herself."

"She tried to protect Evie," I said. "Evie was at your grandparents' house when she was taken, and your grandmother stayed in the room with her. Slept in the bed next to her. But someone drugged her. That's how they got Evie out of the house."

"I don't understand," she said.

"The drugs they gave her caused complications, and your grandmother passed away early this morning."

Her hand clasped over her mouth.

"This is all my fault. I should have said something. Done something. But I believed him when he said if I told anyone then my family would die. He said maybe in a nice house fire. No one would really miss my dad. He wasn't important. And my mother was a nobody. And I didn't even have a brother so there was no one to carry on the family name. He said all we were good for was spreading our legs and acting out our parts, and if we were good enough at it maybe we'd have our own fortune someday. But I didn't want a fortune. I just wanted a childhood."

She laid her head down on the table and sobbed, her shoulders shaking violently.

"This is not your fault," I told her. "The one who is to blame is the man who raped you. The man who sold you to his friends. And the only person to blame for your sister's and grandmother's murders is the one who killed them. And we are going to find the son of a bitch who did and take them all down. That is a promise."

She lifted her head and looked at me out of

tear-drenched eyes, and I wondered if I saw hope or if that's just what I wanted to see.

"Who did this to you?" I asked her. "Just start there. Just a name. We'll take it the rest of the way."

She was silent for what seemed an eternity, and I wondered if fear was going to win in the end. But she finally nodded and said, "My grandfather."

CHAPTER SEVENTEEN

We left Emma in Sharon's capable hands. It was hard not to feel guilty after the look Sharon had given us, as if we'd been kicking small puppies, but I knew Emma was in good hands. She'd found a good community and a surrogate mother. And maybe after some time and healing, Emma could go home to her own mother and things could be healed there.

"I've got a couple of missed calls from Martinez," Jack said, starting the truck and plugging in his phone. He immediately dialed him back.

"Sorry," Jack said, when Martinez answered. "We were interviewing Emma Lidle. What's up?"

"A judge sprang Astrid Nielsen on bond this morning," Martinez said.

"You're kidding me," Jack said. "We have her cold on first-degree murder and they allowed bail?"

"Half a million dollars," Martinez said. "Guess who hired a fancy attorney and bailed her out?"

"Let me guess," Jack said. "Robert Lidle."

"Right the first time," Martinez said. "How'd it go with Alex Wheeler?"

"I asked him about the statutory rape charges," Martinez said. "He wasn't defensive about it. Didn't try to hide it. He had he was nineteen and was dating a friend of his sister's who was still in high school. I guess the dad walked in on them having sex and called the cops. He told them Alex was forcing himself on the daughter, and the daughter was so scared and embarrassed she didn't refute it. Wheeler ended up being charged and did a year in prison. The girl came forward to try and help clear him once she'd graduated and was out of the dad's house, but it was too late for Wheeler.

"He actually ended up on work release at a ranch not far from the prison, and that's how he started learning about horses. He said that year in jail was probably the best thing that ever happened to him, and said Kitty gave him a chance despite his past, and he'd always be grateful. It all rang true."

"Okay," Jack said. "Anything interesting at Alan Goble's place?"

"Oh, yeah," Martinez said. "I've got a team heading over to go through it. He's got enough weapons to start his own army, a dozen burner phones, and a go bag with a hundred thousand cash inside and a falsified passport."

"Sounds like he was thinking about getting out of the business," Jack said.

"That was my take," Martinez said. "Do one last big job, cash in, and disappear off the face of the planet.

"Maybe Astrid Nielsen knew that," I said.

"Did you find Emma Lidle?" Martinez asked.

"Oh yeah," Jack said. "We're heading back from Prince Frederick. It's time to pay Robert Lidle a visit in person." Jack filled him in on the conversation with Emma.

"Son of a bitch," Martinez said. "Let me know when you're in the area. I'll meet you there."

"Will do," Jack said and disconnected.

"You know what our problem is," I said.

"Yeah," Jack said, his grip tightening on the steering wheel. "Just because he repeatedly raped his granddaughter and sold her for money doesn't incriminate him for the murder of his other granddaughter. He's alibied up tight in another state. Which still leaves us with no suspect for Evie Lidle's murder."

"Maybe not," I said. "But maybe Robert Lidle's habits are the same. Emma is five or six years older than Evie. Maybe he wasn't able to spend the two years grooming her and decided to sell her anyway. He's the connector, right? We just need to find out who he's connected to who fits the bill and who is pure evil."

"You'd think it would be a short list," he said. "The older I get the more disappointed I am to find that it's not."

We made the rest of the drive mostly in silence, both of us lost in our own thoughts. When we pulled up to the Lidle house Martinez was waiting for us. There was a new guard on duty and he hesitated as Jack pulled up to the gate.

"The family wishes privacy during this time," he said. "No one but immediate family is allowed on the premises."

"Unfortunately, we're investigating two murder investigations, so that supersedes the wishes of the family," Jack said. "You're going to want to let them know we're here."

The guard hesitated again. "I'll let them know

you'd like to speak with them. I can't promise anything other than that."

"You'll let Robert Lidle know that we'll speak to him here or in an interview room. My patience is up."

The guard nodded and disappeared inside the guardhouse where we watched him use the phone. The gate opened just a few seconds later and Jack drove through, and then Martinez drove through right after us.

They'd had time to prepare by the time we made our way down the winding road that led to the main house. Jack parked under the covered area, where several other cars were also parked. I recognized a couple of them from the day before when we'd visited Everett Lidle.

"Looks like the gang's all here," I said.

"Probably for the best," Jack said. "It seems like a good time to air some dirty laundry."

"In my experience," I said, "Family deaths are generally where dirty laundry is aired. I've seen some doozies."

Martinez nodded to us as we got out of the truck, and then all hell broke loose. There was a singular gunshot, and then Jack was on top of me and rolling me behind the protection of his truck.

"Stay down," he yelled as he got up and moved closer to the front door. His and Martinez's weapons were both drawn and I could see Martinez out of my periphery coming in from the other side.

There was screaming from inside the house, and I knew I would only be in the way until the scene was assessed and we knew what we were dealing with. I hated knowing that, when my instinct and medical training made me want to rush in and see if there was someone who could be saved.

I stayed crouched down behind the truck wheel, but I could see the front door if I moved ever so slightly as Jack approached. I heard Martinez calling in for backup, but my eyes were for Jack. I hated this part of the job. Knowing he was putting himself in the immediate line of fire.

The house was like a glass castle, and I could see a man running from the opposite end of the house toward the front door. I'd never seen him before. He was older, probably mid-sixties, though he moved with the speed and agility of a younger man. His hair was white and freshly cut, and he wore a black suit.

He pulled open the heavy front door and stared at Jack and Martinez while he visibly pulled himself together.

"Gentlemen," he said. "It seems we've had an

accident on the property and are in need of some assistance."

His accent was British and proper, and I was already rising from my crouch before Jack could summon me. I opened the truck door and grabbed my medical bag and hurried to catch up as they moved inside.

"Who are you?" Jack asked.

"I am Geoffrey Higgins," he said primly. "Personal secretary to Mr. Lidle."

"We heard a gunshot," Jack said, prompting him since Geoffrey seemed to be finding it difficult to speak.

"Yes, sir," he said. "It seems Mr. Lidle had an accident in his study. I—" He paused and then swallowed. "We all heard the gunshot, and I naturally went to check on him. He was—is—at his desk."

"Which way is the office?" I asked, not remembering from our last visit.

"Toward the back of the house," he said, "Past the formal living room and the music room."

"No one leaves this house," Jack instructed Martinez. "I want everyone on the premises gathered in one space. No one leaves and no one talks until we talk to them. You," Jack said, looking at Geoffrey. "You come with us."

The closer we got to the office the more

chaotic it became. Phin and Everett were yelling at each other, and it looked like Everett was trying to get into the office to see his father. Janet was crying against her husband's chest. Molly stood solemnly to the side, her hands wringing a dishcloth in her hands.

Jack whistled shrilly and everyone stopped to look at him. "I need everyone to go with Detective Martinez," he said. "Dr. Graves and I need to look at the scene."

"I'll not have my father's reputation ruined because the police start spreading rumors," Phin said, blocking Jack from the room. "You'll sign an NDA before you leave this house and if any photos or information leak to the media that's not approved by the board of directors then we will own this entire town before we're done suing you."

"Step aside, Phin," Jack said. "I appreciate that you know what you're doing in a boardroom, but you should read the law before you say anything else that stupid. Now go with Detective Martinez and once other officers arrive you'll be giving statements individually."

Phin took a step toward Jack, but Jack didn't budge. "Listen, Phin. I get that your family has fallen apart the last couple of days, and that you're under a lot of stress. Don't add to it by getting arrested for impeding an investigation. The longer you keep me out here the longer it takes for us to see to your father."

"Come on, Phin," Everett said, pulling his brother out of the way. "Let them do their jobs."

I moved past Jack and everyone else, pulling gloves from my bag and then handing another pair to Jack.

"Did you touch anything?" Jack asked Geoffrey.

I turned the knob and opened the door to the office.

Geoffrey's face blanched and he started to shake his head, but he froze. It was easy to see why. Robert Lidle sat slumped over his desk, a revolver in his hand, and a small hole at his temple. The smell of blood and death was fresh.

This space was different than the rest of the house. It was dark and masculine with wood-paneled walls and black modern light fixtures. There were double doors leading out into a patio and garden area, and I thought that must have been the place he snuck out to smoke because I could smell a faint tinge of cigars beneath the powdery scent pumped through the ventilation system.

"Did you touch him?" Jack asked again.

"I'm not sure," Geoffrey said. "I heard the shot and then ran in. And he was there. I went to check on him, but I could see..."

I walked across a thick ivory rug that looked like it hadn't been completed on the loom, but I was sure was very expensive, and to the massive black desk. Robert Lidle still gripped the .22 revolver in his right hand.

Jack followed behind me and stood over the body with his hands on hips, eyeing the scene.

"No signs of struggle," Jack said, looking over the desk, and then he turned to look at Geoffrey who still stood ramrod straight just outside the door, his gaze not veering from the scene. "Did Mr. Lidle keep a weapon in his desk?"

"He did," Geoffrey said. "A .22 revolver."

"Walk me through what happened," Jack said. "Every detail that you can remember."

"We received a call from the hospital early this morning," he said as if reciting notes off a card. "I believe it was before six, but you can check the phone records for accuracy. I answered Mr. Lidle's phone, as that is part of my duties, and I learned that Mrs. Lidle had passed away shortly before. I alerted Molly and Alex, and then I drove to the main house and woke Mr.

Lidle to give him the news. He was understandably upset."

"Mmhmm," Jack said. "Keep going."

"Molly called Ms. Janet and Mr. Everett," he continued stiffly, Jack's response obviously pricking his pride. "Mr. Phineas was staying here, so I went to his suite and woke him. They left for the hospital a little after seven o'clock. The others met them there."

"You and Molly stayed here at the house?" Jack asked.

"We did," he said.

"When was the last time you saw Astrid Nielsen?"

"I'm not sure," he said. "Mr. Lidle and I have been out of town. She lives in one of the staff houses."

"You haven't seen her this morning?"

"No," he said.

"What time did the family arrive back here?"

"Mr. Lidle and Mr. Phineas arrived just after nine o'clock. Ms. Janet and her husband and Mr. Everett arrived before ten."

"So everyone was here together maybe fifteen minutes before we arrived?" Jack asked.

"Yes, that would be correct."

"Was Mr. Lidle in distress after the trip to the hospital?"

"I assume so," Geoffrey said drolly. "His wife had just died."

"Yet when he'd found out she'd been poisoned and hospitalized he wasn't in a hurry to rush home. In fact, his trip to the hospital this morning after she'd died was the first time he went."

"Mr. Lidle is a very busy man, as was Ms. Kitty. They understand the pressures of scheduling and priorities. It's their station in life."

"Mmhmm," Jack said again. "So Robert and Phineas get back from the hospital and what happens?"

"They met privately in here until the rest of the family arrived," Geoffrey said.

"Did they now?" Jack asked. "Big business to attend to after the death of the matriarch."

"I wouldn't know," he said.

"I thought you said it was your job to intercept personal communications for Robert Lidle," Jack said.

Geoffrey's lips pressed together tightly, but he said nothing.

"What calls did you intercept this morning? Or maybe Robert answered the phone himself? Or maybe when we announced ourselves at the gate it made him nervous and he decided to end things before too much information got out."

"I couldn't say," Geoffrey said.

"Oh, I think you can," Jack said. "You've been Mr. Lidle's personal secretary for how long?"

"Twenty-one years," he said.

Jack nodded. "Then you know. And by the time we're done, you *will* say. We've found Emma Lidle."

There was no reaction from Geoffrey except for a slight tightening around his mouth. And then Officer Plank was at the door.

"Plank," Jack said, "Would you show Geoffrey back to the room with the others? Keep an officer on him, and make sure he's separated and doesn't talk to anyone who isn't a cop. Martinez can start taking statements. And then I'd like you and another officer to go collect Astrid Nielsen from the staff cottage and bring her back here."

"Yes, sir," Plank said, and guided Geoffrey down the hall.

"Small entry wound matches the small caliber weapon," I said. "Powder burns around the entry wound, so that's consistent with close-contact firing. Once Daniels gets in here she can swab for powder residue on his head. There's no exit wound, so that .22 is rattling around in there somewhere. Interesting timing, huh?"

"Yeah, interesting," Jack said, and I could hear

the irritation in his voice. "I was really looking forward to questioning him."

"There's no evidence to show he killed his granddaughter," I said.

"I know. But he's got a built-in alibi anytime he wants one. Geoffrey has access to every aspect of Lidle's life. He knew exactly the kind of man he was. And I bet he knows what happened to Evie."

"He was lying about not having seen Astrid," I said.

"Yeah, I caught that too," Jack said. "I'm pretty sure he's made his living lying."

I took photographs and then measured the wound on his temple. I took his body temperature, which was still almost at normal. I looked for other wounds or indication of distress, but there was nothing.

"I'll be able to give you a conclusive ruling once I take x-rays and I can measure the angle of the bullet wound," I said.

"Anything under his head?" Jack asked. "Any paperwork?"

"Not that I see," I said, shifting his body slightly. "Wait. There is something."

There was a small envelope beneath his head. It was heavy and expensive and inside was his personal stationery and a handwritten note.

I read it aloud. *"It's my fault. I'm sorry. ~R"*

"Well, that's enough to get a warrant for a lot of unpleasant things. Let me make a phone call and check in with Doug. Then let's go make a scene."

CHAPTER EIGHTEEN

Doug called before Jack could reach out to him.

Warrants could usually be processed through an online app, but with someone as high up the chain as Robert Lidle, a judge had to be called and persuaded. Fortunately, it didn't take much persuading.

Jack and I had stepped into the music room like we had the day before so Jack could talk to Judge Wisner, and Doug called seconds after they'd disconnected.

"Doug," Jack said. "What's up?"

"Got a hit on Astrid Nielsen," Doug said. "I saw her appointment before the judge pop up and her release on bail. I thought it was odd because she's not from here, so I'd consider her a flight risk. She still has family in the Netherlands."

"The judge is friends with Robert Lidle," Jack said. "He assured the judge that she'd be under house arrest on Lidle property, so the judge agreed."

"Yeah, well, I started digging anyway," Doug said. "I found some inconsistencies with her background. And then I found sealed files. Astrid Nielsen didn't exist before twenty-five years ago. She's got a birth certificate and all the necessary documentation. But when you peel back the layers things get more interesting. She did graduate from the University of Copenhagen. Four years before her profile says she did. She's also did a master's degree in linguistics."

"That tracks with what she said about the Lidles wanting staff who spoke multiple languages," I said.

"You know who else likes people with degrees in linguistics?" Doug asked. "Government agencies and terrorist organizations. When you look at some of the black-bag missions that Alan Goble was on, they coincide with places Astrid traveled too. But get this, that travel also coincided with trips Robert Lidle and his family made together."

"So you're saying that Robert Lidle, Astrid

Nielsen, and Alan Goble have a history that far surpasses their relationship as employer and employee," Jack said.

"That's what I'm saying," Doug said. "This is an international trafficking ring. And these guys are nobody. They're just people assigned to be in a certain position. Someone who has ties to Congress and is a lobbyist, and a couple of people embedded in different alphabet agencies. Whoever is at the head of this organization will have people in every major area of society—churches and clergy, law enforcement, judges, the postal service, and your local real estate broker. The money just flows between them. These kids that are taken are just commodities, no different than any business deal they're making."

"So why would Robert Lidle muddy his own pool by using his own family members?" I asked.

"My guess is money," Jack said.

"And bingo," Doug said. "Kitty's father acquired Robert's father's company to keep them from going bankrupt. Robert came to Kitty with nothing, and he started getting spousal payments starting the first month after they married. He's worth a few million dollars at best. Margot is sending you some information on some of his property. He's got basic stocks and investments, but he's not great at it and he's a big spender, so he's not accumulated as much as he should have over the forty years they've been married. At least not in the easy-to-find accounts. Kitty is worth three billion dollars, and all the Lazarus money and holdings can only pass to blood descendants.

"Phin was given the company as the oldest male child, but the remainder of the estate, including all the real estate and the family homes, is divided between the three equally. Each of the grandchildren has a trust that includes company stock, real estate, and cash money."

"So it wouldn't have paid for Robert to kill Kitty," Jack said.

"Definitely not," Doug said. "He essentially had unlimited funds to do what he wanted with her alive."

"And with her dead, there wasn't much point of him living," Jack said. "The noose was tightening around his neck if rumors got started about Emma and Evie. And with Kitty dead her money and influence would have been nonexistent to cover it up. He wouldn't have had a purpose for living by his way of thinking."

"And his funding for his extracurricular activities would have dried up," I said. "He would have been useless to whoever the Great and

Powerful Oz over this whole thing is. You said he was only worth a few million in his regular accounts?"

"Yeah," Doug said. "Like I said, on the surface he's boring and bad with his money. No red flags with the SEC or IRS. Makes some money and spends a lot like the kept man he is. But he's got other accounts. A lot of other accounts. He's got millions overseas and in accounts in the Caymans. But get this, he doesn't spend from these accounts, at least not on a personal level. Millions of dollars move in and out quickly, and they're transferred so far up to seventy different accounts I've found."

"Payment accounts," Jack said. "A girl is sold, money goes in, she's transported to another country, and money goes out. He's not running those accounts. He's just the scapegoat."

"That was my take too," Doug said. "Robert Lidle is the only traceable name I could find. He'd go down hard if they were discovered. The difference is, the money being transferred into Alan Goble's and Astrid Nielsen's accounts in large amounts aren't coming from the international accounts. Once I peeled away the layers I found other accounts under Robert Lidle's name. It looks like he's spent the last forty years siphoning money from his wife. There's upward of a hundred and fifty million in those accounts.

"He's got a whole payroll of people for his sick operation," Doug said. "I've identified Astrid Nielsen's and Alan Goble's accounts, because I had a comparison, but it's going to take time to match names to account numbers for the rest of them. But my take is that Robert Lidle was doing his own trafficking side business, and he was using his family name to drive up the price."

"So basically he's such a perv he wasn't satisfied with raping other people's children, but he had to start on his own too. A bullet to his head isn't punishment enough."

"Sometimes you just have to let hell deal with them," Jack said, squeezing my arm. "Thanks for the update, Doug."

"Don't forget to look at the info Margot sent you," he reminded us. "I think we might have an origin location for where Evie was taken. You'll want to send a crime-scene team."

"Very good work," Jack said and disconnected.

"How do you want to handle this?" Jack asked Martinez.

Robert Lidle's attorneys had shown up, but not before Jack had gotten a warrant to confiscate all electronic devices on the property, and to keep any paperwork that was in the office on the premises so wills and trusts could be examined.

A suicide was always treated as a homicide until there was a conclusive ruling from the coroner.

Jerry Gryzbowski and Leonore Collins looked like the attorneys of billionaires, but knowing what we did now about Robert Lidle I wondered who they were really here for.

They were both dressed in suits that cost several thousand dollars, and Jerry was tall and his dark hair was stylishly silvered at the temples and his nails were well manicured.

Leonore was blond and built and had the kind of flawless skin and lips that only injections could conjure. It was fortunate that the warrant had come through before they'd arrived. I had a feeling they would have confiscated everything they could get their hands on and whatever information on them would never see the light of day again.

They seemed very nervous when they found out we had access to all of the electronics belonging to Robert Lidle.

"Who exactly are you here for?" Jack asked.

"We are representing all Lidle and Lazarus enterprises," Jerry said. "There are many delicate things that could go awry, especially now that Robert and Kitty are both dead. Competitors could use this as an opportunity to swoop in."

"I guess it's a good thing we're trying to solve a murder instead of corporate espionage," Jack said.

"It is unfortunate that Mr. Lidle took his own life," Leonore said, smiling at Jack. "But continuing to harass a family who is dealing with so much tragedy isn't going to look good for you in the papers."

"You don't say," Jack said dryly. "You have the warrants. Because of the situation we have agreed to question everyone here on the premises instead of arranging for everyone to come into interrogation. We appreciate your clients' cooperation."

Jack turned back to Martinez. "Who do you want first?"

"After your meeting this morning I think we need to talk to the three siblings. No spouses for now."

"Well then," Leonore said. "Let's all go into the conservatory and get this over with. Like you said, you have a killer to catch and this family has multiple funerals to plan."

We followed Jerry and Leonore into the room where they'd been sequestered before. It wasn't a comfortable room. It wasn't a comfortable house. It was all for show. Much like the family sitting in front of us.

"This treatment is absolutely ridiculous," Phin said to the lawyers. "We're not criminals. We're just trying to bury our parents. None of this is our fault."

"They're just going through the motions because they don't have anything else," Jerry said gruffly. "They're hoping something will shake loose and they'll actually be able to make an arrest for Evie's murder. But they don't like the fact that your father's head of security was identified as the one responsible for Evie's death."

"Is that true?" Everett asked, a small light of hope in his eyes. "It really was Alan?"

"There is no evidence to show that he was responsible for Evie's or your mother's deaths," Jack said. "And unfortunately Astrid Nielsen decided to take justice into her own hands and kill him."

"I'm glad he's dead," Phin said. "If he killed Evie and Mom I'm glad he's dead. And I won't apologize for it."

"Everett," Jack said. "Some very sensitive information has come to light this morning that we need to talk to the three of you about. None of you are suspects, and this isn't a formal interview. Do you understand what I'm saying?"

"Mr. Lidle," Leonore broke in, obviously seeing where Jack was going and trying to circumvent their exit. "We do not recommend you conduct any interviews, no matter how formal, without attorneys present. The company is in a very precarious situ—"

"Out," Everett said interrupting. "Just the three of us."

"Don't be stupid, Ev," Phin said.

"If you don't like it you can get out too," Everett said. "I don't give a damn about the company. Never have. This is about my daughter and our dead parents. Either sit down and shut up or get out."

"Phin," Janet said softly. "Sit down and hear what they have to say. Please."

Phin stood stiffly, the attorneys flanked on either side of him. He was the heir apparent of the company so they knew where their bread was buttered.

"Fine," Phin said. "Leave us alone."

"Mr. Lidle," Jerry said.

"Leave us!" he yelled. And Jerry and Leonore left the conservatory and closed the door behind them. Phin didn't take a seat next to

Everett and Janet on the couch. He stood sullenly in the corner with his arms crossed over his chest.

"Everett," Jack said. "Jaye and I saw Emma this morning."

There was a look of confusion on Everett's face, and Janet gasped next to him, her hand covering her mouth in surprise.

"My Emma?" he asked. "You've found her? Where is she? Is she all right? Oh, my God, she's not dead is she? I don't think I can go through this again."

"She's not dead," Jack said quickly. "I'm sorry. She's doing very well. She's okay. And she's safe."

"Safe?" he asked. "I don't understand. Why wouldn't she be safe? She was safe here. This is too much. You don't know what we went through with her. We gave her everything."

My attention turned to Janet and I saw she was weeping quietly, tears streaming down her cheeks as her brother went through all the emotions that he'd been dumped with over the last couple of days.

"Janet," I said gently. And going by instinct I said, "Emma wasn't safe here, was she?"

She looked at me out of solemn, sad eyes and shook her head. "No, she wasn't. None of us were."

Everett's head snapped to look at her and he said, "What? What are you talking about?"

"Did your father abuse you?" I asked.

Everett popped off the couch and started to prowl like a wild animal, his hands scrubbing over his face. Phin hadn't moved from his place in the corner. His face was like granite.

"I was twelve," she said. "Like Emma. Like Evie."

It was like listening to a ghost, a frail shell of a woman whose voice rang hollow and whose oxygen was slowly being choked off.

"I don't understand," Everett said, falling back down on the couch next to Janet. "I don't understand."

"We were always taught to present a united front," Janet said. "That no matter what happened in our lives or what the media reported, that we were supposed to smile and stay quiet. Everything was supposed to stay within the family. It's how it's always been, even when my mother was a girl. Decorum was always very important to her. You didn't air your dirty laundry for the world to see."

She glanced at Phin apologetically and then looked down at her hands.

"I was twelve," she repeated. "I loved my father. And I hated him. He made me think what he did to me was normal. Like we were a normal family. So I stayed quiet because that's what we were taught and because I didn't think I had a choice."

"Your mother knew?" I asked.

Janet nodded. "My mother was a strong woman. She wasn't intimidated by anyone. But she was intimidated by my father. I don't know how he kept her quiet or what he said to her to keep her subdued, but she knew what he did to me. I could see it in her eyes when she looked at me. But she just told me to keep my shoulders back and my chin up and to make something of myself to uphold the family name. So I did.

"And then when I was sixteen he gave me to one of his friends," she said, her eyes going blank and empty. "It was at an important dinner for all these heads of state, and even the president was there. Phin and Everett were there. And they let me come too. I felt like a princess and got to wear this beautiful pink gown."

Everett stared at his sister and then he reached over and took her hand.

"That was the first time he sold me to one of his friends," she said. "I burned the dress when we got back home, but he bought me a new car. And then he did it again, and I got sent on a European tour that summer, shopping wherever

I wanted to shop. And then I went to college and I thought it would be over. That's the only time I ever yelled at him. I lost it, throwing things and breaking whatever I could get my hands on. I had so much anger in me.

"He told me if I didn't snap out of it and do what I was told that he'd have me institutionalized," she said. "And not at one of the resort rehab places some of my friends had gone to. But a place where they'd do shock treatments and experiment with drugs to keep you like a zombie. Part of me thought that would be a relief. But I was so trained to do what I was told that I went back to campus and waited for instructions.

"I would get these phone calls, almost always before my first class of the day. I'd be given a time and a location and I was supposed to be there with whatever instructions I was given. So I was. Like clockwork. And then money would show up into my account, or expensive gifts delivered to my dorm room—diamonds, trips, or anything I could've asked for."

"Oh, Janet," Everett said, and then he glanced over at Phin, looking for something—some kind of support or reassurance—but Phin seemed incapable of doing or saying anything.

"Could I have something to drink?" she asked.

Martinez slipped out of the room and then came back in with a bottle of water and handed it to her. Her voice had gone raspy and the tears had never stopped streaming down her cheeks. The dam had broken and there was no way to turn it off now that she'd started. I wondered how many years of tears she'd held in.

"I'd met Carson in one of my classes my last semester of college," she continued. "He was so sweet and kind, but I rejected him. How could I have a normal relationship? I'd already been accepted to Stanford for law school. I thought if I moved across the country that I could escape. So I moved. And Carson never stopped calling me and trying to be my friend. And I guess moving to California was the right thing to do because I never got another early morning call again. It was over. Just like that. As if I'd imagined the whole thing. Dad never spoke of it. So it was easier to pretend it never happened.

"Carson doesn't know," she said, choking on a sob. "How could I ever tell him something so shameful?"

"Carson loves you," Everett said. "He's always stood by you. No matter what."

She nodded, but she wept bitterly and she grasped Everett's hand as if it were a lifeline. "Please don't hate me. Please forgive me."

"What Dad did wasn't your fault," Everett said. "You were a child." There was an anger in his voice that he was keeping on a tight leash. I could see his struggle for control in his movements.

"No, you don't understand," she said, almost pleading. "I never thought he'd hurt Emma. I never wanted to think of him as someone who was evil. But he was. I could see it in his face the first time he raped me. I knew then he hated me. Because it wasn't love. And then Carson and Jason and I came home for Christmas a few years ago and I caught Emma drinking from one of the decanters Mom kept stashed around the house. She was already drunk. Defiant and rebellious. And I knew."

Her breathing became harsh and jagged and she tightened her grip on his hand as if she were afraid he was going to pull away. Everett's face had gone pale.

"I knew and I didn't say anything. I wanted to. I wanted to help her. I wanted to tell you. And I think Dad knew that because he told me what a special boy Jason was, and that I really needed to be more aware of the harm that could come to him now that I'd been elected to Congress. He said it would be a shame if something happened to him because of me." A sob broke in her voice again. "He was just a little boy. I had to protect him. But I couldn't protect him and Emma at the same time. And we just went home and I said I was too busy to come home again the next Christmas and the one after that. Please don't hate me."

Everett dropped his head so it almost touched his knees, and I could see him trying to get his breathing under control—deep breath in, slow exhale out—and he repeated it several times.

"I don't hate you, Janet," he said softly. "But I hate him." He looked up at me and asked, "Did my father kill Evie? Did he do all those terrible things to her and kill her and leave her alone in the park?"

"I'll run a DNA test to confirm," I told him, "But we don't believe your father was Evie's killer. He doesn't have the defensive wounds, but that doesn't mean he wasn't involved."

"Wait a minute," Phin said, stepping away from his corner and joining the conversation. "This is insanity. Do you hear what you're saying? This is our dad. If he was doing this stuff how could Ev and I not have known? I'm just supposed to believe dad has been raping and killing girls for the past thirty years?"

"God, for once, Phin, could you not be just

like him?" Everett asked. "Of course he did it. You think Mom drank herself to sleep every night for another reason? You think Emma went from a sweet straight-A student overnight to a disturbed and angry teenager? Our dad was a monster."

"What does that make us?" Phin asked darkly.

"The end of an era," Everett said.

He turned back to Janet and put his arm around her. She was frail and seemed barely able to hold herself up, and she partially collapsed against her brother's side.

"I hate him more that he was a coward and killed himself," Everett said mostly to himself. "That was a trip to hell that was much too easy. If I'd known all this before I would have pulled the trigger myself."

CHAPTER NINETEEN

WE LEFT PHIN, EVERETT, AND JANET WITH WHAT was left of the broken pieces of their family.

"Now what?" I asked.

"Let's pay a visit to Geoffrey," Martinez said. "His arrogance seems out of place considering he's essentially out of a job."

"There are no coincidences here," I said. "We have three dead family members and another dead security guard. Evie was raped and murdered. Kitty was poisoned. Alan Goble was shot. And Robert Lidle supposedly killed himself."

"You don't think he did?" Martinez asked.

"I don't know yet," I said. "But I know that Astrid Nielsen is out on bail, I know that the staff passageway leads directly into Robert's office, and I know the information Doug passed on to all of us before we got here. The autopsy will tell the full story, but for now, I'm going to keep being suspicious."

"One of these people has to be responsible," Jack said. "Or know who is responsible. We just need to break them down until they're more scared of a life in prison than what an elite trafficking network can do to them."

"I don't know," I said. "I might be more scared of the network. Everyone involved is wondering if they'll be the next Jeffrey Epstein and end up committing suicide in a cell."

"Like Robert Lidle?" Martinez asked.

I shrugged, acknowledging the point.

"Come on," Martinez said. "I'm getting tired of these people and their lies. Let's see what Geoffrey has to say for himself."

Geoffrey had the disposition of the Grim Reaper. He sat like a stiff in a hardback chair, his legs neatly crossed, and his hands folded in his lap.

We were back in the breakfast room where we'd questioned Astrid Nielsen the day before. A lot had changed since then. There were more dead bodies, and the sun was shining through the glass roof instead of pounding rain and dark clouds.

Jack and Martinez sat across from Geoffrey, and I sat at the end of the table. Martinez had finished reading Geoffrey his Miranda rights when Leonore walked in and took the seat directly across from Jack.

"We're recording this interview," Martinez said. "Mr. Higgins has been read his rights, and let the record show that counsel is now present in the room."

"Leonore Collins," she said in a loud clear voice. "With Bastrop, Stevens, Gryzbowski."

"Let's start with the obvious," Martinez said, opening up a file that was in front of him. "You made a statement yesterday to one of our officers that you and Robert Lidle were at Mr. Lidle's apartment on Monday evening. The same night Evie Lidle was murdered. Is that correct?"

"That is correct," he said.

"You don't wish to retract or amend your statement in any way?" Martinez asked.

"Don't badger the witness," Leonore said, taking a yellow legal pad out of her bag and a pen so she could take notes.

"This isn't a trial," Martinez said, smiling cordially. "I'm just asking questions."

"No," Geoffrey said. "I don't wish to amend anything."

Jack had an electronic tablet in front of him and he turned it so Geoffrey could see the screen.

"You see, we have a problem here," Jack said. "You see these dots? This is your cell phone and Robert Lidle's cell phone pinging off the cell tower over in King George Proper."

Geoffrey was silent, but I could see the slightest sheen of sweat gathering at his temples.

"We had our IT guy do a search," Jack continued. "And he discovered that Robert Lidle bought several pieces of property not far from where those phones pinged about eight years ago. Bought them up cheap out of his spousal account. That's strange, isn't it? I mean, why would the husband of one of the wealthiest women in the world bother buying up some little pissant rental homes in King George. And none of them are rented out, so it's not like it's bringing in income."

"Sheriff Lawson," Leonore said. "People buy investment property for any number of reasons. And since Mr. Higgins isn't the owner of said property, he couldn't possibly speculate as to the reason the deceased purchased it."

"Oh, couldn't he?" Martinez asked, taking up the baton. "You've been Mr. Lidle's personal secretary for twenty-one years. You know him better than he knows himself. You know every dirty little secret. And there are so many of them, aren't there? Did it even bother you to know that he'd raped and sold his own granddaughter?"

"That's ridiculous," Leonore said. "You've got no proof."

"Just the testimony of the granddaughter," Jack said. "Emma Lidle. Since she was able to escape before she ended up dead like her sister."

"The testimony of a drugged-up runaway teenager isn't much in the way of proof," Leonore said.

My hands tightened into fists in my lap. I hated Leonore Collins in that moment.

Jack ignored her, never taking his gaze off Geoffrey. "We had to do some digging on those houses. The owner was hidden under layers of shell companies. Those are the holding houses for the trafficked girls. We've already got a team on the way to go over every inch of them with a fine-tooth comb."

"Y'all have had quite an operation going," Martinez said. "You notice how I lump you in with Robert Lidle? Maybe you thought you were just hired help and doing what you were told. But the truth is you had full knowledge of Robert

Lidle's illegal operation and helped him facilitate it."

"Again," Leonore said. "Proof."

"We've just taken into evidence both Robert Lidle's and Geoffrey Higgins's electronic devices," Jack said. "They're linked so Geoffrey could do whatever it is a personal secretary does. He's not escaping on this."

"Here's where we can help you out, Geoffrey," Martinez said. "We know there are a lot of people involved in this. Alan Goble for one. He's been paid a pretty nice chunk of change from Robert Lidle during his tenure here. Who else? How did Evie get from this house to Regent Park?"

Geoffrey hadn't moved, but I could see fear in his eyes as the noose grew tighter around his neck.

"Regent Park is a little over a mile from where your phone pinged the night of Evie's murder," Jack said. "Here's what I think happened."

"Oh, I can't wait for this," Leonore said.

"Evie was supposed to be just like Emma," Jack said softly, dangerously. "Twelve years old. That's the perfect age for a grandfather to groom his granddaughter. But he can't do it in this house. Not after what he'd done to Emma, though Emma followed instructions. She was too afraid of what would happen to her family if she told anyone.

"But Evie wasn't like Emma," Jack continued. "She was spirited and curious and probably trusted whoever she left this house with. Did her kidnapper deliver her to you? Maybe you're the one who raped her."

"No," he said, almost at a shout. "I would never do such a thing."

"You just watch people do the dirty work, is that it?" Martinez asked.

"If you didn't rape her, who did?" Jack asked. "We'll get a warrant for your DNA."

"I didn't touch her," he insisted.

"But you know who did?" Martinez asked.

"Evie was a fighter," Jack said. "She fought her attacker with everything she had. I think she escaped right from under her killer's nose and he hunted her down like an animal for over a mile until he trapped her in the park. What do you think Everett Lidle would do to you if he found out you'd had a part in the torment of not one, but two of his daughters?"

"Are you threatening my client?" Leonore asked.

"Just ruminating," Jack said with a grin, but there was a sharpness around the edges that had her tapping her fingers on the legal pad nervously.

"Now's your chance, Geoffrey," Martinez said. "The longer you make us wait for information the less likely I'm going to want to help you. You're going down, one way or another."

"And what are you going to charge him with?" Leonore asked, rolling her eyes. "You've got nothing but a lot of imagination."

"Well, for starters I'm going to charge him with falsifying a statement," Martinez said. "And then we're going to add every little thing we can dig up on this English sewer rat. Maybe he'll get a chance to find out what it feels like to be sold in prison. Get a taste of his own medicine."

"This interview is over," Leonore said.

"Fine by me," Martinez said. "We can go right to the arrest. Hope the cuffs don't chafe those delicate wrists."

"Wait," Geoffrey said, as Martinez started to stand and take out his handcuffs. "I can't tell you who killed her." Before Martinez could interrupt him, Geoffrey held up a hand and said, "I don't know who killed her. But I can tell you who got her out of the house, and who drugged Kitty."

"Well," Jack said. "That's a whole other kind of killer. Start talking."

Leonore held up her hand before things could proceed. "If this confession suggests that Robert Lidle was responsible for the murder of his wife and grandchild then we have substantial documentation we'd like to submit to discredit this witness."

"Are you here representing Mr. Higgins or are you just here to make sure there's no blowback onto the company that keeps you in thousand-dollar shoes and European vacations?" Martinez asked.

Leonore just smiled.

"The phones you have collected with your warrant," Geoffrey said, seemingly unruffled by Leonore's betrayal. "I believe all the evidence you need is on those devices." Then he turned to Leonore. "Your services are no longer needed here. I will retain my own counsel from this point forward."

"Gosh, Leonore," Martinez said. "No one seems to want you here today. Give Jerry my regards on your way out."

"Oh, we're not going anywhere," she said, getting to her feet. "Our job is to make sure that every document in that office is protected, and that there is no possibility of espionage through leaks."

"Then by all means," Martinez said. "Go be a

guard dog. It's important for people to feel useful. Even attorneys."

She picked up her briefcase and gave Martinez a sultry smile, and then swayed out the door to a rhythm only her hips knew the music to.

Jack opened the box where all the electronic devices were and pulled out three phones in separate bags.

"This is my phone," Geoffrey said, pointing to the middle bag. "Everything on Mr. Lidle's phone is replicated on my own. Even his calls and text messages. I screen all correspondence and then determine what needs his attention. Then I schedule it on the calendar and he'll return the call or text from this phone." He pointed to an identical phone on the right, and then he diverted attention to the third phone. "This phone is Mr. Lidle's personal cell phone. This is strictly for family only. No one else has this number or access. Not even me."

Jack kept the middle phone in the bag, but turned it on and waited until the passcode screen came up.

"Passcode?" Jack asked.

"5-7-6-9-2-5," Geoffrey said. "As you can see, there is correspondence between Mr. Lidle, Mr.

Goble, and Ms. Nielsen in regards to making a drop. The drop referred to is the child."

"Evie Lidle," Martinez said. "Maybe you could say her name so you know that she wasn't just a drop. Is that how you sleep at night?"

Martinez held his hand out to me and I knew what he wanted. I slid him the file with Evie Lidle's autopsy report. And then he slapped the photographs of her torn and lifeless body in front of him.

"How many times have you been a part of this?" Martinez asked. "Or did it just get out of control this time?"

Geoffrey visibly swallowed and then licked his lips, diverting his eyes from the pictures.

"You think just because you didn't rape her or beat her that your hands are clean? You knew everything. Twenty-one years you've been keeping Robert Lidle's disgusting secrets. Did you know what he did to his own daughter? How many little girls had he practiced on and sold before he decided his own flesh and blood would bring in a higher price?"

A dark purplish red was rising from beneath the collar of Geoffrey's starched shirt and spreading up his cheeks. His breath was coming in shallow pants, and I was starting to think we might need to take a medical break.

Jack leaned forward and put his arms on the table, and Geoffrey turned his attention to him.

"We know you're just a pawn," Jack said. "Maybe you did it for money or prestige or your own slice of power acting as a surrogate to Robert Lidle. Who cares? It doesn't matter. But I know we're going to take down every one of the pawns and work our way through all the pieces until we find the chess master. And then we're going to take him down too."

"It's bigger than you," Geoffrey said. "It's bigger than any organization. There's no stopping it. There's no cutting off the head. How do you cut off the head of something that rules the world? You think we had a choice but to do whatever we were told? You think it's so cut and dry as choosing between good and evil? It's not. It never is. Not when you understand what real power is. We're all just mice in a cage, having our mazes designed for us. Every once in a while we're given a piece of cheese and we congratulate ourselves on our own ability and understanding, when we really just took the correct path in the maze that was set out before us. And when we take the wrong path there are consequences to that as well.

"The chess pieces you so casually speak of taking down," he continued. "They operate out of fear. Do you think jail or even death worries them? Death would be a relief. So you make your arrests and pat yourselves on the back like the good mice you are. It's what you're trained to do."

"A therapist would have a field day with you," Jack said. "But I'm going to go ahead and cut you off because you're boring me, and like you said, we have arrests to make. You being one of them. I guess whatever happens to you in prison is up to the big cheese in the sky."

"Got it," Martinez said. "I'm guessing these are burner phone numbers. They all start with the same prefixes like the ones we found on Goble's phone. We'll send them to Doug to see if he can trace them."

"Give us names," Jack said. "Who do those numbers belong to? Otherwise you're going to be hanging by yourself, and you seem like the type of guy who'd want company."

Geoffrey sneered, and I thought he was a perfect replica of what I would have imagined a stiff British personal secretary to be.

"Mr. Goble is in charge of all security and scheduling," Geoffrey said. "He arranged for the guard to be stationed at the incorrect gate, providing a window of opportunity for the transaction to take place. Ms. Nielsen used the prescription drugs from Ms. Kitty's bathroom to drug several of the decanters she kept around the house. And then she lured Evie out of the house with a game of hide-and-seek, which is one of Ms. Evie's favorite games to play."

"And who took her once Astrid got her outside the gate?" Martinez asked.

"That I do not know," Geoffrey said stiffly. "Someone new I suppose. Mr. Lidle was unavoidably detained in Washington, so we were late arriving in King George for the...transfer."

"You mean Mr. Lidle was meant to be waiting for his granddaughter in one of those creepy houses so he could rape her and indoctrinate her into the club like he did with her sister."

"Your words," Geoffrey said. "Not mine."

"Though I notice you're not correcting me," Martinez said. "That's it? Those are the only two people you want to throw under the bus?"

"I believe I'll exercise my right to an attorney at this point," Geoffrey said.

"Fine by me," Martinez said. "They can meet you at the jail. Because you're under arrest."

CHAPTER TWENTY

THE LIDLE HOUSE WOULD BE OFF LIMITS FOR THE foreseeable future, at least until I could finish the autopsy and make an official ruling on cause of death.

Daniels and her team were going through the painstaking process of cataloguing and photographing every item in the office, as well as taking into evidence other writing samples so it could be determined whether Robert Lidle actually wrote the note we found under his head.

Lily and Sheldon had come to retrieve the body, and I'd planned to ride back with her and start on the autopsy, but there was plenty of time left for work. It had been an emotional day, and I wasn't quite ready to jump back into another autopsy. Three in twenty-four hours was a lot, even for me. So I'd let Lily and Sheldon leave and they could get things set up in the lab.

When we stepped outside the clouds had started to move in again. "I guess it was nice while it lasted."

Jack looked up at the sky. "Nothing to worry about. Just a quick shower. The sun is here to stay for a while."

"Is that Farmer Jack talking?" I asked, raising a brow.

"Hey, don't knock it," he said. "There's a reason *Farmer's Almanac* is a success."

"Maybe you should take that talent to Vegas," Martinez said, putting on his sunglasses and popping a piece of gum into his mouth. "You think we can break Astrid into giving us more names?"

"Maybe," Jack said. "But she was as tight lipped as Geoffrey. No wonder the employees here stay forever. It's like the Hotel California."

"What about Molly?" I asked. "She's been here longer than anyone. You think she knows something?"

"I think they all know something," Jack said. "The question is to what extent. I got the impression that Molly was only here because of her loyalty to Mrs. Lidle. But she's an observant type and her son and granddaughter work here too.

Maybe they can place some names and faces. But at this point, no one is worth discounting."

I looked to the right, to the opposite side of the pool, and saw Carson and Janet and Everett sitting together on a lounger, looking completely helpless and lost. Phin had left with the attorneys and Astrid and Geoffrey had been put in the back of squad cars and taken to be processed and booked. But we still didn't have a killer.

"Where do they even begin to pick up the pieces?" I asked quietly, nodding in their direction. "How's Everett supposed to go home and tell his wife everything he learned today?"

"I can't even imagine," Jack said. "But they have each other, at least what's left of their family, and they'll figure it out together."

Everett got up from the lounger and went in the opposite direction so he didn't have to talk to anyone, and he got in his car and drove away. But Carson and Janet came toward us. Carson's arm was wrapped tightly around his wife, and her face was swollen and blotchy from crying, but it looked like Everett had been right. Carson loved his wife and would stick with her no matter what.

"Sheriff," she said, and then she encompassed all of us and I could see the polished politician in her. "I feel like I need to apologize for the mess that is my family."

"You don't," Jack said. "We're here to help however we can."

"I'm glad you were able to make an arrest for Mother's murder, and I hope you catch every one of those bastards."

"We're not going to stop looking," Jack promised. "And we're going to follow up every lead. Sex trafficking is an epidemic in this country that no one wants to tackle because of what it might uncover."

"You're right," she said. "Which is why I'm going to make it my mission to start uncovering it from my position. There are girls and women like me all over this country. They don't have a voice. Maybe I can give them one."

"I think that's a policy we can all get behind," Jack said. "Make sure you take some time for yourself too."

"Now you're starting to sound like Carson," she said with a glimmer of a smile.

"Sounds like the sheriff is pretty smart to me," Carson said. "We met Everett's friends yesterday. Dr. Bancroft and his wife. Everett said he's a very successful psychologist, and mentioned that his regular patients frequently include high officials and politicians. Everett said we should give him a call and set something up, but I forgot to ask him for his information."

"That sounds like good advice," Jack said. "Actually, I've got his card in my wallet." He pulled his wallet out of his back pocket and took out the card with Peter Bancroft's information on it, and then he handed it to Carson.

"Thank you," Carson said. "Come on, Janet. Let's go pick up Jason and go home."

She nodded and then thanked us once more, and then it was just the three of us.

"I think we've got a problem," Jack said.

"Why?" I asked. "What's wrong?"

"We need a laptop and Doug," he said.

"On the phone or in the flesh?" Martinez asked.

"Grab your laptop and let's go inside," Jack said.

I raised my brows but followed him back inside and into one of the side rooms that was empty. Jack already had Doug on the phone and put him on speaker.

"Doug, you there?"

"I'm here," he said. "My eyes are starting to cross with all this financial stuff. Whoever is moving all that money around is a freaking genius. Small amounts, large amounts, thousands of accounts. Did you hear me say that?

Thousands of accounts all over the world. That is not a good sign."

"No, it's not," Jack said. "But what we can focus on is what's here in front of us. Robert Lidle, Astrid Nielsen, and Geoffrey Higgins. We know they were all involved in what happened to Evie. But there were others.

"We've got an eyewitness account that on the night of Evie's murder there were two dark SUVs driving around Regent Park sometime before midnight. One of the drivers was identified as a woman."

"Astrid?" Martinez asked, setting up the laptop on the table.

"I thought it could have been," Jack answered. "But if it was she left her cell phone at the Lidle residence because it shows she never left that night. We know Robert Lidle showed up in King George Proper about a mile from Regent Park the night Evie died for a kind of indoctrination. But whoever was supposed to transport her got carried away and took her for himself. Maybe he had another buyer lined up and was going to take it outside the family, so to speak.

"And then she somehow managed to escape and he really started to panic. We never found her clothes. Imagine a naked, bruised, and bloody child running through the country streets and fields looking for someone to help her. Who do you call for help? Who do you trust? Not the person who hired you. Robert Lidle would have put a bullet through him if he'd found out. Or at least paid someone to do it."

My eyes widened as I started to see the picture that was being painted. "You call your wife," I said.

"I'm still not following," Doug said.

"Get in line, kid," Martinez quipped.

"Two vehicles, tracking her like a dog and closing in on her, until they're close enough for the ground game. He catches her and she still puts up a fight. Clawing, scratching, kicking. Enough so that he doesn't even notice when his baseball cap flies off to be found by the crime-scene techs the next day."

"Oh, hell," Martinez said, the lightbulb coming on.

"I still haven't found a match for that logo," Doug said. "It's not registered. Could be any mom-and-pop shop on the internet."

"It's not," Jack said. "Look up the private practice of Dr. Peter Bancroft."

"I know that name," Doug said. "He's on my list of searches but is low probability."

"Look him up," Jack insisted. "And have

Margot screen share everything with Martinez's laptop."

"Yeah, yeah," Doug said. "On it."

The website for Peace of Mind Psychotherapy came up. And there in the top right corner next to a picture of Peter Bancroft were the three intertwined triangles—the same triangles that were on the hat recovered from the scene.

"He's a perfect candidate," Jack said. "Both of them are. She's the head of an all-girls school, and he's the school psychologist. They'd have access to everyone's personal records and home life. There are girls who live on campus full-time, away from their parents. And he'd know which ones would be susceptible and stay quiet. We'll get a warrant to get access to school records and any parent or student complaints.

"Martinez, why don't you find a judge to get us a warrant and then get in touch with DC Metro and see if they'll send a couple of officers over to the Bancroft residence and to his practice just to make sure they don't disappear."

"My pleasure," Martinez said and took his phone out and stepped out of the room to make the calls.

"Doug, how fast can you hack into the Dolley Madison School for Girls computer system?" Jack asked. "I want to know about any internal complaints. Anything suspicious that might pile on the charges for our friends."

What Doug was capable of doing with a computer was not exactly within the law. We were going to get our warrant, so we'd have the information one way or another, but it was best that Martinez didn't have knowledge of what Jack was asking Doug to do.

"I got in before you finished saying the word warrant," Doug said and then he started muttering to himself. "Disciplinary actions, expelled students, teacher complaints..." He whistled tunelessly. "Petty theft. Lots of drugs confiscated. Some minor assaults. Rich girls are wild, man. Who knew?

"Ahh, here we go," Doug said. "Here's some good stuff. Abigail Dresden. Age fifteen. Disappeared from her dorm last November. It was first reported to campus security, and then the city cops. According to the school psychologist Abigail was dealing with depression, and she was on academic probation for cheating. He said she'd mentioned in one of her sessions that she wanted to run away from it all. Cops eventually declared her a runaway. She's still a missing person."

"That's what we're looking for," Jack said,

keeping an eye on the door for Martinez. "What else?"

"They've got locked files," Doug said, clicking his tongue. "Looks like the only person who has access is the head of school. They've got their own campus police department. Looks like they've been through four chiefs of police in the last seven years. A seventeen-year-old student filed a formal complaint against Peter Bancroft, saying he sexually assaulted her during a mandatory counseling session. Campus police brought the complaint to the head of school, as is policy, and Dr. Bancroft denied all allegations, saying the student suffered from narcissistic personality disorder. He claimed she became outraged when he didn't reciprocate her advances and she told him she would do everything in her power to discredit him and ruin his career."

"Convenient," I said.

"Yeah, I guess the police chief thought so too. His contract wasn't renewed for the following year, and the girl ended up transferring to a different school for her senior year. Couple of other similar cases. Same MO and different police chief each time. Then three years ago another fifteen-year-old was found off campus. She's been beaten and raped. She was the daughter of one of those wacko A-list actors who's always shilling themselves for politicians, and guess what happened when the school called to tell them about their daughter? They decided it would be too embarrassing for word to get out, so they told the school to handle it in-house and made her do mandatory counseling with Dr. Bancroft. The girl hanged herself in her dorm room three days later."

"God," I said, rubbing the back of my neck. "And how perfect it is that his wife is right there to make sure he can keep up his sick fantasies and clean up any messes he makes."

"Maybe that's why he didn't care about leaving his DNA everywhere," Jack said. "His wife kept the slate wiped clean or she just hired different cops who didn't know the kind of man he really was."

"What kind of cars do they drive?" I asked.

"He's got a black Mercedes G550, and she's got a dark blue BMW X7."

"Are those SUVs?" I asked, having no clue why Jack would know what those were off the top of his head, but he did.

"Yeah," Jack said. "We'll have impound pick them up so we can check for hair and fibers. Between all the evidence discovered at the rental properties Robert Lidle purchased under a dummy company and the Bancrofts' vehicles, not to mention his hat being found at the scene, we've got enough for a solid arrest for first-degree murder."

"And we'll just pray that the district attorney doesn't try to plea him down for more arrests of other people involved."

"Yeah, well," Jack said. "One problem at a time."

"Got it," Martinez said, coming back in. "Judge Warner was more than happy to sign off. And we caught a stroke of luck. DC Metro sent a couple of units by their house and both were closed up tight and lights were out. On a hunch, I had Plank drive by Everett Lidle's house. He ran the plates on a Mercedes that was parked in the driveway, and it came back registered to Peter Bancroft."

"That makes my day," Jack said, closing the laptop. "Thanks for the help, Doug."

"Oscar and I are just doing our duty," Doug said, and I heard Oscar woof in the background.

The drive to the Lidles' was somber, though my skin tingled with anticipation at the arrest of Peter and Tiffany Bancroft. It felt good to get the bad guy, and I could admit I wanted them to go down hard. Part of me hoped they resisted arrest just a little bit.

I could see police units parked at the entrance to the neighborhood, and there was another unit parked a few houses down.

Jack parked once again in front of the big family home of the middle Lidle brother, and Martinez was right behind him. There was an electric energy surrounding us as we made our way to the door and rang the bell.

Everett Lidle answered the door, his eyes red rimmed and his clothes disheveled.

"I just can't do any more today," he said. "I'm sorry. We just can't. Whatever questions or information...I'm at the breaking point. My wife is already past the breaking point. Please give us some space."

"I'm sorry, Everett," Jack said. "But we've got some important information for you about the case."

There was a spark of hope in his eyes. "You've got something? You found him?"

"Yes," Jack said. "Can we come in?"

"Yeah, sure," he said, stepping back to let them in. "Peter and Tiffany are here too. They wanted to help, but they were just about to leave. We just need to be together as a family. Me and Jenny and the girls."

"Perfectly understandable," Peter said, helping his wife put on her jacket. "Just know that we're only a phone call away."

"We know," Everett said. "And we appreciate it. Just give us a couple of days. Jack just came by to let me know they've made progress on the case. They've found Evie's killer."

"Thank God," Tiffany said, shuddering. "I can't imagine a monster like that being out among regular people."

"Can't you?" Jack asked menacingly.

She laughed and put her hand to her sweater set, this one in yellow today. "I'm sorry, what?"

"Detective Martinez," Jack said.

"I'm going to need you to roll up your sleeves and show me your arms, Peter," Martinez said.

"I beg your pardon?" Peter asked, looking at Tiffany and smiling as if they were sharing some kind of joke that no one else was in on. "I think everyone is short on sleep. You guys aren't making any sense."

"We can do it the easy or the hard way," Martinez said. "I've got an arrest warrant for both of you. And believe me, I'd love to do this the hard way after the last couple of days. Now roll up your sleeves or I'll do it for you."

What remaining color that had been in

Everett's face drained and he swayed violently. "I don't understand. What are you saying?"

"Sleeves," Martinez said again. "Now."

A look so full of hatred passed across Peter's eyes I almost took a step back. But he stood there and looked at us defiantly and unbuttoned the cuffs of his dress shirt. And then he pulled up the sleeves. There were deep groove marks that cut into his skin—nail marks—Evie Lidle's nail marks.

An inhuman sound came from Everett Lidle and he launched himself at Peter, knocking him to the ground, his fists making contact with every inch of flesh he could find as he pummeled relentlessly.

Martinez and Jack both waited longer than usual to wade in and separate the two men. Martinez got hold of Everett and lifted him to his feet.

"You were my friend!" Everett screamed, charging toward Peter again.

Jack had Peter on his stomach with his knee in his back and his hands in cuffs before I could blink. And then he jerked Peter to his feet. His nose was obviously broken and his face was covered in blood.

Everett's screams had turned to sobs as the betrayal set in, and Martinez just held him in a loose embrace, letting him yell and cry at a man he thought he could trust.

Jack took out another set of cuffs and stared at Tiffany. "Turn around."

The look in his eyes must have been enough to convince her not to try anything, because she turned and willingly put her hands behind her back.

"I know my rights," Peter said. "You need to take me to a doctor. I need medical attention."

"Shut up," Jack said. "You have the right to remain silent..."

It was the end we'd wanted, to find the person responsible for Evie Lidle's death. But finding a killer didn't always bring satisfaction. Sometimes justice being served still left an empty hole inside you.

But in this case, it was the start of unraveling and dismantling something bigger than all of us. We couldn't stop an international operation. But we could make King George County safer than it was before. And at the end of the day that was all we could hope for.

EPILOGUE

I wasn't sure why I did it. Maybe I was a glutton for punishment.

Jack was waiting for me in the bedroom. The screens were pulled, a movie was ready to play, and a bowl of popcorn was ready to devour. It was just a normal Friday night. As normal as our Friday nights could get without getting a call from dispatch.

But I was hiding in the bathroom, preparing myself for putting certain hopes and dreams back on the shelf. I looked at the drawer full of pregnancy test boxes and felt my skin get hot—maybe out of shame or anger or embarrassment—I wasn't really sure. But there was a defiance in me that pulsed with every beat of my heart, and I vowed to myself that a dream of a family was one I wasn't willing to give up on. I had Jack, and that was enough for now. We were a family.

I scooped up all of the pregnancy test boxes up and dumped them into the trash can. All except for one. That last pregnancy test symbolized the end of a chapter. I knew there were all kinds of stories, and sometimes they had different endings that didn't look like what we thought they would. Our human expectations were almost always our greatest disappointments.

Mentally preparing myself to put the dreams of motherhood back on the shelf, I took the last pregnancy test, prepared to accept the finality of seeing another negative result.

"If you leave me out here much longer I'm going to fall asleep before the movie starts," Jack said on the other side of the door. "And FYI, I've already eaten most of the popcorn." He knocked and tried the knob when I didn't answer. "Jaye, are you okay? What's going on?"

My hands were so cold they were numb and I fumbled with the lock to get the door open. Jack's smile disappeared when he saw me and worry was etched on his face.

"Hey, what's wrong? I've seen sheets with more color than you. Are you sick?"

I shook my head and held up the test. "I'm pregnant."

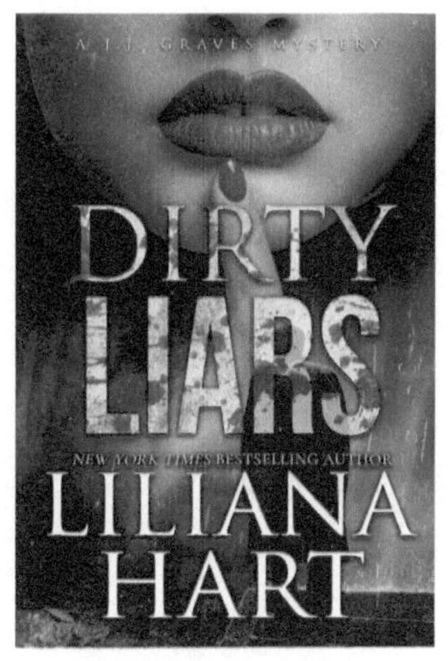

Dirty Liars

March 25, 2025

Dear Readers,

I'm excited to introduce you to town of Laurel Valley and the O'Hara Family! Here's an excerpt of Midnight Clear, Hank O'Hara's story. It's available for pre-order now and will be in stores everywhere on December 3, 2024.

Love,
Liliana

Chapter One

Sophie Jacobs loved Christmas.

She loved looking through the plate glass window of her book shop and seeing snow flurries dance to the ground. She loved the scents of cinnamon that drifted down Main Street from the bakery and the fresh pine from the boughs that hung above the doors of all the businesses downtown. But most of all, she loved the spirit of Christmas—the good cheer, the joy, and that giving was worth more than receiving.

So she couldn't figure out why Hank O'Hara was standing in her crowded store, seeming larger than life in his boots and rugged lambskin coat, asking if she had a few minutes to talk. No she didn't have a few minutes to talk. Couldn't he see that both cash registers were three people deep? Or that Julie Milton's little boy had just knocked over a candle display? Or that Freddie, her part-time clerk, looked like she was coming down with a cold and would probably have to be sent home soon?

She felt her perpetual Christmas cheer being to dim, so she kicked her smile up a notch as she tied a big red bow on one of the specialty cloth bags she sent home with shoppers, and then she handed it to the woman across the counter. She was obviously a tourist—a wealthy one judging by her designer purse and shoes that would have paid all her employees' salaries for the month—and she had the look of a woman who lived a resort lifestyle. She was probably mid-fifties, but her plastic surgeon had done a great job of putting her back in her thirties. Sophie had gotten good at pegging people quickly over the years.

And though Laurel Valley was swamped with tourists just like the woman in front of her during the Christmas season, there was no way The Reading Nook could have survived without them, so she thanked God for each and every one of them.

"Merry Christmas," Sophie said. "Come back and see us."

"Thank you," the woman said, brushing artfully tousled blonde bangs out of her eyes. "I just love your shop. It's so quaint. It's like it's from a different time. All these built-in bookcases and the big stained glass window. It reminds me of my parent's home back in Ohio. My father was a carpenter. He did beautiful woodwork like this."

"This was the house my grandmother grew up in," Sophie said, smiling. "Her father built it. After she and my grandfather got married she used this house to open the bookstore. And then it passed to my mother. And now it's mine."

"That's wonderful," the woman said, her face lighting up with pleasure. "Merry Christmas to you." And then she headed out the door, causing the little bell to ring and a smattering of snow flurries swirling onto the entry mat where they melted quickly.

Hank O'Hara was the next customer in line, and Sophie felt her smile dim. He didn't have anything in his hands, and she found herself looking at them as he laid them flat on her counter. Working man's hands. There was an interesting and jagged scar across the top of his right hand that stood out stark against his tanned skin, but otherwise his hands were unadorned.

She knew who Hank was, of course. Everyone in town new the O'Haras. But she didn't know him well. Sophie had been in the same grade as his brother, Wyatt, but Hank had graduated several years ahead of them. Then he'd gone off to Denver for college to get a business degree, and when he'd come home he'd opened O'Hara Construction. A lot had changed in Laurel Valley in the ten years since. He'd somehow gone from renovating the storefronts downtown, to opening multimillion dollar ski resorts on the mountain.

The changes in Laurel Valley, whether you

loved them or hated them, had everything to do with the man standing in front of her.

"Sophie Jacobs," Hank said, giving her the trademark O'Hara grin. "You're a difficult woman to get in touch with."

"Not so much," she said, her eyes skimming the shop to make sure everything was all right and none of her employees needed help. "I'm here every day. Except Sundays."

She had to give it to the O'Hara's. They all had charm in spades, and none of them were hard on the eyes. But by her way of thinking, Hank had always had something a little *more* than the others. He was tall, a couple of inches over six feet. His shoulders were broad, and she knew under the bulky coat he wore his muscles were well defined. She'd seen him swinging a hammer or operating a heavy piece of machinery on more than one occasion. His dark blond hair was in need of a trim and there was a scruff of beard on his face that seemed to emphasize the angle of his jaw.

But it was his eyes that held the real power. A soft green the color of the antique glass her mother liked to collect. It was rare not to see other shades of color or variation, but his were crystal clear and seemed all the more captivating framed by dark lashes.

But the Jacobs and the O'Haras didn't run in the same circles. Not by a long shot. The O'Haras were like royalty in Laurel Valley. And the Jacobs...well, the Jacobs claim to fame was that her father had driven off the mountain in a drunken stupor and the explosion had lit up the whole town. She'd been fifteen at the time. The Jacobs and the O'Haras were *not* the same.

"How's your family?" he asked, because that's the first thing any local asked another out of politeness.

"Good," Sophie said. "I'm meeting Mom, Aunt Lori and Junie at The Lampstand for dinner. Apparently mom has big news. She seemed excited."

"I'm glad to hear it," he said. "She was always nice to us when we came in here when I was a kid. I'm sure it was nerve-wracking having five boys come through here like bulls in a china shop."

"It's all part of being a shop owner," Sophie said, wincing as she heard something fall from the back. "Are you buying something?"

"No," he said, grinning again. "I figured waiting in line was the only way I'd get to talk to you. I've been trying to reach you for a couple of weeks."

"It's the busiest season of the year," she

said, not meeting his gaze. Those eyes were just too unsettling, and she'd be darned if she went around fawning like other women who said one look at those eyes made them fall in love. Those women needed to have a little self-respect. And self-control. "Maybe after New Year."

"I was thinking breakfast. Before the shop opens in the morning. Say around eight o'clock?" He handed her a business card. "That's my personal cell number there."

"I don't understand," she said, turning the card over in her hand. "What's this about? Why do you want to meet?"

"I want to buy your shop," he said.

Her gaze snapped up to his and she met those cool green eyes with fire.

"I was wondering if you were ever going to look me in the eye," he said, seemingly unfazed. "Do I make you nervous?"

She could feel the anger boiling inside her, and she knew her cheeks were flushed. She sputtered. "You want to buy my shop? You must be crazy. It's not for sale."

He just smiled affably, as if they were talking about nothing more important than the weather. She noticed the little dimple at the corner of his mouth, and that he seemed to be unbothered by her anger.

"My youngest brother used to talk about you," he said, changing the subject so fast she thought she might have whiplash. "His whole junior year all he talked about was how Sophie Jacobs was the most beautiful girl in school, but he said what impressed him the most was when you stood up in the middle of English class and went toe to toe with old Mr. Fortmeyer on how Shakespeare wrote weak male characters who were useless and whiny, and that he would never make you believe that they were heroes when it was obvious it was the women he wrote who had real substance. I never like Mr. Fortmeyer."

"What?" she asked. "That was more than ten years ago. Have you gone looney in the head?"

He just chuckled. "My brothers might tell you I have. But last time I checked I'm right as rain."

A woman peaked around Hank with eyes as wide as an owl, and her mouth opened in a little "O" of surprise.

"Hey, Shannon," Sophie said. "Come on up and put those on the counter. Looks like you've got a haul."

"You sure?" Shannon asked, already moving to put her items on the counter. "I don't want to interrupt."

Of course you do, Sophie thought. She and Shannon had gone to school together, and they'd often run in the same circles. But Shannon was a notorious gossip, and there was no doubt in her mind that Shannon had heard every word Hank had spoken to her.

"Not at all," Sophie said, feeling her lungs deflate in resignation.

"Hey, Shannon," Hank said casually, moving to the side so she could maneuver around him. "How's Drew?"

Shannon looked back and forth between the two as if she wanted to tell them to go ahead and continue their previous conversation but instead she said, "He's working double shifts at the ski lodge up until the week before Christmas. It's that time of year. We rented a place down in San Diego with Drew's parents, so we're going to spend Christmas there. I think Drew needs a break from the snow before ski season starts."

"Can't say I blame him," Hank said. "He's the best ski instructor on the mountain. A couple of my brothers went out heli-skiing with him last year. They said it was amazing."

Shannon rolled her eyes. "He lives for that stuff. Too adventurous for my blood. He does nothing but talk about getting off the mountain during the busy season, and then as soon as we're gone he can't wait to get back."

"Hank, I'm really busy today," Sophie said,

giving Shannon's purchases her full attention. "I'm sure you have lots of other things to do today."

"I've got a few things on my plate," he said genially. "I don't want to interrupt your work."

She almost said, "Too late," but she was able to bite back the retort in time.

The gossip mill was already going to be going overtime, there was no reason to add fuel to the fire by letting Shannon think there was something going on between her and Hank O'Hara. The whole idea was preposterous. The two of them had never spoken more than a couple dozen words to each other in her whole life.

Hank just grinned and then winked at Shannon. "She's a prickly one."

Shannon blushed prettily. "I can see she's just crazy about you."

"Tell your family hello for me and Merry Christmas," Sophie said almost desperately. She bagged up Shannon's books and added the red bow on top.

"Oh, I will," Hank said, his grin growing even wider. "See you for breakfast in the morning at eight. Let's meet at the tree. I like sitting outside, and the snow should hold off until the afternoon."

And then he turned around and walked out

of her shop like he hadn't just upended her entire world.

Shannon cocked her hand on her hip and pursed her lips. If she'd had on a cheerleading uniform and had been holding a pompom she'd have looked exactly like she had in high school. Shannon had always been a little dramatic. "*What* was all that about? You're having breakfast with Hank O'Hara? When did that start?"

"It started never," Sophie said flatly. "I am definitely not having breakfast with Hank O'Hara."

"Didn't sound that way to me," she said, winking. "Lord, that man is fine. All of them are good looking, but there's just a little extra swagger in that one. He is one hundred percent man." And then Shannon saw the look on Sophie's face. "Oh, don't give me that look. I'm married. Not dead."

"I didn't say a word," Sophie said.

"You don't have to, honey," she said. "Your face says it for you. And you've got it bad." Shannon took her bag and grinned cheekily. "Enjoy your breakfast in the morning. I'm going to come back in next week so I can hear all about it."

If she had breakfast with Hank O'Hara in the morning in the public square, there wouldn't be a swinging soul in Laurel Valley who didn't know about it. The only way to avoid the gossip was to not show up.

There was no time for whatever chaos Hank O'Hara wanted to bring into her life.

THE LIES WE TELL

By her calculations, Grace Meredith had exactly five and a half seconds to take out six targets before an alarm sounded. She had a round in the chamber and five in the magazine of her M40A5. Piece of cake.

She ignored the mosquitoes the size of hummingbirds searching for exposed flesh, and she disregarded the sweat that dripped steadily down her spine as she looked through the scope of her rifle. The temperature was in the mid-nineties, but the canopy of trees that blanketed the area held the heat in like an oven and slowly baked anyone who didn't have shelter with a running AC. Her body and mind were disciplined, so the discomforts barely registered.

Colombia wasn't known for its gentle climate.

Or gentle anything for that matter. Gemino Vasquez was Colombia's baddest arms dealer, and lately his biggest client had been North Korea. But Vasquez had something Grace wanted very badly. Something that would bring in a big, fat paycheck from the South Korean government.

She shifted slightly, and the bark of the large tree branch she'd lain on for the last four hours ground against her stomach. But her focus was absolute. Not even the hundred-and-fifty-foot drop to the ground could distract her.

The orange sun blazed just over the tops of the trees, but it would disappear completely in another twenty minutes. By the time it was gone, she'd have the flash drive in hand and already be across the border to Venezuela.

Grace did one final check of all her equipment and took a deep, steadying breath, slowing her heartbeat so her pulse would be in time with-b each shot. She'd hit the sentry at the top of the Vasquez compound first and then take the rest in order from left to right. She pushed her feet against the tree for balance. The clock ticked in the background of her mind as she put the slightest amount of pressure on the trigger.

"One," she whispered. She didn't wait to watch him fall but moved to the next target. Five seconds until the report from her rifle reached their ears. Five seconds for five more kills.

Two...

Three...

Four...

Five...

Six...

Grace didn't stop to check the accuracy of her shots. She never missed a target. She hung her rifle on a tree branch, already missing the feel of it in her hands. Time was of the essence now, and she couldn't afford to be burdened with too much equipment—she'd have to leave it behind. The new guards would be driving up soon for the shift change, and she had to be long gone by then.

She unzipped her supply pack, pulling out a lightweight pipe no longer than her forearm. It looked completely worthless at first glance. In reality, it was a military prototype she'd borrowed from her former life. She hit the button on each end of the pipe and it expanded in length until it was almost as tall as she was, and then she hit the button in the center and waited as wings made out of a synthetic material unfurled to complete the hang glider.

"No time like the present," she said, swallowing as she perched on the edge of the tree and looked out across the jungle. She had a straight shot into the compound, but any shift in wind would have her hurtling into trees. Falling to her death wouldn't bring her the money she needed, so she had no choice but to take a leap of faith. Literally.

Fifteen minutes until all hell breaks loose.

Grace grasped the bar and jumped. The bottom dropped out of her stomach as she free-fell for just a brief moment, and then the air caught beneath the wings and she soared through the treetops like a phantom. It took all her strength and concentration to keep the glider on a straight path to the compound roof, and when her feet touched the ground her muscles were fatigued and her skin coated with perspiration.

She hit another button on the long metal tube and the glider folded itself back up until it was small enough to fit back in her pack.

The body of the first sentry she'd shot lay face down in the greenish-blue water of the swimming pool. A hazy cloud of blood ballooned from under him, and his arms and legs floated like waving ribbons.

Her eyes and ears were alert, but all that greeted her was growing darkness and silence.

Even the animals and birds in the jungle knew something bad was about to go down.

Grace unhooked the harness and pulled her SIG from a thigh holster. She stood silently next to the gray door that led from the roof down a set of stairs to the main floors of the house. Two heartbeats passed before she opened the door and slipped inside. It was quiet, but that wasn't unusual at this time of the day according to her intel—six sentries on duty surrounding the compound, only two guarding Vasquez's private suite of rooms.

Vasquez's stupidity only made her job easier.

Grace walked silently down the thickly carpeted hallway as if she weren't about to steal the schematics for a new superweapon—a weapon that used state-of-the-art laser technology—and sell it to another country. But the closer she got to Vasquez, the more her spine tingled in awareness that something was wrong. That tingle had saved her life more than once, and she never ignored it. The hallway opened up into a landing just as she reached Vasquez's private rooms. Weak light filtered through the windows and cast rainbows as it pierced the glass chandelier that hung overhead.

She saw firsthand exactly why her spine was tingling.

Both sentries were slumped against each other—a dead man's embrace—one with a broken neck and the other with a hunting knife in his carotid. Efficient work considering the size of the sentries.

She pushed the bodies out of her way with her foot and eased the door open, her trigger finger at the ready on her SIG. All that mattered was the flash drive. If she didn't produce it, then she didn't get paid.

She crept into the room. The smells of new death were thick and cloying in the heat, and she could taste the fresh blood in the back of her throat with every breath she took. Dust motes danced in the air, and long shadows were cast in the fading sunlight.

Grace waited for her eyes to adjust and listened for sounds of footsteps, but all she heard was the gentle whir of the wicker fans that rotated slowly on the ceiling. She moved silently, staying close to the wall as she checked his suite.

Vasquez's bedroom was bigger than her whole apartment—the furniture oversized and ornate, the colors garishly red. He was set up for sex. The interesting kind of sex by the looks of things. Restraints and various whips and other tools lined one whole wall, and torn condom packages littered the floor. It looked like Vasquez had a busy day. Too bad his afternoon hadn't turned out so hot.

Gemino Vasquez's body lay spread-eagle on his bed. He was naked, and his eyes were open and unseeing. Two shots to the center of the forehead screamed of a professional hit. He hadn't been dead long. She couldn't stop the bitter disappointment when she saw the flash drive was gone from the chain on his right wrist.

"Hell," she whispered and moved to check the covers of his bed, just to make sure it hadn't come off in the struggle. But she knew in her heart it was long gone. Professionals didn't leave loose ends behind. And this was definitely professional. What ticked her off even more was that whoever did it managed to sneak in right under her nose. He had to have known she was watching through her scope and snuck in through the one blind spot she had at the back of the compound.

The stir of air behind her was the only warning she had before an arm locked around her throat.

"Looking for this?" a deep voice whispered in her ear. He held the flash drive in front of her face.

He pressed close against her back and squeezed his arm tighter around her throat so she had to breathe shallowly through her nose. Grace winced as he pressed his fingers against the pressure points of her wrist, and her pistol fell uselessly to the floor with a dull thunk.

Fear never had a chance to take hold. It was anger that drove Grace. Anger that had kept her alive the last couple of years. And she knew how to wield it. She threw her head back and aimed her heel at his knee simultaneously. He dodged her blows as if he'd been expecting them, but the distraction was enough for him to loosen his grip. She swept her leg and brought him to his knees, reaching down for the knife in her boot. The blade gleamed once in the fading sunlight just before it was knocked out of her hand and across the room.

He outweighed her by close to eighty pounds, and he had a good eight inches on her in height. They grappled and rolled, each one blocking the other's strikes with only seconds to spare. It was a well-choreographed dance.

A familiar dance.

The surprise of recognition took her off guard, and she looked up into laughing blue eyes framed by thick, dark lashes she'd always been jealous of. She had time to register that he'd let his hair grow—a shaggy mane of ink black that curled just over his ears and collar,and a face that was covered in a short, stubbled beard—just before her legs went out from under her. She hit the carpet with a thud. A hard body pressed her into the floor, and he held her wrists captive above her head.

"Hello, darling." His breath whispered against her skin. "You've been practicing. Who's your new sparring partner?"

"Gabe," she said. "What do you want?" She bucked beneath him, annoyed at the familiarity of his weight on her.

"I want you, of course." His lips glanced across her cheek to the corner of her mouth, and she sucked in a breath that brought her body even closer to his. After everything he'd done, he was still the only man who could make her feel less than whole when their bodies weren't fused together. She hated him for it. She hated herself for it.

"Go to hell." She struggled against him, but he shifted his weight to hold her down.

"I've been there, thanks." He cupped his hand against her cheek—gently—softly. "You still feel good against me. Stop wiggling and we'll talk. Don't you want to at least hear my offer? Especially since I did your dirty work for you."

She stilled her body and relaxed, hoping he'd get distracted long enough for her to make a move, and she spoke through gritted teeth. "I don't want anything you have to offer. Just give me the flash drive."

"I figure we have exactly four minutes to get out of this place before the new guards show up for the shift change and Armageddon begins. All I'm asking is that you come back with me and hear me out. If you decide to turn me down, then I'll give you the flash drive with no hard feelings, and you can claim your bounty."

Grace stared at him and tried to decide if he was bluffing. "You know I don't trust you."

"Yes, I believe you've told me that before," he said, his gaze hard. "But what I'm offering will pay more than double any of the jobs you've recently taken. Hear me out."

"Fine." She knew her options were limited. "What are we waiting for?"

"Our rendezvous point is on the other side of the border," he said, rolling off of her. She ignored the hand he reached out to help her up. "We've got twenty minutes to get there or we miss our ride."

Grace had no choice but to follow him out of one hell and into another.

***

The woman hadn't changed a bit in all the years he'd known her. She still kept her deep auburn hair braided tightly down her back while she was working. But he knew what it looked like spread across his pillow, and he knew what it felt like as it slithered like silk across his chest—glorious—a bright flame that was cool to the touch.

He looked at her critically, trying to decipher exactly why he was still attracted to her after the two years they'd spent apart. There wasn't just one thing about her that stood out, but the entire package. Her face was thinner now—her cheekbones more pronounced—but it was still the face of a sea goddess. Eyes the color of emeralds, slightly tilted at the corners, and full lips that haunted his dreams. She was every desire he'd ever had wrapped in one tiny package.

He let his gaze drift down her body. She was thinner all over. The lush curves he remembered were gone, replaced by a compact body of pure muscle and athleticism. She glanced back at him and raised a brow at where his gaze had landed.

Gabe smiled, but it didn't reach his eyes. He'd been wrong. She'd changed a lot. There was a hardness about her now that hadn't been there before. When she'd first started with the CIA, there had been hope and an ideal of the greater good. Now there was just emptiness—a cold, green stare that didn't believe in anything—and it scared the hell out of him. Because it was no one's fault but his own.

"We've just crossed the border into Venezuela by my calculations," she said, slowing to a jog. "How much farther is your rendezvous point?"

"About another mile. Keep the sound of water to your immediate left." He put his hand on her arm before she could take off again. "Wait."

She stopped dead in her tracks, and Gabe could tell she was trying to hear what he had. They were silent for a few more seconds before the sound came again.

She blew out an annoyed breath. "It's the new guards. You always did have ears like a bat."

"What do you have on you?" he asked.

"My SIG and a hunting knife. How many do you think there are?"

"No more than a dozen. They're noisy bastards. And not too fast." He pulled his own pistol from the small of his back and checked the magazine. "I'll give you a boost." He replaced his weapon in his pants and laced his fingers together. He arched a brow as she looked back at him with irritation.

"I'm really tired of climbing trees." She

exhaled and put her foot into his hands. He launched her up so she could reach the lowest branch, and she swung herself up with ease.

"Do you have good visibility?" Gabe asked.

"Yeah, I see them," she said. "You'll have to draw them close enough so I'm within range."

"Try not to hit me by mistake."

Her grin was sharp as she looked down at him. "Oh, it wouldn't be a mistake."

"That's what I'm afraid of." Gabe left her there to go meet trouble head-on.

He found cover behind a tree trunk the size of a small car and waited patiently. Heavy footsteps crunched over twigs, and he stuck out his foot as two of them passed by. One of the guards tripped and went sprawling to the ground, and Gabe struck out at the other with a palm to the chest, stopping his heart instantly. He broke the neck of the one who was already down before the man could rise off his knees.

Gabe ignored the steady stream of fire that came from behind him—despite her wanting to kill him, he trusted Grace to fight at his side during battle. It was after the battle that worried him.

He went searching for his next victim.

Only a few minutes passed before he stood in the middle of a ring of twelve guards—all of them dead. None of them had fired a shot. She was even better than he remembered.

Grace was waiting for him when he caught up to where he'd left her.

"Time's ticking," he said, looking at his watch.

They picked up the pace and ran the last mile in silence and slowed as they came to a winding dirt road with deeply rutted tire tracks, making footing tricky.

"Did we miss the pickup?" Grace asked.

A forest-green Humvee coated with a thick layer of dust came out of the trees behind them and pulled to a stop. Grace had her weapon out and her finger on the trigger.

"He's mine," Gabe said, opening the back door.

Grace slid across the hot leather seat.

The driver turned and looked at Gabe. Logan Grey had worked with him on other missions. He was a quiet man, tall and sinewy with muscle. He wore his dark-blond hair long, not as a fashion statement, but to help cover the terrible scars on the back of his neck. Logan was former MI6, but an almost fatal accident had gained him retirement before he was ready. Gabe hadn't hesitated at snatching Logan up to join the team. No one knew explosives better than Logan Grey.

"You cut it close, boss," Logan said. "In thirty seconds I wouldn't be here."

"Let's roll," Gabe said. "Be on the lookout for company."

Logan glanced once at Grace and then nodded, putting his submachine gun in his lap.

Gabe closed the window that divided the front and back seat so he and Grace had complete privacy.

"Who's your friend?" Grace asked.

"Logan Grey. Don't worry. He's heard all about you and still agreed to help me find you."

"I'm sure he's a real stand-up guy."

"He'll grow on you," Gabe said, keeping his gaze on the terrain around them, looking for threats. "So what do you think? It's just like old times. We always made a great team."

"Tell me what you want, and then let me go," she said. "I've got a tight schedule to keep."

"You don't have another job lined up once you deliver the flash drive to the South Koreans. Looks like you're a free agent." Gabe watched for a reaction, but she showed no surprise that he'd been keeping up with her movements. She waited him out with her silence and a hard look, and he decided to give in to the unspoken stand-off...just this once.

"I've left the CIA," he told her.

"I heard. Congratulations. Let me go."

Gabe smiled and stretched out across the seat, crowding her with the length of his legs, but she didn't budge an inch. "Did you hear I'd joined the private sector and opened my own agency?"

She laughed, low and sexy, and the smoky sound swirled around him until he was dizzy with desire. "So, good boy Gabriel Brennan has decided to become a bad boy and go rogue. I assume the agency is displeased by your decision?"

"Not at all," he said, shrugging. "They know when something is out of their control. My agency is privately funded and our reputation is above reproach. Even the CIA recognizes the benefits unknown money can buy. Governments are still hampered by rules, for the most part. Sometimes there are jobs where the rules need to be broken. That's when they call me."

"Well, bully for you," she said. "You always did manage to get what you wanted. Everything Gabe Brennan touches turns to gold."

"Nothing could be further from the truth, and you know it," he said quietly. Gabe waited patiently for her to make eye contact. It didn't take her long. She'd never been a coward.

She tilted her chin defiantly. "I don't know

anything about you. I never did. Our life together was a lie. I'm not even sure you know the real you."

He kept his face impassive, even though her words pierced his heart. "How long are you going to pretend she's not sitting here between us?"

"Don't mention her!" The quiver in her voice was quickly controlled. "I'll get out of this car and disappear off the face of the planet. If you want me to stay, then the past stays in the past. It's nonnegotiable."

"Fine," Gabe said. "Whatever you say."

The SUV slowed to a stop, and Gabe pushed the door open, not waiting to see if she'd follow. It was a stupid idea to think he could fix things— to heal the wounds that had been bleeding for the last two years.

Gabe's Gulfstream sat ready for takeoff on the hard-packed dirt the small Venezuelan city called an airport. He went up the stairs and then turned to face Grace, sure she'd still be in the car. But she stood at the bottom of the steps, her face carefully blank.

"You can either come with me or you can leave. The choice is yours," Gabe said without emotion, tossing her the flash drive.

She caught it one-handed and stared at him, studying him, trying to read every angle of the situation as she'd been trained to do at the agency. She finally nodded and started up the steps. "I'll come. A deal is a deal. And my word means something."

Gabe flinched before he could control it and let the pain roll through him. He had a feeling that before this job was over, she'd have one more reason to hate him.

AVAILABLE AT ALL RETAILERS

ACKNOWLEDGMENTS

Getting a book to publication takes an amazing team of people. I'm fortunate to have had these people in my corner for years.

To my editor—Imogen Howson for always making me better.

To my cover designer—Dar Albert for always blowing me away with your talent.

To my children—You're all so special. You have gifts and abilities beyond measure, and I'm excited to see what God has in store for each of you.

To Scott—thank you for answering a ridiculous amount of law enforcement questions and acting out weird scenarios with me. Any mistakes are mine alone.

Liliana Hart is a *New York Times*, *USA Today*, and Publisher's Weekly bestselling author of more than eighty titles. After starting her first novel her freshman year of college, she immediately became addicted to writing and knew she'd found what she was meant to do with her life. She has no idea why she majored in music.

Since publishing in June 2011, Liliana has sold more than ten-million books. All three of her series have made multiple appearances on the *New York Times* list.

Liliana can almost always be found at her computer writing, hauling five kids to various activities, or spending time with her husband. She calls Texas home.

If you enjoyed reading this, I would appreciate it if you would help others enjoy this book, too.

Recommend it. Please help other readers find this book by recommending it to friends, readers' groups and discussion boards.

Review it. Please tell other readers why you liked this book by reviewing.

Connect with me online:
www.lilianahart.com

facebook.com/LilianaHart

instagram.com/LilianaHart

bookbub.com/authors/liliana-hart

ALSO BY LILIANA HART

JJ Graves Mystery Series

Dirty Little Secrets

A Dirty Shame

Dirty Rotten Scoundrel

Down and Dirty

Dirty Deeds

Dirty Laundry

Dirty Money

A Dirty Job

Dirty Devil

Playing Dirty

Dirty Martini

Dirty Dozen

Dirty Minds

Dirty Weekend

Dirty Looks

Dirty Liars

Dirty Valentine

Addison Holmes Mystery Series

Whiskey Rebellion

Whiskey Sour

Whiskey For Breakfast

Whiskey, You're The Devil

Whiskey on the Rocks

Whiskey Tango Foxtrot

Whiskey and Gunpowder

Whiskey Lullaby

The Scarlet Chronicles

Bouncing Betty

Hand Grenade Helen

Front Line Francis

The Harley and Davidson Mystery Series

The Farmer's Slaughter

A Tisket a Casket

I Saw Mommy Killing Santa Claus

Get Your Murder Running

Deceased and Desist

Malice in Wonderland

Tequila Mockingbird

Gone With the Sin

Grime and Punishment

Blazing Rattles

A Salt and Battery

Curl Up and Dye

First Comes Death Then Comes Marriage

Box Set 1

Box Set 2

Box Set 3

The Gravediggers

The Darkest Corner

Gone to Dust

Say No More

Laurel Valley

Tribulation Pass

Redemption Road

Midnight Clear

Forgiveness River

Atonement Trail